"MAN" (dictionary defir
high degree the qualities
malehood...

"MAN" (every woman's definition!): Someone who won't tell you what he's feeling, but still expects you to figure it out!

Abby Van Patten on men: "I'll admit it, cowboys are my weakness. Even if they are always riding off into the sunset, leaving you with a broken heart! And Beau was the worst kind of cowboy—he looked long and lean and as good as his word. But he never thought he was good enough for me, when truth is, *I'm* probably not good enough for *him!*"

Carolyn Cole on men: "Men! They come strolling back into your life, expecting you to drop everything. Take my ex-husband. For ages he was married to his job, forgetting that his real wife—*me*—was waiting for him at home. Now, of course, he says he's changed—and my body's actually telling me to believe him. But could I be making a big mistake?"

Catherine Courlaine on men: "I always dreamed of a strong, dark and dangerous man who'd sweep in on a giant steed and rescue me. Then I met Tamar Fallah Haj. This is definitely a case of 'be careful what you wish for....'"

KATHLEEN EAGLE

is a transplant from New England to Minnesota, where she and her husband, Clyde, make their home with two of their three children. She's considered writing to be her "best talent" since she was about nine years old, and English and history were her "best subjects." After fourteen years of teaching high school students about writing, she saw her own first novel in print in 1984. Since then she's published many more novels with Silhouette Books and Harlequin Historicals that have become favorites for readers worldwide. She also writes mainstream novels and has received awards from Romance Writers of America, *Romantic Times* and *Affaire de Coeur*.

JOAN HOHL

lives in southwestern Pennsylvania, where she was born and raised. The bestselling author of over forty novels, including twenty-five for Silhouette Books, Joan has won numerous awards, including the Romance Writers of America Golden Medallion Award and two *Romantic Times* Reviewer's Choice Awards. One of the industry's most popular authors, Joan writes both historical and contemporary romance.

BARBARA FAITH

believes that love is a rare and precious gift. Her work shows an endless fascination with the attraction a man and a woman from different cultures and backgrounds have for each other. Her long marriage to an ex-matador she met when she lived in Mexico proves the truth of such an attraction. Barbara has written more than thirty novels, including a June 1996 Special Edition title, *Happy Father's Day*, and an August 1996 Intimate Moments novel, *Long-Lost Wife?*

KATHLEEN EAGLE
JOAN HOHL
BARBARA FAITH

Summer Sizzlers

MEN OF Summer

Silhouette Books

Published by Silhouette Books

America's Publisher of Contemporary Romance

SILHOUETTE BOOKS

ISBN 0-373-48319-8

MEN OF SUMMER

Copyright © 1996 by Harlequin Books S.A.

ALL-AROUND COWBOY BLUES
Copyright © 1996 by Kathleen Eagle

GONE FISHING
Copyright © 1996 by Joan Hohl

THE SHEIKH'S WOMAN
Copyright © 1996 by Barbara Faith

Printed in U.S.A.

CONTENTS

ALL-AROUND COWBOY BLUES

Kathleen Eagle

To Leslie Wainger, editor extraordinaire, mentor and
dear friend—

I ain't trying' to butter you up or nuthin', but after
twelve years I oughta know: you're the best.

Prologue

Beau Lassiter swung his long leg over the black gelding's rump and sank his boot heel into a foot of wet snow. Simple move. He'd done it ten, twenty, fifty times a day nearly every day of his life. But these days, especially cold, wet days like this, it was a move that nagged his joints with pain. He would sooner live in the saddle all day, any day, *every* day, never get down. He always felt better riding than he did walking. A man on horseback was the king of his world. A man on foot had to deal with his common blisters, and April's untimely chill had burrowed deep into Beau's abused, bronc-buster-blistered joints.

But aching joints were nothing new. He flipped the reins over the black's ears and bit back a groan as he knelt beside the source of a bad hurt, worse than physical. With a gloved hand he uncovered the frozen hindquarters of another dead calf.

Damned spring blizzard had played hell with calving season. He'd been battling scours before the snow hit, treating the calves out in the pasture, putting his championship roping skills to good use and forcing his aunt Kate's cure—her wondrous "pinch of this and that" beaten up with vitamins, raw eggs, electrolytes—down his bawling babies' throats. But a sudden shift in the wind had brought hock-high snow and piled it into chest-high drifts. Winter blizzards were a given in South Dakota. Spring blizzards—calving season blizzards—were a rancher's worst nightmare.

And *this* calf—the poor little white-faced black bull calf Beau hadn't reached in time—was the last straw, the one that promised to sink his operation deep into the hole. He was either going to have to borrow more money or find another source of income. The notion of more borrowing stuck in his craw. But then, so did the notion of moonlighting for an hourly wage, especially since he had things to do during his moonlit hours. Like sleep.

He'd been offered another option. The money was damn good for a job that wouldn't demand much effort, certainly no brainpower. A little brawn was required, but only for show. Which, of course, was the kicker. Getting paid to show off clothes sounded pretty stupid. He'd done a couple of endorsements during his pro-rodeo days, but he'd turned down the offers that didn't suit him, and getting duded up didn't much suit him.

But this deal did have its attractive aspects to consider, which was exactly what Beau did as he climbed into the saddle. The number one attraction was easy money. He had his back to the wall on that score. For the right price, he figured he could swallow a little pride and dress up like a picture-pretty cowboy. It wasn't like he'd have to pose naked.

The number two attraction was a sweet memory. Abigail Van Patten. In her letter she'd wondered if he remembered her. He smiled wistfully as he gave the gelding its head, letting the horse make its own way out of the snow-filled draw, lunge through a drift and head for higher ground. The bleak brown ridge above had been blown clear.

Just like Beau years ago, knocking around in the wind, blown from here to Texas at the drop of a hat. It had been about ten years since he'd met her in the Colorado Springs airport. It was the kind of chance encounter only the wind could devise, but he remembered it well. And he remembered her *very* well. Every rich auburn hair, every inch of creamy alabaster skin, every graceful step. It had taken him five weeks, but he'd memorized every detail. He figured the reason he remembered so well was that she was the woman who'd gotten away. But the time they'd had together... man, oh, man. He could still hear Abigail's sweet sigh.

Or was that the wind? One was about as elusive as the other.

You probably don't remember me, she'd written, and he'd laughed out loud when he read it. It was just something to say. She knew damn well he would remember. A man wasn't likely to forget the first and last woman he ever allowed to break his heart.

But I've read about you, and I know that since I saw you last, you did realize your dream of winning the

All-Around Cowboy Championship. How wonderful for you!

Damn straight. He'd won his trophy buckle just the way he'd told her he would.

I wonder if you would be interested in lending your name . . .

Lending his name? She was really asking him to *sell* his name, which was pretty funny, considering there'd been a time when he'd dreamed of giving it to her outright. He'd never said so, not in so many words, but he'd told her how he felt. Pretty much.

A young cowboy's dreams were a lot like his money. Easy come, easy go, at least mostly. He'd won a whole lot more go-rounds than he'd lost, so he wasn't about to start complaining about unrealized dreams. He wouldn't even mind seeing her again, but he would rather no favors were asked and none owed.

This wasn't a favor, he told himself. This was business, pure and simple. She wanted to hang her designer duds on him and use his name, and she was willing to pay for the privilege. If the price was right, maybe he would just let her.

He could think of tougher ways to make a buck.

Chapter One

"Have I got a surprise for you."

Jackie Turnquist waggled her heavy eyebrows, grinning at her partner like the proverbial canary-fed cat as she closed the office door behind her. With a pointed glance she indicated that she'd left the surprise in the clothing store out front. She edged closer to the desk, moving as though she was half afraid her surprise might escape while her back was turned.

"I've found our All-Around Cowboy."

Abigail Van Patten straightened her tired shoulders and welcomed the excuse to roll her desk chair a few inches backward. She needed a break from her columns of numbers and pages of plans.

"A real one?"

"He's got the right face, the right body and the right trophy buckle," Jackie reported eagerly.

"At the right price?"

"Well...let's just say Mr. Right doesn't come cheap, but he's worth his price." Jackie jerked a thumb over her shoulder. "And he's here, in the ever-lovin' flesh."

Abby pushed her fingers through a nearly straight hairdo that, this late in the afternoon, was almost as worn-out as she was. "And you're dying to introduce him."

"Actually, you've already met."

Abby lifted her chin, then one brow, inviting Jackie to divulge the name. She'd met lots of cowboys since she and Jackie had started their high-fashion Western-wear business, but unlike Jackie, she couldn't recite pro-rodeo stats chapter and verse. And knowing Jackie, she wouldn't get to the name until she'd listed his accomplishments first—record calf-roping time, first cowboy ever to ride some notorious bull, number of first-place scores in a single season. Abby waited to be regaled so she could reward her partner with the appropriate awe-filled response once the name was finally announced.

But Jackie stepped back, folding her arms and tucking her chin in a petulant pose that spelled trouble.

"Actually, you sort of signed the letter we sent offering him the job." Big brown eyes offered an apologetic glance that skated past Abby's mystified expression and landed on the wall calendar behind her. "That is, your name...was signed."

Abby stiffened. She never signed anything she hadn't read. "We advertised," she recalled calmly. She had placed the ads herself before she'd left Denver to come to Rapid City and help with the opening of the new store. "We didn't send out any personal—"

"We wanted a *real* Professional Rodeo Cowboys Association World Champion All-Around Cowboy," Jackie recited. "There aren't that many around, you know."

"So you wrote personal letters?"

"Just one."

Just one.

Then there was only one possible name. One man. The only cowboy whose name Abigail would never confuse with any of the others. The one name she never dropped. The one man she hadn't seen or heard from or run into since she'd started her business. The one she never talked about except that one time when she'd mentioned, just *mentioned*...

"Abby, you know him *personally*," Jackie crooned covetously. "Our store is All-Around Cowboy Blues. Our catalog is going to be called All-Around Cowboy Blues. You know him *personally*."

"Jackie, I could just—" Abby searched the ceiling for inspiration. Throttle? Strangle? Scream?

Just stare. Dumbfounded.

Or nearly so. "You wrote to him and signed *my name?*"

Jackie nodded.

"What did you say?"

"It was very businesslike. You just said—" She shrugged and offered a wan smile. "Well, you knew it had been a long time, but you hoped your name might ring a bell."

Abby rolled her eyes, tsked, then heaved a mighty sigh.

"You hoped he'd fully recovered from his injuries."

Double take. "What injuries?"

"Just a banged-up leg. I know all his scores and stuff, and I knew he retired two years after he won the championship, but I had to do a little research to find out why. He had one real bad run-in with a chute-fighting saddle bronc." Jackie smiled reassuringly. "But you wouldn't know it to look at him. He looks..." She cocked her head toward the door and crinkled her whole face up into a visual plea. "Go see for yourself. He's out there waiting."

Abby closed her eyes, and there he was. Never far from her mind's eye. Always the irresistible smile, the quick and easy wink. *Out there waiting.*

"I can't believe you did this."

"I had to." Jackie tried to nod away Abby's scowl. "I did, I *had* to. He's perfect, Abby. And it's not like we're hitting a friend up for a favor. This is business. He wants the job, and we're paying him." She smiled tentatively as she laid careful claim to Abby's arm. "Although I think he's really looking forward to renewing an old acquaintance."

The scowl was still there.

"Please back me up on this, Abby," Jackie wheedled as Abby allowed herself to be pried from her chair. "He's out there waiting."

Good conservative sense had flown the coop since Abby had gone into partnership with Jackie Turnquist. But there was no denying that All-Around Cowboy Blues had expanded rapidly. "If you weren't such a marketing genius..."

"More brass than brains," Jackie admitted, gently pushing her friend toward the door. "After the two of you shake hands, kinda make nice with each other and generally get the ball rolling in the right direction, then I'll own up to my little scheme, and we'll all laugh about it, and everything will be fine. We're buying him dinner. I already offered."

"I'm busy." Abby straightened her pleated, pearl-gray skirt and claimed the matching jacket from the wooden hat tree in the corner by the door.

"No, you're not. I already checked your calendar." Jackie arranged the collar of Abby's white blouse, smoothing it over her lapel. "You look great, as always."

"So?"

"So." A fleeting smile, a naughty-girl shrug. Jackie knew she'd already been forgiven simply because she was Jackie. "Just an observation." Then the truth flashed in bright, hopeful brown eyes. "He's perfect, Abby. Just what we need. King of the Cowboys."

"That's Roy Rogers," Abby muttered as she opened the door.

She took a deep breath. There was no need to scan the store. Sitting on the counter by the cash register, flipping through a magazine, he drew her eyes like a magnet.

"Roy's stepped down from the throne. There's his successor," Jackie whispered from behind—the angel or the devil on Abby's shoulder, she didn't know which. "He's perfect, Abby."

Perfect, indeed. That was what she'd thought when she'd first laid eyes on him ten years ago. Perfect. A real cowboy. Tall and tan, lean and lanky. She remembered the way he'd moved with the unhurried grace of a mountain cat, adjusting his Stetson—or tipping it, she wasn't sure—as he'd leaned down to pick up the bag she'd dropped in the airport terminal. Half a dozen people had hurried on by. Beau Lassiter had stopped to help her.

He hadn't changed much. A little brawnier, perhaps, more weathered. He looked up, and she saw more self-assurance in his smiling blue eyes. He set the magazine aside, slid off the counter and touched the brim of his hat as she approached.

Same endearing gesture. Same warm flutter in the pit of her stomach.

"It's good to see you," she said as she extended her hand and watched it disappear in his. She could feel his eyes on her, and she knew she had to be stingy with her eye contact, at least initially. His eyes had a way of consuming whole people at a glance with the same kind of warm-blanket feeling his hand applied to hers.

"Same here," he said. "Nice surprise, gettin' that letter from you."

"Well, I . . ." She nodded, smiled. "I've thought of you often. You did what you said you were going to do. Proved you were—what was it? 'The hot-damnedest cowboy on the rodeo circuit'?"

He chuckled and hung his head so that his hat shielded him briefly. She was sure he blushed.

"I saw your picture in one of the Western magazines," she explained.

"You made your dream come true, too." He surveyed the racks and shelves. "You said you were going to open a clothing store. You never said you were going to sell cowboy boots, though." He glanced at her gray pumps. "Where're yours?"

"Mine?"

"You didn't outgrow them, did you? The ones I bought you?"

"No. I probably still have them." She noticed the cover of the magazine he'd been reading and recalled the dreams they'd traded. "I never got my horse, though."

"Why not?"

"Same problem I had before." She shrugged, surprised at how easily the words came despite the fact that her throat had gone dry, how easily she smiled despite the attack of butterflies. "No place to keep one."

"You've come to the right place. Space is something we've got plenty of in South Dakota." He nodded toward the front door, where a would-be customer had paused to read the Closed sign in the window. "You got a nice place here. All-Around Cowboy Blues. I like the name."

"You don't think it sounds sad? The blues part refers to denim, of course, but we had a lot of discussion about it sounding a little depressing, like a sad cowboy or something, which might not be the most effective way to market..." He was looking at her with that bemused smile, the one that said he was reading something else in her eyes. "What?"

"Nothing. It's a good name either way." He hooked his thumbs in his belt, tipped his head to one side, still reading her. "I thought you'd be married by now. Jackie said you weren't."

The easy words skittered away. Abby slid a hard glance at the crack in the office door, which quickly disappeared. "I really haven't had time."

"Ten years?" Beau laughed and shook his head. "Me neither. Been real busy."

Abby stiffened. "Beau, I know this crazy idea took you by surprise, and I don't want to impose on you. I don't want you to feel any obligation because of our past—" she offered a meaningful look and took firm control of the word "—friendship. I know this must be a very busy time of the year for you."

"You do?"

"Well, I just meant..." She turned away, confessing quietly, "I guess I don't. This whole thing was kind of a shot in the dark. Now that you're retired, you probably don't have—"

"I still do a little team roping. I'm not completely washed up. A few people might remember my name." Her distressed look only amused him. "That's what you're lookin' for, isn't it?"

"I just meant that..." She shook her head quickly. She hated floundering in what had started out as someone else's deception. "I would never want to...

I mean, I'm sure you've had a parade of people who knew you when coming out of the woodwork.''

"Not lately." He eyed her speculatively. "You and your partner offered me a job, right?"

"We...I..." She gave a tight nod. "Yes, we did."

"I've done a couple of endorsements. I know how they work. You're not asking me to recommend smokeless tobacco to the little buckaroos, right?"

"Of course not."

"You just want me to say I like your clothes." His gaze slid to her pumps, then slowly back to her face. One side of his mouth turned up, topped off with his signal wink. "I like your clothes."

She steeled herself against that old feeling and rose to the occasion with an urbane quip. "You've taken a good look?"

"Oh, yeah."

She swept her jacket back and postured, hand on hip. "You wouldn't mind coming out of the chute wearing something like this?"

"Gotta wear something."

Inside her head, Beau's voice called, "Outside!" The gate swung open, and a horse plunged forward carrying a cowboy wearing Beau's hat, Beau's boots hooking the shoulder points, Beau's chiseled face... and a gray kilt.

"True enough."

They drank in the sparkle in each other's eyes for a moment before sharing a laugh.

"Your partner found my terms agreeable," he said finally. "How about you?"

"Jackie's busy putting it all in writing as we speak. But it's more than just an endorsement. You know there's some modeling involved."

He laughed again. "A guy's gotta do what a guy's gotta do." On second thought, he pulled a serious expression. "You don't sell underwear, do you?"

"Not for men." It was her turn to smile. "But we will have night-wear in our catalog."

"Like pajamas?"

She nodded, still smiling.

"What, with little pictures on them?" Another nod. "Damn."

"They're silk."

"Silk?" He stepped closer. "First time I ever touched silk..." She glanced away, and he chuckled. "They were real pretty. Pink. Soft as—"

"We have robes, too," she said quickly. "Tell me your middle name and we'll monogram the pocket with your initials. That'll be a nice touch, I think."

"You mean I get free samples?"

"We want you to wear the All-Around Cowboy Blues brand. Not only in pictures, but around the fairgrounds, out on the town..." She gestured with a flourish, indicating the shirts and pants on display. "We're hiring you to help us sell clothes."

"People see me in my cowboy pajamas, they're sure gonna want a pair just like 'em." He reached around her, ostensibly to examine a tooled belt hanging among several on a rack. She stepped to the side. He dropped the belt, cocked an eyebrow. "They come in his and hers?"

"Not exactly."

"Who's wearing the women's clothes for you? Which Miss Rodeo America? Better be careful who you pair me up with."

She dismissed that particular non-worry with a graceful hand. "We're only hiring one rodeo personality. For obvious reasons we wanted a World Champion All-Around Cowboy. The others will be professional models. I'm sure they'll meet with your approval."

Neither of them had noticed when Jackie had emerged from the office, contract in hand. "You'll probably want to have your lawyer look this over," she suggested, turning the paper over to Beau. "It's pretty straightforward. The terms we discussed, the standard—"

Beau scanned the figures and nodded. "Where do I sign?"

"There's no rush," Jackie said. "Take it with you, talk it over with your attorney. Is he in town?"

"Office just down the street."

"Check it out now, and then you can bring it with you tonight. Supper's on us."

"No, thanks. I can read the numbers myself. Write my own name, buy my own meal." He snatched a pen from a cup with an Indian motif around the rim, tossed the contract on the counter next to the cash register and signed his name on the bottom line. Then he glanced at Abby. "Just for the record, there's no middle initial. Beau Lassiter's all the name I've got and all the name you're buying."

"It's a big name," Jackie assured him as she accepted the contract and offered a handshake. "Everyone remembers that ride you made in Fort Worth, Beau. You scored a ninety on Tailspinner. Nobody could stick that horse, and you scored a ninety. I mean, that was..." At a loss for words, Jackie shook her head. "You're very well respected, Beau, and this is a privilege for us. If any of our designs don't suit you, we'll find something else."

"Fair enough."

"I'm glad we were able to work something out," Abby said.

With a hint of a smile, Beau slid her one of his irresistible winks on his way out. "Wasn't even all that complicated, was it?"

Complicated wasn't the half of it.

Ten years ago Beau Lassiter had stopped Abby in her tracks, thrown her completely off track, made her wonder, at least for a time, whether her life ought to have a track beyond the next butte, or a plan other than hitting the road, or a schedule more restrictive than showing up in time for the Grand Entry at the next rodeo. She'd lost herself in his world for the better part of one romantic summer. But even a starry-eyed child soon figured out for herself that Frontierland was all a dream. Nobody really lived there.

Nobody except dyed-in-the-wool cowboys like Beau. She'd believed him when he'd said he loved her, but she knew he'd loved the rodeo more. And there had been no way she could compete. It hadn't taken her long to realize that. Five weeks, to be exact. Five glorious weeks, which was a very long time for a man who never looked at a calendar and didn't own a watch.

He lived his life in seasons, and he plotted it on a tattered road map. A series of towns circled in pencil, the date for a rodeo jotted beside each one. That was his plan. He was headed for the PRCA National Finals someday. All he had to do was win enough go-rounds, rack up enough prize money, and he would be a world champion.

She'd hooked up with him under circumstances just as unlikely as their ill-fated romance. An Eastener, just graduated from Rhode Island School of Design, a woman who had planned her every move since she'd taken her first careful baby step, suddenly heading for Colorado on a whim. A cowboy who never went anywhere without his pickup suddenly taking to the air.

And a flight to Denver, sidetracked by bad weather.

She always tried to handle too much carryon baggage. There was always the danger of lost luggage—it had happened to her once—and there were important things she didn't want to be without when she arrived. And then there were the breakable things, like the apothecary jar that was to be a gift for Aunt Mellie. Fortunately, that wasn't what she'd dropped. The portfolio was awkward to carry, but she wasn't going to trust it to a baggage handler.

Trust it to a cowboy?

"Let me help you with that, ma'am."

He picked up the portfolio and reached for her tote bag. A boyish thatch of sandy blond hair escaped his Stetson when he pushed it back. His blue eyes demanded nothing, simply offered. And his smile was as easy as an old porch swing. The tote bag slid from her hand into his.

"I checked all my stuff," he said. "Got another free hand, if you need it. Where you headed?"

"Um...those seats by the window." She pointed to an empty waiting area facing an expanse of glass, smeared with rivulets of water. Huge puddles were gathering on the tarmac around the plane they'd just vacated, and the downpour showed no promise of letting up.

"When we take off again," he clarified. "Where you headed?"

"Denver."

"Me too. So close and yet so far away."

Abby glanced out the window. "In this weather, it would seem so. You'd think if we could land here, we could've landed there."

"Mountains are great weather machines. Why don't we watch the rain through that window over there?"

He nodded toward a small bar. "I slept through the meal they served on the plane."

"You didn't miss much."

"Let's get a sandwich, then." He claimed the handles of the hot pink shopping bag containing the fragile apothecary jar, along with a pair of presentable shoes—she was wearing her power-walking sneakers—and the "minnie-apple" salt and pepper shakers she'd picked up at the Minneapolis airport to add to her collection. But she let all those treasures go, and she followed him to the table by the window.

He ordered a chicken-fried steak sandwich and a beer, and he made no comment about her diet cola and onion rings. He did say that he was glad the rodeo he was headed for would be held indoors, and that if he won the saddle bronc event he was going to put a new transmission in his pickup so he wouldn't have to depend on anybody else for transportation.

"I guess you're right. It's probably a lot worse than this in Denver," she said, shivering as lightning turned the world beyond the window into a big, gray cracked plate. Thunder was a Mack truck, rumbling after the flash's fading tail. "Do you think they'll keep us here overnight?"

"Not if your boots are made for walkin'." He sipped his beer, then grinned. "With a line like that I could be singin' in the rain. Care to join me?"

"*Walk* to Denver? In *this?*"

"Maybe hitch a ride?"

She shook her head like the good girl she'd always been. "Hitchhiking is dangerous."

"Not if we're looking out for each other. I'd get a ride a whole lot faster with you along, and you'd have a bodyguard."

"You're the bodyguard?" she asked dubiously.

"Me or the driver. Chances are at least one of us is honorable."

"I think I'd rather take my chances with the airline pilot."

"Suit yourself," he invited with an easy shrug. "Tell you what, though, pilots are a dime a dozen. Real old-fashioned cowboys are damned hard to find these days."

"I seem to have found one quite easily."

"Only because you weren't looking." He leaned back in his chair, spraddle-legged, a bold grin, quick as lightning, brightening his eyes. "If you'd been looking, you'd'a scared me away."

In the end he talked her into renting a car and splitting the cost. In the pouring rain he loaded up her luggage, his duffel bag and bronc saddle, and they were off.

He was off to ride in a rodeo.

She thought she was off to visit Aunt Mellie.

But it had been more complicated than that for both of them.

The small parking lot behind the store was dark when Abby finally closed up shop. Jackie had left, disappointed that their new company spokesperson had turned down her invitation. Secretly Abby was, too. Not that she wanted to go out with Beau, not socially. Jackie would have been along. It would have been business. But they could have talked. She could have sat across the table from him, a safe distance, safe circumstances, and she could have listened to the sound of his voice, enjoyed his ready smile. She was just curious to know more about what he'd been doing for the past ten years. That was all.

"You always work this late?"

Her ankle turned over her spike heel as she gasped, jumped and tried to turn around all at once.

He caught her by the arm, then, amazingly, caught the keys that had fallen through her fingers.

"Beau!"

"Sorry."

"You scared me."

"Didn't mean to."

Her heart was pounding, he was smiling, and they were both whispering, like two thieves in the night.

"Just heading for my pickup." With a nod he indicated the vehicle parked beside the compact car she'd leased shortly after she'd arrived in South Dakota. "I had time to do some thinking. Guess I was kinda rude about supper. Thanks for the offer."

"Jackie means well, but she can be presumptuous sometimes." Abby collected herself and took a deep breath, nodding her thanks as he dropped her keys into her palm. "She probably didn't even bother to ask if you already had plans."

"She didn't, but I wouldn't have had any trouble telling her if I did." He stepped back, then studied the toes of his boots for a moment. "This wasn't your idea, was it?"

"Jackie always wants to celebrate every transaction. She's just a very fun-loving—"

He pinned her with a shadowy stare. "You didn't write that letter."

There was a brief, heavy silence, a moment of utter paralysis. Then she shook her head.

He nodded. "It didn't sound like you. Didn't sound like any of the letters I imagined you might write to me."

"You never wrote to me, either," she reminded him softly, and ten years fell away, exposing disappointment that seemed suddenly fresh. "You never called."

"I had my cowboy pride to protect." His dry chuckle echoed in the alleyway. "It's still intact. That much of me, anyway."

"How much isn't?"

"Couldn't say." He glanced away. "Guess you'll have to figure that out for yourself."

"Ordinary people just ask. They say, 'How are you, Beau?' And you answer..."

"Doing just fine, Princess." He tipped his head to one side. "You believe that?"

"Should I?"

He shrugged. "Do you want to grab something to eat? I'm kinda hungry."

"You turned down my earlier offer."

"It wasn't your offer." He took a wider stance as he shoved his hands into his back pockets. "How long has it been since you've had yourself half a chocolate milk shake?"

She smiled. "Quite a while. They only tempt me when I see someone else having one." Especially someone whose mouth, whose lips, always had a way of making everything that touched them look so delicious.

"You're kinda hungry, too. I can tell." He laid his hand on her shoulder, turning her toward the vehicles. "Let's take my pickup."

He took her to a roadside café where he ordered a corner booth, chicken-fried steak, a milk shake and onion rings. "Best in the country," he promised.

"Oh, I gave those up," she said, patting her flat stomach as she slid into the booth.

"Something else for you to try off my plate," he predicted. "None of the food they serve here is good for you, so you might as well order strictly for taste."

"Grilled chicken," she told the waitress. "Baked potato."

"Double the onion rings," he added. "And bring an extra straw. We'd share, but you know how it is. It's been a while since we were on kissing terms."

Abby admonished him with a look.

He responded with a wink. "But that could change real soon."

The waitress went away laughing.

Abby shook her head. "I can see that *you* haven't changed."

"Don't be too sure," Beau warned. "I'm older and wiser. The older part you can sure see, and the other, well..." He reached across the table and pulled two napkins from the dispenser near the wall. He handed her one. "That shows, too, if you're looking for it."

"You were never short on intelligence."

"I was always smart enough, but wisdom..." He studied the small napkin. "This wouldn't do a damn bit of good hangin' over a guy's leg, would it? I'm leaving it on the table." He smiled at her. "But I do remember what I'm supposed to do with it. A *real* napkin, anyway."

"You haven't changed your mind about the hat?"

He glanced up at the gray brim. "Remembered those rules you taught me a couple times. One time I found myself staring at an empty peg where my favorite hat had been. Another time I walked off and left it on the seat of a chair. I was lucky that time, though. Pretty little waitress had saved it for me." He fingered the brim, tipping it from his face. "They take some shaping. Hate to lose a well-broke hat."

"I remember." The way he looked in a cowboy hat had shaped her own designs. In her mind she was always dressing Beau Lassiter. She would picture him wearing only his hat and boots and build a complete outfit from the skin out.

Which gave *her* a secret to smile about. "What are you doing now that you're not following the rodeo circuit?"

"I'm still punchin' cows. I still do some team roping. That's pretty easy on the legs."

The naked Beau was displaced by an injured Beau, and her smile faded. "How badly were you hurt?"

"You mean when I tore up my leg?" He shrugged it off. "Wrecked my knee, mostly. They pieced it back together pretty good." He leaned back, squaring his shoulders. "I limp a little sometimes, but it's a real cowboy limp. Doesn't bother me. It suits the image."

"But it ended your career."

"Not before I reached my goal," he reminded her. "I'm a retired champion. Nobody beat me out of my title. I went down in a blaze of glory."

"Cowboy style."

"Cowboy style," he confirmed. "That's what your business is all about, isn't it? All-Around Cowboy Blues. Sounds like cowboy style to me."

"It is."

"Serves us both well."

"There has to be more to it," she said. "More than just the look."

"You got that right."

"The quality has to be there, too."

"Cowboy quality. Rugged material, tough construction." He chuckled. "Can't be fallin' apart at the seams."

"Are you?"

"You always were direct. Like I told you..."

He paused while the food was served. After the waitress walked away, he offered Abby an onion ring.

"Finger food," she acknowledged as she made pincers of her thumb and forefinger.

He shook his head as he held the batter-fried hoop to her mouth. "*My* food from *my* fingers. Careful. They're hot." He leaned closer to answer her question while she let him feed her. "I'm gettin' along just fine, Abby. Found out I wasn't invincible, but I also found out I could live with it." He nodded, smiling when she used her tongue to haul in the onion's tail. "I'm doin' just fine."

"It's good to see that." She swallowed, nodding. "To know that you're well."

"Did you wonder?" Slowly he poured the thick shake, served in an old-fashioned malt tumbler, into a tall glass. "I've wondered about you," he said as they both watched softened ice cream fall in clumps along the sweetened milk flow. "Over the years I've wondered often." He speared the chocolate froth with a straw, then looked up.

"About what?"

"About you. What you were up to." He sipped from the straw, then pressed his lips together as he looked into her eyes. "Who you were with."

Abby smiled. She was enjoying this immensely. Granted, her mouth was watering. She could almost taste that chocolate.

"But I won't ask," he said quietly.

"Promise?"

He shook his head. "Don't have to ask. Right now you're with me. That tells me there's no one else. Not right now."

"Men's intuition strikes again."

"Am I wrong?"

"Are you asking?"

They locked each other's eyes in a contest, a stare down. Without looking away, he slid the glass her way. "She forgot the extra straw. I could have been a gentleman and given you first taste." He parked the glass beneath her chin. "Guess I'm still a little rough around the edges."

"You probably always will be."

"Probably." His voice dropped to just above a whisper. "How long has it been, Abby?"

"Quite a while."

"Care to risk it?" His blue eyes challenged hers. His mouth twitched. He slid the glass back and forth a little. "Real old-fashioned shakes are damned hard to find these days."

"I wasn't looking."

He grinned. "See how that works?"

After she got her laughter under control, she took a long, deep pull on the straw, letting her eyes meet his, letting him see how much she enjoyed the taste, the company, everything about this moment.

"I like it when you laugh," he confessed. "I like the sound. I like the way your eyes light up."

But he'd almost forgotten how it made him feel.

Chapter Two

Beau's favorite chore was riding his own pasture on a summer morning, checking on his own cows. His big black gelding followed the fence line on a loose rein while Beau surveyed the draw below, counting heifers as they grazed, noting the improved condition of an older cow that had wintered hard, spotting the calves nestling in the grass under the watchful eye of the "sitter" cow, noting ear tag numbers, assuring himself that all was in order. He'd done this job countless times with his father when he was growing up, nodding dutifully on cue when the old man described the place they would have of their own someday, the brand he'd already registered in both their names, the kind of horses they would ride. That day had never come for his father, not in his lifetime, but Beau liked to think that he'd made it happen for both of them. He'd stuck with the Double B Bar brand, paid handsomely for the right stud, hung the sign across the gateposts, exactly the way his dad had envisioned a thousand times. He'd made it happen today, *this* day, for a father who had stuck by his son.

And what a day it was. The hills and meadows were as green as Beau had ever seen them, replete with purple and yellow wildflowers, lush with tall green grass, and the creeks that sprang forth from the Black Hills were still running swiftly, deep and clear. The spring snowfall had been good for something besides killing calves. It had blessed his land even as it cursed his livestock. Such was the bargain any rancher made when he bought into the business. Take the bad with the good, work harder, put in longer days. It was more than a job; it was a way of life.

It was a place he could finally call his own.

It was a place that had been worth busting broncs, busting his butt and half his body for, and now it was worth taking on an extra job for. Sure, it was a crazy job, but no crazier than trying to ride an animal that didn't want to be rode, proving that any fool cowboy could get himself throwed.

And it gave him a chance to see Abby again.

He had loved her from the moment he first saw her. She was the princess his dad had described in one of those fairy tales he used to spin when they'd been fixing somebody else's fence or riding herd on somebody else's livestock. The old man never could keep a story straight, but Beau never minded when the mean stepmother got baked in the oven by the green giant, even when he knew better. There was always a princess, and the princess was always too fine for this world, too precious to last.

Abigail Van Patten, struggling through the airport terminal with her huge portfolio and her three unwieldy bags, had struck him that way. Too fine to be carrying such a load. Too pretty and precious to give a cowboy the time of day. Ordinarily he would have given her a hand, tipped his hat and gone on his way. But ordinarily he didn't fall in love the moment he looked into a woman's eyes.

This woman was different. She'd been different ten years ago, and she was still different, and there wasn't a damn thing he could do to change that. Seeing her again had his head in a spin. His princess. For the short end of one glorious summer he had courted her as valiantly as he could manage, and then he'd watched her go on her way. He'd covered his disappointment in hard-core style. He'd never seriously wished for anything, not even on the candles of the birthday cakes the old man had always managed to scrounge up, and he wasn't about to start in wishing the day Abby decided it was time she got back to what she'd been doing before he'd so unexpectedly interrupted her. Talk was cheap, promises meant to be broken and bus-stop appeals just too damned humiliating, so he'd said goodbye with a kiss he'd told himself she could never forget. A guy couldn't ask a princess to keep following him from one rodeo to another or to settle down with him in a two-bedroom trailer house. So he'd kissed her goodbye, then camped out on a bar stool for a week.

But what a time they had shared that summer. She loved horses, but she'd never had one of her own. Horses were his life, and that had been his trump card. He'd played it to the hilt. He was magic on a horse. He'd been her champion, and she'd been his lucky charm. He couldn't get bucked off with her watching. He couldn't drop his heels too soon and miss his horse out. He couldn't miss dropping his loop on his calf. There had been nothing he couldn't do on a horse that summer.

Well, almost nothing. But not for lack of trying...

From the first ride he'd made knowing she was in the stands, his princess had brought him a windfall of luck. He called Rusty Durant, the buddy left to watch over the old blue bomb, and told him to overhaul the engine and drop in a brand-new transmission. While the transformation was in the works he hung around Denver, doing a little roping to pick up extra cash. Doing a lot of heavy-duty charming on Abby's Aunt Mellie.

By the time he hitched a ride to Rapid City to claim his rehabilitated pickup, Beau was one lovesick cowboy. On his way to Denver he racked up two speeding violations, but, damn, it was worth it to hear Abby say she'd missed him, too. He counted the day she agreed to ride along with him to Pocatello as the first day of the sweetest five weeks he'd ever known.

They traveled light—he talked her into leaving all but one bag at Aunt Mellie's—and they took one day's journey at a time. After each rodeo, she agreed to tag along to one more. At first she insisted on staying in motels, separate rooms, but that became expensive for both of them. They spent a couple of nights charting stars in his pickup bed. Then he borrowed a tent. He kept wanting more of her. She kept giving in a little at a time, just like a true princess. When the time came, he promised himself he would love her well.

He'd left her standing in line at a campground shower facility just outside Cheyenne. He'd burned last night's supper, so tonight it was her turn to cook after he did the shopping. She was still gone from the tent when he brought back steaks and beer on ice, so he slipped off again to round up his real surprise.

"Hey, Princess," he called from his bareback mount. The huge gray Percheron wouldn't have been his first-choice model for impressing his lady, but it had a nice, broad, two-passenger back. "Wanna go for a ride on a stout, trusty stud?"

"Where in the world did you find...?" She gave the beast a wide berth as she took a slow turn around its substantial hindquarters. "My God, he's big. He doesn't buck, does he?"

"This guy buck?" Beau leaned over the draft horse's huge neck and coaxed a quick lift of the head by scratching under its cheek. "Is this the face of a bucking horse?" He flashed Abby a smile. Damn, she looked cute in her pink T-shirt and skimpy cutoffs. "Come on, now, are these the eyes of a widow maker?"

Examining those eyes required her to stretch her lovely long neck. "He looks pretty placid. I think he's falling asleep." She raked her fingers through the coarse, wavy mane. "Are you a gentle giant? Hmm?

I love horses, big or little. Would you let me ride you?"

"All you have to do is wrap your legs around my back and I'll give you one hell of a ride," Beau promised suggestively, waiting until she cast him that royally prim look before adding, "*he* says."

She took another visual measure of the situation. "I'll need help getting up there."

"At your service, Princess." He swung his leg over the withers and used the horse's hide as a slide. Handing her the reins, he laced his fingers together and gallantly offered his hands as a stirrup, easily lifting her onto the horse's back. Then he vaulted into place behind her, put his arms around her and took the reins, which were threaded through D-rings on the big harness collar.

"Drive us over to the pickup and I'll get a pair of jeans," Abby suggested. Beau nudged the horse into a hulking walk. "This isn't exactly regulation riding attire I've got on."

"Perfect for this horse, Daisy Mae." His knuckles grazed the inside of her thigh. They were headed straight for a meandering cow path he'd checked out. River bottom, quaking aspens, cool breeze, red-orange sunset. "Perfect for this cowboy, too."

"He's a workhorse, right? Like for plowing?"

"He's part of a team. Belongs to an old farmer I met up with at the store where I got all the stuff you ordered—steaks, beer, charcoal..."

"I didn't ask for beer."

He snuggled himself right up behind her, like two spoons in a kitchen drawer, and leaned close to her ear. "Got you some marshmallows."

"Mmm."

"Got you some liniment."

"Did I ask for liniment?"

"You will."

"I knew I should've put on some long pants. I know *that* much about riding." She rested her palms on the big leather collar as the horse negotiated the slope of a cut bank. "I hope I can have a horse of my own someday."

"I'll be glad when I can afford a good roping horse so I don't have to pay other guys to mount me," he said.

"*Mount* you!"

"Let me use theirs," he clarified. "What kind of horse would you like to have?"

"Not this kind." She patted the mane-tufted withers. "No offense, fella, but you're a little too big. Sixteen hands is about all I can handle."

"Then you'll probably hardly notice my two." He'd freed just one for stroking her silky, clean-shaven thigh. So that was what had taken her so long in the shower.

"Eyes on the road, hand on the steering rein, Mister."

"You're in the driver's seat, honey."

"I don't know where we're going."

"Neither do I." Wherever the river-bottom path took them, he figured. Draft horses were good at following the road. Beau knotted the reins and dropped the knot over the harness collar. "Guess we'll leave it up to him."

"Beau..."

"I'm not asking you to trust me. Hell, I'm a cowboy. You'd be crazy to trust a cowboy. But this horse is guaranteed solid and dependable."

"Says some anonymous farmer."

"Come on, now, farmers are the salt of the earth. Swing your leg over here." He guided her right leg over the horse's neck while she rubbernecked, questioning his sanity with a look.

Oh, he was quite sane. "I just want to make you more comfortable," he explained when he had her sitting sideways.

"Now, slide your leg through here." The move would take some flexibility on her part, maybe more than she thought she had. He would show her. He put her hands on his shoulders and guided her left leg, coaxing her to bend it like a chicken wing. "Hold on. Just don't kick me."

She giggled as she let him thread her leg through the space between them, dragging her sneaker across his lap. He squirmed, then smiled boyishly. "See how I trust you?"

"I'm riding backward!"

"Put your legs around me. I saw this in a movie once, and I've always wanted to try it." It was like posing a rubber doll, tucking her heels behind his butt, situating her so that the brim of his hat sheltered her face. "That's better, isn't it? My back's not as broad as his is."

She looked at him, wide-eyed with astonishment. "But I can't see where I'm going."

"You can see me. You're going where I'm going." Her hair was still damp at the temples. She smelled good enough to eat. He couldn't stop grinning. "I can see you."

"And the road, I hope."

No more than a path, but the big, surefooted gray plodded along.

"I know it's there. I know you're here." He leaned closer, nuzzled her cheek and flicked his tongue over her earlobe. "You smell like lemon and taste like sunshine."

"It's soap and...and—" his light nibbling at the side of her neck trapped a bubble of words in her throat "—and so much outdoors, which I'm not..." And momentarily distracted her from his hands, which were slip sliding over her sides, bracketing her breasts, closing in, sensitizing.

"Beau..."

"Hang on to me tight. I don't want you to fall." He secured her arms around his neck, slipped his hands over her bottom and tucked her firmly against him. "Closer," he pleaded. He was hard as a rock with her sitting on him like that. Delightful torture. "I don't want to lose you."

"You won't, but, Beau . . . the horse might . . ."

His thumb wandered under the frayed edge of her cutoffs. "The horse is wearing blinders," he whispered.

"Might get scared . . . Beau?"

"Nothing to be scared of," he promised on the breath of a kiss. "I'm a professional rider." He loved the way she said his name when he was touching her and she was enjoying it in spite of, maybe *because* of, the unusual circumstances. Teasing her with his thumb, testing a bit of elastic, he smiled as he nuzzled her soft cheek. "One hand holds the reins, the other reaches for heaven."

"Oh, my . . ."

"All yours, sweetheart."

And he was. She probably thought it was just sweet talk, but in his heart he knew he was going to be all hers that night. And on more nights to come . . .

Jackie had scheduled the fitting before the store opened in the morning, which meant, whether she wanted to be or not, Abby was there. She had to be there by seven, no matter what. It was her custom. Besides, she knew what she wanted in this catalog, what she and Jackie had discussed and settled on. Jackie would likely veer off course if some new brainstorm suddenly hit her.

Abby wasn't sure why it made her uncomfortable to ask Beau to keep changing his clothes. Maybe because it reminded her of a lion tamer's act she'd seen on television. She'd felt oddly embarrassed for the lions, required to perform tasks that must have seemed pointless to them. She'd felt even more embarrassed for the man for putting those magnificent animals in such an outlandish situation. The last thing she would ever want to be was a lion tamer.

But Beau did what was required of him without growling, maybe because he wasn't alone.

"I see you got Gayle Browning," Abby remarked to Jackie. She'd told herself that she was simply going to make her wishes known, then stay out of the way and let Jackie handle this, but she had to see how the dress suits looked. They were two of Abby's favorite designs. Both black, the men's suit in a traditional Western cut was a striking counterpoint to the looser cut of the woman's slacks and matching jacket. Hers was a masculine look made to set off a feminine face and figure like those of the willowy model who was making a production of adjusting her black cowboy hat according to Beau's instructions.

"They'll make a nice pair, don't you think?" Jackie returned as the partners stood back and observed. "Her strikingly dark hair and delicate features complement his bold, sort of Nordic—"

"It's a great combination, Jackie." Exactly the way Abby had pictured the suits would look on just the right people. All man, all woman, thoroughly Western. "Inspired, I'd say."

"Don't they just look darling in those outfits?"

"Just darling," Abby agreed airily. Gayle was straightening Beau's collar, which didn't need straightening. It was really kind of a cute gesture, Abby told herself. It would make a nice picture.

"Remember how I told you I wanted to use a black horse in the shot with that white-on-white outfit? Beau says he has a black horse."

"Gayle's afraid of horses," Abby recalled, having worked with the woman before. "Right, Gayle? I'm almost surprised you agreed to this." The slim, perfectly manicured hand smoothing the fine-textured lapel, *his* lapel—that was a nice touch, too. *Almost.*

"I nearly turned this shoot down just because it was Western, and I knew what that meant." Gayle smiled as she dragged her gaze away from Beau's. "But Beau was very reassuring about the horse."

Reassuring, Abby mused. Yes, he could be that. She'd almost decided her comparison to the caged lion had been unwarranted when Jackie asked to see how the two models would look without hats. To Abby's surprise, the hats came off easily. No complaints about feeling naked without his hat.

"You've got quite a farmer tan, Beau," Jackie observed. Beau grinned as he raked his thick hair from his pale forehead. "A little makeup should take care of that easily enough."

"Makeup!" The grin vanished. Beau jammed the black Stetson on his head, pulling the brim down low. "Sorry. I don't do makeup. I'm wearing a hat."

"Not with pajamas," Abby said, feeling unusually devilish.

"I'd sooner wear a hat to bed than pajamas." He folded his arms over his broad chest and cast her a pointed glare. "A hat and a workin' man's tan."

"Hmm, I wonder where those tan lines would be." Smiling, Gayle was quick to lay a conciliatory hand on his arm. "We can use a tanning bed, Beau. I've already scoped one out where I got my nails done yesterday. I use a tanning bed a couple of times a week, just to keep up."

"You mean one of those lighted coffins?" Beau returned his pretty new colleague's smile. "Now you've got *me* scared."

"I'll hold your hand, sweetie."

He glanced at Abby. "Maybe I'll just leave my hat off for a couple of days, huh? I tan pretty easy."

"We wouldn't want you to get sunstroke." Abby favored her models, each in turn, with a mock-motherly smile. "Or star struck. Or any of that sort of thing."

"Abby, come on," Gayle demurred. "I'm not a star. Not yet, anyway. That cosmetics contract hasn't turned my head one bit. I'm not doing too many little catalogs anymore, but when Jackie called and told me about this job..." She looked at the man whose powerful stature made her look far more petite, Abby thought, than she truly was. "Beau's the star. He's a real cowboy and an honest-to-God world champion." She squeezed his arm. "I think that's so excit-ing."

"Former champion," Beau amended, but he was basking in the compliment all the same. "It's been a few years."

"Once a champion, always a champion," Gayle said.

He smiled. "You're as easy on the ego as you are on the eyes, ma'am."

"Ma'am," she cooed as she flashed her winning smile toward the back of the store. "Don't you just love the way he talks?"

"Oh, yes," Abby agreed. "Cowboy charm. It's nearly irresistible." Unlike this whole ridiculous scene and the way it was making her feel. The cure was to behave like the woman she was, the woman in charge.

And do it with an unflagging smile. "You look wonderful, both of you. I can't wait to see you to-gether on a horse." She turned to her partner. "What are you doing this afternoon, Jackie? I know I said we'd use that parkland west of town, but it's not quite what I want. Shall we scout the area for some better outdoor settings for tomorrow's shoot?"

"Can't fit it in today." Jackie was suddenly en-grossed in the list Abby had made of shots that would be required for the catalog. "The artsy stuff is your department, anyway. I don't have much of an eye for that sort of thing. Why don't you—"

"I'll ask Tom to go with me," Abby decided. It was good to have a purpose other than watching, admiring . . . senselessly gritting one's teeth. "He's the photographer. He'll know exactly what we need."

"Tom's busy this afternoon, too," Jackie reported as she removed two shirts from the rack of outfits she and Abby had selected and steamed earlier. "In fact, we'll be busy together, shooting jewelry and accessories."

"I guess I'll mind the store, then."

"Wanda's coming in this afternoon, so the store's covered. You go on out and take a look around." Jackie glanced at Beau, who was taking advantage of the opportunity to get rid of the suit jacket. "I mean it, Abby. You've hardly been out of the store since you got here."

The hint wasn't lost on Beau. After the fitting was over, he appeared in the open office doorway. Abby didn't hear him, but she knew he was there. It was his move.

"I might have a pretty good idea of what we need," he said as he propped his shoulder against the door frame. "Care to let me show you?"

"What we need?" She stared at him, myriad possibilities leaping to mind. Space, she told herself firmly. An understanding. "Oh. You mean scenery?"

"Isn't that what you were talking about before?" He offered a knowing smile. "I live here, remember? I know all the best scenery. Would you like to see some of it?"

"Are you free this afternoon?"

His smile touched his eyes. "I won't cost you a dime."

At Beau's suggestion, Abby put on a pair of sneakers, but when he told her how much he liked her softly shirred summer dress, she thought better of taking the time to change into a pair of jeans. The decision had a familiar feel to it.

They drove to the top of a narrow, pine-shaded road made up of hairpin curves and switchbacks, where Beau parked his pickup, then escorted Abby down a sun-dappled path that led to the glistening blue waters of Sylvan Lake. They strolled the granite-lined shore for a while, saying little, listening to the water lap the rocks. A hawk called to its mate across the lake. The two glided toward one another, then wheeled and circled, dancing on air.

"South Dakota was one part of the rodeo circuit I missed that summer," Abby mused. They paused near a pink granite shelf at the water's edge. "Why didn't you show it to me then?"

He shrugged as he adjusted his straw cowboy hat against the sun. "It wasn't on the schedule."

"But it was your home. You had family here." She wrapped her arms around her waist, just above the billowy umbrella the breeze had made of her dress. "A small detour would have been nice."

"I thought of it more like home base," he said quietly, gazing at the tranquil water. "I didn't have a home back then. Not what most people would think of as a home, anyway.''

"Do you have one now?''

"Sure.'' He rested his backside against the rock and grinned, one eye squinting against the sun. "I've got a place to park my pickup.''

"And a place to keep your horse.'' She returned his smile.

"Which is more than you can say.''

"That's true. Sadly, I have no place to keep a horse.'' She glanced over her shoulder toward the path they'd taken through the woods. "This is a nice backdrop, but can you get a horse trailer up that road?''

"Better to leave the trailer and ride the horses up.''

"Gayle's afraid of horses.''

"You're not. You and I could ride a couple of horses up and meet the rest of the crew at the top.''

She turned to him. The breeze lifted her hair from her face. "Tom would want the morning light for the shoot.''

"So we ride up the day before the shoot. Camp out.'' His voice dropped. "Remember the Cheyenne rodeo?''

"Of course I remember,'' she answered defensively. The tone of his voice echoed the intimacy of that night as though it had just happened, as though the past ten years had been no more than a day.

It might have been true, as vividly as the moonlit images sprang to mind. The images and the troublesome yearning that accompanied them. Pure, unadulterated nostalgia was all it was. After an idyllic ride on an impossibly huge horse they had pitched a borrowed tent at the edge of the campgrounds and made love for the first time. *Of course* she remembered.

But she put the bittersweet memory in its cool, dark place as she moved to his side, then leaned against the rock.

"Why did you take this job, Beau?"

He stared at her for a moment.

Because I thought it was you asking me. Surely she knew that.

But he wasn't going to say it. He was going to give her an easy smile instead. "Because it's good pay for a few hours of standing around looking the part, and I can use the money."

"I don't do much camping anymore. I mean, I haven't since…" Finally she permitted herself to smile wistfully as she remembered. "Okay, that was my one and only camping experience. That time in Wyoming."

"One and only, huh?" He chuckled. "We camped a few more times, didn't we? Before and after."

"But that was…"

"That was the ground breaker," he finished for her. "Now you're more of a room-service kind of a girl."

"Not necessarily." She folded her arms, and her smile turned cute and sassy. "A restaurant with a view is always nice."

"You can't ask for a better view than this." He pressed on against his better judgment. She was going to turn him down, sure as hell. Still, he smiled. "And I'm a much better cook than I used to be."

"I think we want our catalog to have more of a ranch feel," she said, as if she thought they were really talking business. "Someplace with rustic buildings, weathered fence posts, wildflowers popping up out of the pasture. I was going to use that place in the park where they give trail rides, but that's not the right feel. Would you happen to know a rancher who wouldn't mind letting us take a few pictures on his property? Some discreet rancher," she hastened to add, "who won't give you a hard time about your modeling job."

He turned the corners of his mouth down and shrugged casually. "I might."

"We'd pay the going daily rate for the use of private property. Maybe the man you work for would be interested."

"The man I work for?"

"Didn't you say you were punching cows?"

"Oh, yeah." He chuckled. "What makes you think I'm working for a man?"

"You're right. I presume too much." She looked away and accused him gently, "But so do you, Beau. I'm not the same girl who lost her head when you turned on the cowboy charm. I'm not going to spend the night with you in a tent or the back of your pickup, or your buddy's girlfriend's apartment or—" She searched the sky, probably smiling less for him than for herself, for who she wasn't anymore and for who she was now. "I was just lucky I came to my senses when I did."

"It was a real hardship tour, huh?"

"It was..." She shook her head, slid him a quick glance and chose her words carefully. "It was a hard lesson."

Interesting choice of words. "What did you learn?"

"That I'm no Bobbie McGee," she quipped off-handedly.

"She left, too, didn't she? Isn't that the way the song goes?" It had been one of his favorites, back in his footloose days.

"Who really left, Beau?" She gave him a moment to answer, then sighed. The memory of facing each other in a bus station in some long-forgotten Texas town seemed to be floating out there in the middle of the lake. They saw it from different angles, different attendant feelings, maybe, but they saw it together, plain as day. "We both did, I guess," she said, answering her own question with a princess's studied diplomacy. "We went our separate ways."

"I asked you to give me some time, Abby. To hang in there with me just a little while, so I could—" He looked to her to know, to understand. She was looking at him, waiting, knowing he was about to repeat himself, a soft echo from the past. He glanced away before doing so. "Make something of myself."

"Hang in there with me," she quoted, dragging the phrase out like a rubber band. "What does that mean, Beau? I still don't understand."

"It means—" Hell. Pure hell.

There was nothing to do but pull her into his arms and show her, cover her protest with a hard, heavy, insistent kiss.

It started out that way, but the taste of her intervened. The sweet taste, soft scent and softer feel of her gentled him quickly. He drew back, then dipped his head at a new angle, less eager to show than to be shown. He had no idea what "hanging in there" meant, really, beyond the fact that he was willing to do it, doing it now. He was twisting in the wind, hoping she would accept the next kiss, and the next one. He was hungrier now for having tasted her, needier now for having taken her in his arms. He held her closer, breathed her warm breath, slipped his tongue between her lips and sought the shy greeting of hers.

Like coming home, he thought wildly when she put her arms around his waist and held him, too. After so much time had passed, so much loneliness, this was like coming home. When the kiss was over, they simply held each other for a time, her temple pressed against his cheek, his nose in her hair. He felt the butterfly kiss of her eyelashes as she blinked once, twice.

"It means be with me," he whispered, eyes closed as though daring at last to make a wish, even when it wasn't his birthday. "Wherever I am."

"I can't."

His heart fell to his too-often worthless knees.

"I mean, I *couldn't*. I couldn't just..." She drew back and looked into his eyes. "I couldn't live like that, Beau."

"I know. You had your own dreams."

She nodded. "Our dreams didn't fit together very well, did they?"

"I guess not." He smiled, bemused by the sadness in her eyes. "But everything else sure did."

She closed her eyes and uttered his name in a way that sounded more like an appeal than a denial. What could he do but answer with another kiss? And then another.

And then, because he could still taste her appeal on his lips, a reminder. "You loved me once."

"I... thought I did."

"Thought?" He touched her silky straight hair and smiled. *Thinking* didn't quite cut it. "You would have slept with me in a ditch beside the road."

"If I'd stayed with you..." She sighed as she pulled away from him. "I guess I would have."

He released her. The turnabout didn't work for him. He wanted her to acknowledge that once she had been willing to love him anytime, anywhere. *Willing*. Not doomed to.

"Is that what you think I had in mind for us?"

"I don't think you had anything in mind." She looked at him apologetically, as if she'd forgotten to give him due credit. "Except the next rodeo."

"And you had a lot on your mind. You were *thinking* you loved me." He laid his hands on her shoulders, squeezed lightly, insistently. "You know you loved me, Abby. You look at me now and you remember how it was. And it scares the hell out of you, because you *know* you loved me. Otherwise you wouldn't have slept with me at all."

She glanced away. "That's true."

"What's true?"

"I loved you." She sighed and put her hand on his shirt pocket, studying her fingers as they stirred, just slightly, as though testing the feel of him. "I fell in love with you much too hard, much too fast. I wasn't thinking at all."

"The thinking came later."

She nodded. "We've both made something of ourselves, Beau. You had to do it your way, and I had to do it mine."

"Guess so." He smiled, unconsciously rubbing her upper arms, his hardened hands abrading her smooth, sun-warmed skin. "Funny how what you've made of yourself and what I've made of myself just happened to cross paths again."

"I guess my interest in cowboy style is no coincidence." She patted his pocket, returning his smile as she backed away. "I admit it. I owe you that one."

He laughed. "You never saw me dressed in any shirts as fancy as the ones you're selling."

"You don't like them?"

"They're a little too pricey for a working man."

"You get to keep whatever we photograph you in." She reached out to him as she continued to back away, palms up, like a beneficent Madonna. "We want people to see that you really endorse the line."

"That's a pretty nice bonus."

"It's the only one you'll be getting."

He looked at her skeptically, but he was too much of a gentleman to point out that he'd just sampled the bonus he wanted. He reached for her hand. She slipped it readily into his, as though they'd been walking hand-in-hand without a ten-year interruption.

"So you're really not into camping anymore, huh?"

She laughed. "Give it up, cowboy."

"But you did love me, and you still like my style."

"I still *love* your style." She swung their hands between them as they walked. "I've invested in it heavily."

"And it's paid off," he concluded, his foolish heart swelling. "So you wanna see where I work? Meet my boss?"

"Do you think it's a place that would suit our needs?"

"Suits mine." He ducked a pine bough, then pushed the next one aside for his princess. "You'll have to see it and decide for yourself."

Chapter Three

The sign that topped the tall standards flanking the approach to the big log house read, Double B Bar Ranch. The gravel road traversed a pale green meadow bursting with purple and yellow wildflowers. Corrals and a big red barn were visible behind the house, which, Beau informed Abby as they approached the split-rail yard fence, was three-quarters of a mile from the road. Tall ponderosa pines marching up low-lying hills formed the backdrop.

"This is beautiful," Abby declared, alighting from Beau's pickup after he'd parked in the driveway next to a small white car. "Where do you stay? In the bunkhouse with the rest of the crew?"

"I get to stay in the house," Beau informed her. "I *am* the crew."

He ushered Abby up the steps to a small side porch, through the mudroom, where he tossed his hat on a wall peg next to a pair of chaps, then led her into an airy pine-and-white kitchen.

"Kate? You home?" The rapping of boot heels on hardwood echoed as he disappeared down the hallway beyond the kitchen, calling out, "Got somebody here wants to meet you, Kate. You decent?"

The door to the half bath off the kitchen popped open, and a stout, gray-haired woman emerged, towel in hand. "Of course I'm decent. It's the middle of the day." She noticed Abby, still standing near the back door. "Well, I'll be. He brought a lady friend."

"I hope we're not . . ."

Beau reappeared in the doorway.

"I've been out in the garden," the woman explained as she worked her hands over with the towel. "I've got dirt all under my . . ." She cast a scolding glance. "You should have warned me, Beau."

"I just did. Where's your hat?" He surveyed the top of his aunt's head as though she might be hiding something in her straggly gray updo. "Out in the sun without your hat again?"

"I must've left it outside somewhere." With a spotted, leathery hand she stuck a damp, stringy tendril behind each ear. The sun had long ago had its way with the lines in her face. She'd clearly spent the better part of a century outdoors. "You should have told me you were—"

"Abby, this stubborn woman who refuses to take it easy is my aunt Kate. She's the boss around here." He laid a hand on the old woman's stooped shoulder. "Kate, meet Abigail Van Patten."

"Abigail . . ." The old woman repeated the name slowly, the light gradually dawning in her eyes. She flashed Beau a look of surprise. "Is this that girl—"

He nodded once. "The lady who owns the new Western wear store, designs the clothes, hired me to be her poster boy. That's right, this is the one. I don't know if I mentioned it, Kate, but we're old friends, Abby and me.''

''Mentioned . . . ?'' Kate was both amused and confounded by his choice of words. ''I think you might have mentioned it once or twice, boy. Once or twice.'' She extended a well-dried hand. ''It's a real pleasure to meet you, Abigail.''

''We were just thinking,'' Beau began, hooking his arm around Kate's shoulders. ''Just wondering if you'd mind if we took some of the pictures for Abby's catalog out here at the place. Use the barn, the corrals, maybe a few cows for background.''

''Why would I mi—''

''Wouldn't get in the way of anything, and I'll make sure to get my chores done early, have everything looking just so.'' He winked at Abby over the top of Kate's gray locks. ''She's fussy about how the place looks when people come calling.''

''Me!''

''You,'' he insisted, squeezing her shoulder.

''I don't blame you,'' Abby said. ''If someone wanted to come barging in and interrupt my—''

''Abby's willing to pay for the use of the place for . . . I don't know.'' He shrugged. ''A day or something.''

''Pay?'' Kate reared back and peered at him as though he'd cursed. ''She's already paying you to be in the pictures. I don't see why—''

''Because that's the way it's done. Right, Abby?''

"Yes, that's standard practice. This is private property." Abby turned, tipping her head to take a look out the window over the gleaming stainless-steel sink. "And that old barn is just perfect. So much character."

"Well, it's, uh . . ." Kate traded another look with Beau. Hers was puzzled, his pointed. "Beau's been fixing it up. He's worked real hard shaping this place up."

"Just doing my job," Beau said. "'Course, you can let Abby off the hook on this rent thing if you want to, Kate. It's up to you."

"Have you gone loco?"

"That's what I thought. Business is business."

Kate shook her head as she ducked out from under Beau's arm. "He's gone plumb loco. As far as I'm concerned, you can take pictures of anything you see around here except for me." Mumbling, Kate reached for the handle on the refrigerator door. "I surely think you've lost your mind, boy."

"Hospitality," he quipped with a grin. "It's the code of the West. You're welcome to use the ranch free of charge, Miss Abigail."

"The ranch *hand* is another matter," Abby noted.

"Altogether another matter. He don't come cheap, on account of him being such a rare commodity." A groan erupted from behind the refrigerator door. Beau nudged the door, rattling the contents of its shelves. "Humor me, Kate. I thought I'd saddle up a couple of horses and show Abby around."

"Beau, I'm not dressed for—"

"That never stopped you before." He peeked over the door. "Kate, you got a clean pair of jeans Abby could borrow?"

"If she's not fussy about the fit." Brandishing two plastic bowls, Kate bumped the door closed with her backside. "How about showing her a sample of that Western hospitality you've been bragging up? Here's some leftover chicken and fixings that might make a nice picnic supper."

"How does a picnic supper sound, Miss Abigail?" Beau leaned against the counter, folded his arms and grinned. "We'll find us a nice little ditch by the side of the road."

"Ditch? What kind of devil's gotten into you today?" Kate set the bowls down and jerked a drawer open. "He can do better than that. This boy's got a beautiful—"

"Sense of humor," Beau interjected. "Abby's a city girl. It's fun to tease city girls. They think we're really roughing it out here in the sticks."

"You mind your manners, Beau. You don't be giving this lady a bad time." Kate wagged a serving spoon under Abby's nose. "You let me know if he does. I had a hand in raising him, and I can still give him what for."

They rode separate horses, which was no advantage over the first time they'd taken a ride together as far as Beau was concerned. He invited Abby to take the black so that she could see for herself how well-mannered the animal was, even if its owner was a little rough around the edges. He slung the canvas bag Kate had packed over his saddle horn and tied a plaid stadium blanket and a jacket behind the cantle. He was secretly eager to show Abby the rolling pastures tucked into the valleys among the pine-covered hills that made up his ranch.

His ranch. He would tell her that sooner or later, after she let him know what she thought of it. He wasn't ready to tell her just how big a piece of himself he was exposing on this outing. He might just as well have turned himself inside out for her inspection. This was it; this was his whole life now.

Beautiful, she kept saying.

Beautiful, yes, but beautiful enough? Enough for what, he couldn't say. Or wouldn't. Wasn't ready. Right now all he knew was that he wanted her to see that it was beautiful. Perfectly beautiful.

They shared their picnic on the blanket beside a swirling stream in the evening shade of a stand of lodgepole pines. There was a mountain chill in the air as soon as the sun went down, so he dropped the denim jacket he'd brought along over her shoulders, his hands lingering a moment longer than necessary.

She tipped her head to look at him, acknowledging his gesture with a smile. "What exactly did you tell your aunt Kate about me? That we were lovers once?"

"Lovers?" He smiled back and gave her shoulders a quick squeeze before returning to his spot on the blanket. "That's just between you and me, Abby."

"She knew *something* about me."

"I showed her your letter. *Jackie's* letter, but at the time I thought it was yours." He shrugged. "I just told her you were the most beautiful woman I'd ever met, and that I couldn't believe you were actually offering to *pay* me to get into your clothes."

She groaned. "Still incorrigible, despite your aunt's good intentions. Are you working for her or looking after her?"

"We're looking after each other, I guess. She lost her husband about a year ago. He was working out in the field, got struck by lightning."

"How awful."

"Maybe not." He pushed his hat back, one finger under the brim, and stared into the shadowy grass on the far side of the stream. "Carl never knew what hit him. He was seventy-eight years old, still active, didn't suffer from much besides a little arthritis, died at home at the end of a day's work. But Kate..." He felt his insides listing a little with the recent memory of seeing the old woman through a half-open door, sitting on her bed with a box of old pictures in her lap. "She misses him something terrible. That's the part that hurts. Being left behind."

Abby touched his knee.

He pretended he didn't notice.

"You never told me much about your family."

"Not a whole lot to tell." He stretched his legs out in front of him and leaned back on one elbow. "Carl and Kate were married for more than fifty years. Lived in the same house all that time. Never had any kids of their own."

"But she helped raise you?"

"I stayed with them off and on when I was a kid."

"I mean, who was she helping?"

"She's my dad's older sister."

"I remember you told me your father died when you were in high school," she said. "What about your mother?"

"I don't remember her very well." And it was a damn good time to change the subject. "Your parents still living back East?"

"They retired, sold the house and moved to Tampa," she answered quickly, determined to keep scratching around in barren ground. "Did your mother—"

"I don't know." He stared at her in the waning light, chafing at her notion that these were simple questions with obvious answers and that he was holding out on her. It embarrassed him that there was nothing to hold, annoyed him to have to repeat, "There's nothing to tell. I don't know much about my mother."

"I'm sorry." Her words came to him timidly, like the shrinking daylight. "I didn't mean to—"

"It's okay," he said abruptly. Then, in the gentle tone he'd intended, "It's okay."

She drew his jacket close around her shoulders and sat with him quietly for a while as twilight's rosy flush dissolved to purple. One by one the early stars appeared.

She turned her head toward the gurgling water. A bullfrog sang from somewhere along the bank, and another answered. Abby smiled. "It really is so beautiful here."

His spirits lifted. "You like it?"

"Very much. I fell in love with the West ten years ago, when we..." She acknowledged him with a look. "Well, when you showed it to me."

"We covered a lot of territory, didn't we?"

"I was hooked. I...didn't want to go back. So I got a job and stayed. I have a fabulous view of the mountains from my living room." She glanced away. "In Denver."

"Denver," he repeated with a curt nod. "These are just little hills here, compared to what you're used to."

"This is beautiful country."

"So when are you heading back?" He leaned back, crossing one booted ankle over the other. "To Denver."

"When I have everything I need to put the catalog together." She tipped her head, eyeing him speculatively. "And how long will *you* be here?"

The question took him by surprise.

"Working for your aunt," she clarified. "Don't look now, cowboy, but there's grass growing under your boots."

"Maybe I oughta take them off." He raised the top leg, stacked the heel of one boot on the toe of the other. "You cold?"

She shook her head.

"That water looks mighty tempting on a summer evening, doesn't it?"

"Tempting as in, wouldn't it be nice to shed our clothes and take a swim?" She had him grinning, remembering when. "No, it doesn't look that tempting."

"Just the footgear, then. It's too shallow for a swim, anyway, but we could wash the trail dust off our feet." He had his right boot off by the time the suggestion was out.

"Trail dust off our *feet?*" She watched him peel his sock off, then laughed—a bright, tinkling sound—and made short work of toeing off her tennis shoes.

"You don't have to worry about the pants," he assured her. "They look so damn cute on you, I wouldn't take 'em off you even if you asked me to."

"Not even if I—"

"Not even if you *begged* me to." But he claimed the honor of rolling the voluminous pants legs up to her knees. "Wanna try me?"

"I know better. Help me up." She let his jacket drop behind her and extended her hand.

He pulled her with him as he stood.

She groaned from the ground up. "I'm already sore. I feel like an old lady."

"It's just the pants, but don't even *think* about takin' 'em off." He stripped off his shirt, then bent to roll his pants legs up, giving her another once-over from his new vantage point. "Yep, they sure look cute. Kinda grannyish."

She hmphed. "Not as grannyish as those dough-boy-white legs of yours."

Laughing, he snatched her hand and towed her from the blanket. "Lady, you're asking to get wet."

It was a shallow stream, but the rocks were slippery, and the pants they'd carefully rolled up were soon soaked. Their laughter rolled back the years while the pale moon rose above them in a dusky Dakota sky. They splashed in cool water, teasing each other like fresh, innocent children, but they savored each other's teasing like a man and a woman long seasoned in the intimate knowing of each other. Both fantasies were liberating. Both fit just fine.

She slipped. He caught her, but she sagged like a sling, water sloshing around her waist, and they laughed as he dragged her up. "Your pants are drooping," he taunted.

It was true. She shrieked and giggled, pulling the waistband up and down to show him not her white silk panties—though she did that, too—but her slim hips and slimmer waist.

"Well, of course, they are. They're too big!"

"Don't take 'em off, now, jeez." He grabbed a fistful of waistband as he hauled her up against him. "Let's have a little modesty here."

"Easy for you to say, since you're wearing your own pants. These stayed on me better dry."

"Shoulda kept them dry, then." Grinning, he lined her hips up with his. "You brought this on yourself, makin' fun of my legs. I may not look it, but I'm a very sensitive guy."

"If I had a belt..." She tucked a forefinger into his belt and coaxed sweetly. "Maybe I could borrow yours?"

"And have my pants falling down, too?"

"Yeah, right, they fit you like..." She tugged playfully. "A true gentleman would offer a lady his belt."

"That's a new one." He slogged backward a couple of steps as he unbuckled his belt and jerked it through the loops of his jeans. "Come get it."

She sloshed toward him, smiling, inhibitions gone the way of her dignity. It was hard to be dignified with droopy drawers.

"Here, let me help you with this." He grasped the ends of the belt, lifted it over her head, looped it around her bottom and used it to pull her to him again. "You wanna borrow my belt, huh?"

Tucking her thumbs into his side belt loops, she nodded. "If you'd be so kind."

"This is a very special belt. There's a trick to buckling it."

"I know clothes like you know horses. I'm a professional."

"You look like a professional." With little tugs he bounced her against him. "What are you gonna give me for the use of my belt?"

"You said you wouldn't cost me anything today."

"I said *I* was free," he reminded her. "But not my belt. This is a *very* special belt."

"So you said."

"How 'bout a kiss?"

"One kiss."

"From your lips to mine." He leaned closer. "But it's gotta be the right kind of kiss."

"What's the right kind of kiss?"

"Slow and juicy."

"Okay, it's a deal." She lifted her face, closed her eyes and presented her soft, full, irresistible lips.

But he resisted.

"You have to give *me* a kiss. You think I'm giving you my belt *plus* a kiss? What the hell kind of horse tradin' would that be?"

She pouted. "Belt first."

He tugged on the prize, bouncing her against him, hipbone to hipbone. "I'd say you're in no position to dictate terms."

"Get your mouth down here, then."

"Make me. It's your move."

She put her arms around his neck, drew his head down and touched her lips to his. He didn't make it easy for her. He didn't move his lips at first except to smile and tease and call for more juice.

So she gave it to him. She parted his lips with her tongue and used it to tease him. To please him. To ply her wiles on him and ply the recesses of his mouth with as delicious a morsel as ever he'd tasted.

His belt slid into the water with a soft plunk. Her baggy jeans drooped below the fullness of her hips. His hands spread over damp silk panties, cupped her bottom as she arched against him. They became a column of flame, surrounded by water. And it burned high and long. He let her end it when she would, wishing—well, *hoping*—that would be never.

"How was that?"

She sounded as breathless as he felt. His eyes were still closed, his mouth tingling, his heart hammering in his chest.

He swallowed, nodded, let his eyes drift open. "Not bad."

"Worth your belt?"

"What belt?"

"Your very special belt."

"Oh, yeah." He sighed. "Definitely. I'll even fish it out of the water for you." Which he did, thoroughly enjoying the fact that while he was fishing, her hand lingered on his bare shoulder even as his lingered at her hip.

"I'll even put it on for you." He took his time threading it through her loops, doing it by feel, letting his eyes smile unabashedly into hers. "Kinda tricky to buckle."

"So you said."

"You know what?" He touched her nose. "I think your nose is getting red. You need a hat."

"Do I really? " She giggled. "Am I getting moon burn?"

"Now this . . ." He touched the brim of the hat that rarely left his head. "This is a very special hat. What am I bid for the use of this hat?"

They set up the first outdoor shoot near a stock tank. They used corral panels, barbed wire fence, the water pump, a calf and a horse as props, prairie grass and purple hills touching blue sky as backdrop and a tent for a dressing room. It would have been perfect, in Abby's estimation, except that photographer Tom Banks wanted to "feel the attraction" between his models in every shot.

"Smile for him," Tom kept saying. "He's just dying for a kiss, but all he gets is a smile, so make it count, Gayle. Nice one." Click. "*Niiice* one."

Abby studied the list on her clipboard. They did look cute together, she had to admit that. Which was exactly what she wanted. But she and Beau had gotten a little silly the other night, a little drunk on moonlight and mountain air, so it irritated her now to watch another woman put her hands on him. Simple hangover. Beau Lassiter's charm was notoriously intoxicating. Even now, Gayle Browning was showing all the symptoms.

Little sips, Abby wanted to warn her. *You don't want to get addicted. He's one of a kind, and he's only passing through.*

"Too much shade on his face," Tom told Jackie. "The hat."

Jackie motioned to Beau for an adjustment. "And while we're at it, Beau, let's fix that shirt."

"Did I miss a snap?"

"I'd say you did up one too many." Gayle slid four fingers into his shirtfront and flicked a pearlized snap open with her thumb. "Maybe two too many."

"You're on the right track, but, uh..." Jackie stepped behind Tom to get a camera-lens view. "Just the one. We don't want to ruin the line."

"Try it both ways," Tom suggested, his camera whirring as he snapped shot after shot.

"There." Gayle patted Beau's shirtfront. "Now let's spice it up a little." She slipped her fingers inside the shirt, caressed the snap with her thumb and coyly peeked at him through her thick lashes. The camera kept clicking. "There, just a hint of spice. Just a touch."

The horse at Beau's back snorted.

"This is a catalog, not a soap opera," Abby grumbled. "Even the horse is losing patience."

Beau laughed, and the camera clicked again. "He'll hang in there as long as I do."

"I can stroke *his* chest, too."

"That's good," Tom said. "Do that again, Gayle."

"So many chests," the pretty model crooned, attending to Beau's. "So little time."

"Exactly." Abby checked her watch. "I don't know what I'm doing here. I have work to do. This is—" She handed Jackie the clipboard. "I leave it all in your capable hands. Yours and Gayle's."

"It's time for them to change, anyway. Maybe we ought to break for—"

"Let's get on with it," Beau said. "Take as many pictures as you want and quit when you're done."

Gayle laughed. "This man is obviously not union."

"I'm used to setting my own hours, and they're generally sunup to sundown when there's a job to be done." He jerked his shirttail free of his belt. "What's next?"

"Abby has a list here," Jackie said, perusing the notes.

Abby was heading for her car.

"Hey, boss lady," Beau called as he strode through the grass to catch up with her. "Before you take off, how about giving me a rundown."

She turned, questioning his purpose with a look. He grinned. Stopping her might have been part of it, but it was silly to let that notion tickle her fancy.

It did, though.

He propped his elbow on the roof of her car, which was parked on the shady side of the dressing-room tent. "I've never had a woman around to tell me what to wear. Always wondered what it would be like."

"Not your style, I'm sure."

"Why not?" He nodded toward the tent, where they both knew she had clothes waiting for him. "Most guys don't have much of an eye for putting clothes together. You've got all those shirts in there, half a dozen hats. I only own two hats." He started popping open the snaps on his shirt. "When you first met me, I only owned one. You changed my luck. I started winning. Then I bought more hats. But now I'm down to two—" he took the white Stetson off and set it carefully on her head "—very special hats." He paused to give her a meaningful look. "Gayle's the one who's not my style."

"Poor Beau." She ignored the claim, clearly meant to butter her up. "The truth is, you were doing just fine before we met and even better after we parted company."

"How do you know?" He adjusted the hat, cocking it to one side, then tipping her chin up to see how it looked. "Fact is, you changed my luck. You should've stuck around. For a while there, I was dressin' pretty fancy. Hats to match my pants. Belts to match my boots. Shirts to match my eyes." He smiled when she automatically looked into his eyes as though checking to see if they'd changed. "Remember that one you picked out for me? You said it matched my eyes."

She glanced away. Of course she remembered. He'd said the embroidery on the yoke was "pretty damn fancy." He'd looked gorgeous in it.

"I still have it."

She wasn't about to ask him whether he ever wore it. It didn't matter. "I made a list. There are—"

"Abby." His hands felt warm and heavy on her shoulders. His voice was achingly deep, touching her deeply. "What's wrong?"

"Nothing."

"Was I was out of line the other night?"

"No," she said quickly. "I was."

"It was just a little kissing."

He'd wrapped her in his jacket and built a fire after they came out of the water. They'd sat beside it, watching the flames dance while they held each other and talked. And then they'd kissed a little more. It had been hard to keep it at that. Hard and sweet and full of false promise.

His hands stirred on her shoulders. "Surprised the hell out of both of us, didn't it? Just like it did the first time. We never expected—"

She shook her head. "It was easier to surprise me then."

"Easier than what?"

She couldn't say.

"It wasn't hard or easy, Abby, it was natural. It just *was*. No games, no putting on some kind of show. It just was."

"Exactly. It just was." She took the hat off and plopped it on his head. "The gray hat goes with the red shirt, and the black one goes with the blue shirt."

"The one that matches my eyes?"

"Perfectly." Eyes that would not release hers, but she refused to let him see how weak in the knees she suddenly felt.

"What really surprises you is that it still comes just as easy. Just as natural. And it feels just as good as it ever did."

"Cowboy modesty," she observed. "I think the reason it's so effective is that it's unabashedly transparent, even when you forget to say, 'Shucks, ma'am.'"

"The way it felt surprised you, didn't it?"

"No, it did not. Kissing is one of my favorite pastimes. I wish I had more time for it, but I—"

He put a stop to her sarcasm with the kind of kiss she would always have time for. He came away smiling, having tasted the truth.

"But you don't?"

She took a deep breath, unwilling to admit he'd stolen hers. "Rarely."

"Let's make time," he insisted. "For as long as you're here."

"You've got work to do." She stepped back, allowing herself a glance at his beautiful, stout, smooth chest. "Sunup to sundown, remember? A cowboy's work is never done, and your other boss lady deserves to get what she's paying for, too."

"Women can be real slave drivers," he complained as he stripped off his shirt and handed it to her, as though the look in her eyes had given him a command.

He reached inside the tent and snatched a blue chambray shirt off the line they had rigged up. "This looks like a work shirt. How many snaps do you want open?" He slipped it on, then took a wide, challenging stance, hands on hips. "Show me. You're the professional here." To her reproving look he replied, "Gayle wouldn't hesitate to show me."

"Neither would I." She started with the second snap. "And this isn't a work shirt. It sells for seventy-eight dollars. No one in his right mind would round up cows wearing it." Two snaps and her mouth had gone dry, but she did up the rest, then backed away.

Then she watched his hands disappear under the long shirttails, listened to the chink of his belt buckle, the click of a snap, the hum of the zipper on the jeans that bore her label. All he was doing was tucking in his shirt. But she was fascinated.

And he knew it, damn him. She didn't even have to look at his face. She knew he was smiling.

"Just wear it whatever way you would naturally wear it," she said needlessly as she started to turn away.

"I'd probably roll the cuffs, save 'em from getting frayed." He demonstrated on the left side, baring a powerful forearm.

She was mesmerized. There was something about the softer side of a man's forearm.

"Unless I was roping or riding rough stock," he continued as he attended to the other cuff. "PRCA regulations. Long sleeves."

She nodded. "It looks good on you just like that."

"Would you consider going out with your hired man?"

She looked up, waiting.

"Fourth of July rodeo," he explained. "I need a date. Around here, it's bigger than New Year's Eve. It really looks bad if you don't have a date. Pitiful, in fact."

She lifted her brow. "Worse than a woman going out with the hired man?"

He lifted a shoulder, offered a crooked, cocky smile. "Better than no man at all."

"And squiring the boss lady is—"

"Some might say a guy would have to be hard up, especially if she's got some age on her. With you, more like he'd have to be pretty uppity." He laid a finger on her chin, touched his thumb to her lower lip. "But, hell, I've always been long on nerve and short on sense."

"I only seem to have that problem when I'm around you."

"Catching, is it? Guess it's too late to worry about that now." The backs of his fingers skimmed her neck on their way to tracing the edge of her scoop-neck blouse. His voice caressed her. "Make time for me as long as you're here."

"All right."

"We've got a date for the rodeo, then?"

She smiled. What could it hurt? "A date for the rodeo."

Chapter Four

Abby hadn't been to a rodeo in ten years. In one of her few foolish caprices, she had regarded rodeo as her rival, but she'd carefully guarded her jealousy. She'd been able to name her business for the master of the sport, design clothing celebrating its events and still tell herself, if you've seen one rodeo, you've seen 'em all.

But it wasn't true. When Beau regaled her with his little surprise—that as a former world champion he'd agreed to ride exhibition in the saddle bronc event at the Rapid City Fourth of July Rodeo—she realized that rodeos were not all the same. With Beau on the program, the whole show was suddenly bigger and better. More exciting. More dangerous.

He was wearing one of her shirts—blue on blue, to match his eyes—and Tom Banks was on hand to shoot some pictures. Beau told her this was a bonus. No hazardous duty pay required. He was going to do it anyway, just for fun, so he figured, why not lend some authenticity to her catalog? She was skeptical, worried about him getting hurt, but he dismissed her worries with a confident smile.

He sat with her in the outdoor bleachers through the bareback event. They laughed at the clowns' jokes even though Abby remembered hearing some of them ten years ago. Beau reminded her that the clowns' role as comedian was secondary. Like the two mounted pickup men, they were part of the cowboys' meager safety net. The clowns' real performance came during the bull riding, the final event, when their red bulb noses and baggy overalls would suddenly seem incongruous with the perilous role of bullfighter with no weapons except agility and wit.

"That was my first ambition in life," Beau told her. "My dad took me to a rodeo when I was five or six, and I got to be part of this one clown's dog trick. For years after that, I was gonna be a rodeo clown when I grew up."

She tried to picture a plastic red nose stuck in the middle of his ruggedly handsome face. She told him the image warred with his cowboy pride. He told her to hold that thought and give him a kiss for luck, and he left her to watch the steer wrestling event without him. He'd never taken her behind the chutes before a ride. It was enough to know that she was there with him, he said, but seeing her might break his concentration.

The announcement of his name nearly brought down the house. He'd been their champion since he'd won his title. But long before that he'd been *her* champion, and his name rocked her house, too. The house that held her heart.

She joined in the thunderous applause, then held her breath and clenched her hands between her knees as she watched him risk his precious neck to ride his

wild horse. The fringed chaps she'd seen hanging in
Aunt Kate's mudroom flapped about his knees as he
leaned back and spurred his bucking mount. Which
leg had he injured? she wondered, suddenly realizing
she'd never asked. Did it hurt now? She counted the
seconds until the signal sounded and Beau bailed out
of the saddle.

It was the landing that undid him. He went down on
his right knee, the *wrong* knee. She could tell by the
way he took his time dragging himself to his feet despite the fact that the horse's hooves were still flying
through the air not far from his head. The pickup rider
interceded, releasing the bronc's bucking strap as he
hazed the animal toward the far side of the arena. One
of the cowboys working the gates started toward Beau,
but he waved the man away, tipped his hat in defer-
ence to the applause and made a slightly gimpy exit.

Abby met him behind the chutes. He didn't see her
at first. He was leaning against a portable corral panel,
catching his breath, collecting himself, mentally beating back pain. She battled her initial instinct to take
him in her arms. In front of his fellow cowboys, he
would hate that. She laid her hand on his back instead, and she could feel him trembling.

"Are you okay?"

"Sure." He straightened, pushed his hat back and
managed a smile on a face emptied of its normally
healthy color. "That limp is an important part of the
show. Haven't you noticed? About half the time the
cowboy limps out of the arena." His gesture took in

an array of men and women behind the chutes, most of them dressed in hats and boots that would have fit right into the All-Around Cowboy Blues catalog. "See all these girls, ready and willing to say—" His eyes said this was her cue. " 'Here, honey, lean on me.' "

"They're *women,* not..." But the solicitation in his eyes was too appealing to resist. She slipped her arm around his waist, secretly pleased to carry out her first impulse. "Okay, okay. Here, honey, lean on me."

"Yeah." He put his arm around her shoulders and smiled, his color returning. "See how that works?"

"What do you need? Heat? Ice?"

"What I need is a damn good kiss." Her doubtful look made him laugh. "I ain't kiddin' ya. Right here, right now, what I need is one of those long, slow—"

She slipped her free hand around the back of his neck, drew his head down and obliged him.

An appreciative whistle from somewhere in the periphery thwarted the long and slow part of the order.

"Hoo-whee! Nice one, Lassiter."

Beau came up grinning. "Hey, Dallas, how've you been?"

"Not *that* good, but gettin' by." A wiry, quick-talking cowboy with the number twenty-eight plastered across his back slapped Beau's shoulder. "I'm on deck now. Like the lady says, that was a nice ride. Ever think about turning pro?"

"Pro rodeo?" Beau laughed. "A guy'd have to be crazy to do that for a living."

"Better watch yourself, ma'am." The man's thick mustache twitched in a lopsided smile. "Any guy who'd do it for love is crazier yet."

"Hell, that's the mark of a *real* cowboy," Beau cheerfully averred as the man hurried away. "Hang in there till they blow the whistle, Dallas."

Beau's smile faded. He glanced at Abby.

"Ice or heat?" she repeated.

"Ice. After the fireworks."

"Now," she insisted, discovering a motherly tone in her repertoire. "Otherwise it won't do any good."

"Let's try something new." He started loosening the chap buckles on the back of his right thigh. "Compromise."

Abby set to work on the left side.

He smiled. "What do you say we pick up some ice and go someplace where we can watch the fireworks and lick my wounds in private?"

"I'll apply ice to your wounds, cowboy, but that's as far as I go."

"No kisses?"

"Depends. How bad are you swelling?"

"'Bout ready to bust." He waited until she glanced up, her hand still working the top buckle. "Oh, you mean my knee? Not too bad."

They bought a bag of ice and some cold drinks and drove into the hills. Beau had an isolated spot picked out high on a ridge, close to the stars. He took some pills from a bottle prescribed for the occasional flare-ups in his joints, and they settled down together on a blanket in a nest of tall grass.

"This is beautiful," she said of the site and the night and the arm that served her as a pillow. "Quite a plan you came up with."

And then came the flash, the shattering, the shower of glittering gold fragments followed by a crackle and a diffusion of pink shards, dazzling in an inky sky.

"Ooooh, look at that one."

"Some plan, all right." He cuddled her close to his side, grunting with the pain of shifting his right leg. "That's exactly the way I planned on hearing you sigh."

"That's what fireworks are for." She laid a comforting hand on his flat abdomen. "Oohing and ahing. Are you okay?"

"The sighing was part of the plan. My groans of complaint were not." His hand settled over hers. "Sorry I made you miss the rest of the show."

"I saw the best part. The hot-damnedest cowboy on the rodeo circuit."

He groaned again. "Did I actually say that?"

"You surely did, and I believed every word. You miss it, don't you?"

"I was about ready to hang it up anyway. My plan was to quit while I was on top. As it turned out, I entered one rodeo too many, but that would have been my last season anyway."

"Really, Beau, why did you ride tonight? I know it wasn't for the catalog."

"For old times' sake, I guess." He chuckled. "Ah, hell, I was showing off. For you."

She lifted her head abruptly and turned until she could see his face. "For me?"

"It's a holiday." He smiled sheepishly. "I was celebrating."

"Celebrating independence?"

"Celebrating summer. *This* summer." With a hand on her head, he urged her to settle down while he elaborated. "I saw this movie once. Guy and a girl stretched out on a blanket on a summer night, holding each other, fireworks exploding all around them in the night sky, and they were just lovin' it up."

"The fireworks?"

"Each other. Kissing like crazy." A burst of pink sparks morphing into a splash of green gave him pause while she hummed appreciatively. "Just like in the movie," he said. "I was about twelve when I saw it, and at first I was thinking, 'Maybe Dad would let me get some Roman candles.' Then I noticed how the girl opened her mouth a little just before their lips touched, and I had this weird sensation deep in my gut. All of a sudden I was thinking, 'Maybe kissing a girl wouldn't feel half bad.'"

"Did you see this movie with a girl?"

"I wasn't *that* far along," he said with a chuckle. "My dad used to take me to the show once in a while. Drive-ins, mostly." He sought her hand again, tucked it against his chest as he spoke. "My ol' man always worked long hours in the summertime. The drive-in shows didn't start until dusk, and kids got in free. He'd hook the speaker box on my side of the pickup, and I'd always have to wake him up when it was time to go.''

''It's usually the kids who fall asleep at the drive-in,'' she mused, hoping to keep his reminiscences coming. ''Did you wear your jammies? I always did.''

''You kiddin', lady? Cowboys don't wear *jammies*.'' He jiggled her with a playful hug. ''Anyway, I never had any trouble staying awake. My dad was usually asleep by the time the singing popcorn box and dancing candy bars came on. Usually had his eyes closed, anyway. But you got your cartoons and your two shows for the price of one. Hell of a deal, those drive-ins. My dad was—''

A double, triple, quadruple technicolor feature burst forth in the night sky.

''Damn, that's a beauty!''

''Mmm.'' Abby was eager for more details, but she tried not to show it. She waited a moment. Two, three. ''Your dad was what?''

''My dad was a cowboy.'' While neither of them was looking, he laced his fingers through hers. ''He didn't rodeo except for amateur, backyard stuff, but he could ride anything with four legs, rope anything that moved. He was a real working cowboy. Dying breed. Made his living working cows.''

''Did he ranch?''

''Never did. He always hired out. Slept in a bunk-house or spare room, took his meals at some other man's table." Absently, lightly, he rubbed the inside of her wrist with his thumb. "He kept me with him as much as he could, whenever his boss would allow it. Lotta times they would. If they didn't have room, I'd stay with Aunt Kate. But I learned a lot from my ol' man."

"So you've always been a gypsy," she concluded.

"In a way. I changed schools a lot, but I got through." He sighed and pulled her closer. "We always wanted a place of our own, him and me. We were gonna be partners. But you get your own place, you take on the boss's problems. Instead of him, it's you battling with markets and weather and bookkeeping mistakes. Real life instead of movies." He chuckled. "Who needs more headaches, right?"

"You and your movies," she said, rising over him.

"I learned some things from movies." He smiled wistfully as he tucked one arm beneath his head and traced the line of her jaw with his forefinger. "I learned about taxis and subways, what a house in the suburbs looks like inside...." He drew a path from the middle of her chin down her neck and over her chest to the first hint of cleavage, where her Western blouse halted his progress. He arched an eyebrow. "I learned all about what women wear under their dresses."

"There are lots of sources for that information." She heard the click of a snap, felt the slack in her shirt, the quick flutter in her throat. "Catalogs, for instance, or magazines."

"I grew up around men, mostly. They were big on *Western Horseman* and *Playboy*. Not a true picture of the average female." They drank anticipation from each other's eyes. His fingers feathered over the swell of her breast. One corner of his mouth turned up slightly as his little finger tested the elasticity of the trim on her bra cup. "First time I ever touched silk..."

"True or not, I like the idea that it was mine."

"I wouldn't lie to you about a thing like that." He lifted his head and flicked his tongue where his fingers had been. "You were my first silk. First lady, my first..." Another snap came apart, and another, at his urging. He kissed her squarely between her breasts and whispered, "My only lady."

There was no stopping the thrill that started in her epicenter and zipped through her veins.

"I want to make love to you tonight, Abby."

"I know."

"I want to let you feel those fireworks."

"I do." She could hear them, still popping above her, and she imagined them showering her, sizzling her. He nuzzled her bra cup aside and nibbled at her breast, which felt tingly and tight and terribly confined. "I already do."

"Just sparklers." Her bra's front fastening went slack. "Let me light one here." He pushed her bra aside with his cheek, brushed a kiss over the swell and touched his tongue to her nipple.

"I've always loved sparklers." She closed her eyes and savored the sparks, the pins and needles created by his lips and tongue. Her nipple tightened more. She drew a deep, shaky breath.

"You watch the sky." He reversed their positions, careful to keep his weight off his injured leg as he laid her down beneath him. "I'll give you sparklers first, then Roman candles."

"What I want is cowboy lovin'," she said.

"You got it, honey." He smoothed her hair from her temple. She turned her face into his palm and heard the catch in his breath when she kissed the tough-skinned heel of his hand. "As much as you want me to give you."

"As much as you have," she said. She unsnapped his shirt, unhooked his belt buckle.

"Don't tease me, now."

"I want to," she whispered against his mouth as she unzipped his jeans. "And I want you to tease me."

A little teasing went a long way, driving them both to distraction. They made love the way the teenagers in the drive-in movie might have—the ones on the screen or the ones fogging up the windows of their cars. Once the fireworks got started, they had little patience with clothing. They tugged denim and silk as far out of the way as necessary to get to each other, to touch and be touched, pleasure and be pleasured. By turns each was bold and bashful, each giving, each grasping for more of the other, creating sensations as wondrous as the kaleidoscopic starbursts that filled the night sky with enchantment.

He filled her the same way, his love spilling into every part of her body and mind so that, when it was over, she still needed his arms around her, his voice and his heat and his breath around her, to hold her together for a while, to protect this thin-skinned, ripe, full-to-overflowing creature he had made of her. For the moment she was content to stay that way, enmeshed with him under the stars.

On the day Jackie had scheduled for taking pictures at the stockyards, Abby went to visit Aunt Kate. The old woman was pleased to see her. She offered a long list of treats—iced tea, pop, cookies, rhubarb cake. Abby accepted the tea.

"But I really came to ask a favor," she said as she followed Kate from the kitchen down the hallway. "We're going to do an indoor shoot. I'd like to use a real living room, one that has a lived-in feel, and this is perfect." She took a seat on the leather sofa, which faced a massive stone fireplace.

Kate set horseshoe-shaped coasters on the rustic pine coffee table. "Have you talked to Beau about this?"

Abby shook her head. "I thought I'd come directly to you. I really would want to pay you for the privilege, for the inconvenience."

"You like this living room?" Kate glanced at the exposed pine beams as she settled herself into a big easy chair, relying heavily on its arms for support.

"It's lovely," Abby said on the tail end of a sip of very sweet tea. "Lovely probably isn't a good word. It's bold, striking, warm and comfortable. It feels protective, like an inviting refuge."

"Like a man's embrace?" Kate gave the comparison a moment to sink in. "Beau's, maybe?"

"It has a masculine feel to it, yes. Beau told me about your husband. I can't imagine what it would be like to lose a man after fifty years together. It must be—"

Kate shook her head. "I can't imagine what it would have been like to have spent those years without him. I'm glad I didn't have to."

Abby noticed the absence of photographs and mementos on the walls. Western art hung in heavy frames, an antique rifle above the fireplace mantel. The shelves held mostly books. Maybe looking at family pictures was still painful for Kate.

"How old is this house? It doesn't look..." Abby shrugged. "But you lived in it throughout your marriage, didn't you?"

"Does this look like fifty years' worth of memories to you?" Kate laughed. "Carl used to say that I was a pack rat, but I'll tell you what, it took me months to go through all the stuff that man had saved over the years."

"I'll bet that was hard."

"It was hard at first, until I let the joy take over from the sorrow. His belongings weren't him, but they were friends of his. Companions while he was here. He left them behind. Now *me,* it's gonna take more than a bolt of lightning to shake him loose of me once I..." The old woman's eyes brightened at the prospect. "I know I'll see him again."

"I'm sure you will." Abby noticed an elaborately appointed silver-trimmed saddle displayed on a tall stand in the corner of the room. "Was that your husband's?"

"That's Beau's."

"Oh." It looked like a collector's item, and she didn't take Beau for a collector. Must have been a rodeo trophy. "What about the old rifle?"

"That's Beau's, too." Kate's odd stare was beginning to make Abby uncomfortable. "You beginning to get the picture?" the old woman asked.

"Beau's more like a son to you than a nephew," Abby inferred.

Kate sighed, then smiled, her old head brimming with fond memories. "His dad was like a son to me, and Beau's a lot like Billy. Prideful. Stubborn. Head full of dreams." She leaned forward in her chair, her eyes twinkling. "A hopeless romantic from the get-go, like all cowboys."

"Charming and free-spirited," Abby added.

"And tenderhearted. Beau's got him a tough hide, but that boy's about as tenderhearted as they come. When he loves somebody..." Kate's smile turned melancholy, her attention drifting to a tall window and beyond. "A cowboy will carry a torch to his grave. Did Beau ever tell you about his mama?"

"He says he doesn't know much about her."

"Only what Billy told him, and Beau's got sense enough to know about half that's the stuff fairy tales are made of. Billy met the love of his life when he was laid up in the hospital, after he got stepped on by a bull. Charlotte, her name was. Beau's mama," Kate explained, "not the bull."

"I got that," Abby said, smiling.

"See, now, you can catch on when you're workin' at it," Kate instructed with a wag of her finger. "Anyway, Charlotte was my little brother's angel of mercy."

"A nurse?"

"She was some kind of a hospital volunteer, I think. Anyway, she was a college girl. She came from a different world. But that Billy, he was a real looker. Well, you can just imagine from lookin' at his son. And he was a cowboy. Charm that wouldn't quit."

"I can just imagine."

"But I'll tell you what, Miss Abigail." Kate's eyes glistened as she leaned forward again, punctuating her revelation with a firm nod. "He loved that woman till his dyin' day, and nobody ever dared criticize her for leaving him and the boy, not while Billy was around. She was his princess. She belonged in a castle."

"His p-princess?" The beginning of the word stuck to Abby's lips.

"That's what Billy used to call her."

"And she deserted Beau?"

"And Billy," Kate said, nodding. "They weren't married, you see. Billy wanted the baby. Charlotte didn't. So..." She reached across the coffee table and slammed her glass on the coaster, sloshing the tea. "It's unnatural, if you ask me. A woman going off and leaving her little boy. But Billy never asked me, and neither has Beau. So I don't say anything." She eyed Abby long and hard. "And I'm only telling you because...well, you seem like the kind of woman who might want to know about something like that. The kind who might take it into account and try to understand."

"Knowing a cowboy is one thing. Understanding him is something else."

"That's because he keeps a lot inside. Always has, always will." Kate tapped a wrinkled finger to her saggy breast. "But you got to know it's here. You got to feel it in him. And *for* him." She peered hard through her spectacles. "I can see you do."

"Where...where do you think he'll go after he leaves here?"

"He won't leave here. He'll never leave here, unless something..." The old woman sat back, watching Abby, taking a moment to choose her words. "Beau's had a hard year. He won't tell you that, either, but that's why he needed the extra job. He's had a hard ten years. He's had a hard *life*. But he'll hang on here because this is his home." She waited for Abby's reaction, but all she got was a smile for her kindness. "It's *his*, Abigail. Not mine. He saved up his winnings to buy his dream, his and Billy's. The ranch belongs to Beau.''

Beau's ranch? "He said he worked for you, that you were his boss."

Kate laughed. "I'm more than willing to turn that job over to the right woman."

"But... why didn't he just tell me?"

"That the place is his?" Kate shook her head and sighed. "Who knows? Pride, maybe."

"Pride?"

"Like I said, he's had a hard year. Who knows what he's thinking, what he might be afraid of? Losing it, maybe, losing you. He don't talk much about his fears, but since he's human, you can be sure he carries a few, somewhere deep down inside himself." Instructively she added, "Free-spirited don't necessarily mean fancy-free. Beau's always wanted a home."

"So have I," Abby said. "With a husband and children."

"Did you happen to mention that to him?"

"We've talked about dreams. His dream of winning a PRCA championship, and mine of designing and selling—" The answer was no, she hadn't. She had her pride, too. She laughed and plucked at her skirt "Clothes. *Clothes,* of all frivolous things."

"We all need clothes," Kate allowed. "Looks like you both did what you wanted. Happy?"

"It's good to realize those ambitions. I'm sure Beau would agree." But she was willing to admit what the old woman already knew. "It's good to see him again. Really good."

Kate nodded. "His heart is as true as you'll find, and I'm guessin' it belongs to you."

"He's never said that."

"Men don't always know what needs to be said," Kate pointed out. "I'm not saying you two wouldn't have a lot to work out between you. You try to put two lives together to make a marriage, you always got a lot to work out. That's just the way it is. But I'm here to tell you, it's worth putting in some lifelong effort." Remembrance warmed her gray eyes as she cautioned, "If you love each other enough."

"That's the question, isn't it? How much is enough?"

"You really like this house?"

"Very much."

"You tell him that." Kate reached for her glass again and raised it in salute. "When you tell him I said you could come on inside and take your pictures."

Chapter Five

It had been her own idea, and a good one, but it made Abby uncomfortable to stand around watching them carry it out. She saw Beau and Gayle through two clothing changes before she joined Kate at the kitchen table for a glass of lemonade. "They're taking the romantic shots in front of the fireplace, and it's hotter than blue blazes in there," Abby explained after she'd sucked down a third of the glass.

Kate chuckled. "Got a fire going?"

"Roaring, which is, I'll admit, just what I asked for."

"I mean you. You've got a fire going." Kate pulled at her own boat neckline, pumping it as if to create a breeze. "A little hot under the collar, aren't you?"

"Oh, Gayle's such a flirt," Abby admitted disgustedly.

"She's pretty, too."

"She's beautiful." A curt gesture diminished the compliment. "Well, she's a model. What do I expect?"

"You could be a model yourself."

"Cameras hate me," Abby claimed. "And, of course, the feeling is mutual."

"They don't do me any favors, either, but then I'm—"

Jackie stuck her head in the door. "Abby, we need your opinion on something. Your support, actually." She included Kate with a nod. "Yours, too, Mrs. Bristol. Beau's giving us a hard time about baring that wonderful chest of his."

The pajamas were made of silk, the color of red earth, and the only Western motif was a rope worked into the monogram along with the two initials of "all the name she'd bought." And the man looked gorgeous in them.

But he was not happy.

He stood his ground before the fireplace like the King of Siam, greeting Abby and Kate with a stern warning finger. "Now, you two stay out of this. Go back in the kitchen and try to figure out what those pots and pans are for."

"That settles it, Jackie," Abby said. "Whatever the problem, we're on your side."

"I don't care what kind of reinforcements you bring in, I don't do nudity." He grabbed two handfuls of unbuttoned silk shirt. "This is bad enough."

"You obviously go out without a shirt sometimes, Beau," Gayle injected from the post she'd taken up on the sofa. "You have a great tan."

"I work outside. It gets hot, nobody's around, I take my shirt off. Took my hat off a few times lately, just to make you guys happy. But I am not—" He glared directly at Abby and shook his head. "It's not in my contract, and I'm not doin' it. I hardly know this woman."

Abby gave Jackie an incredulous look. "Wait a minute, what—"

"We just thought it would be cute if she wore the top and he wore the bottom."

"Cute." Abby considered the idea. She looked at Gayle, who was dressed in a robe, then eyed the pajamas. Not him. Just the pajamas. Finally she lifted one brow, turned the corners of her mouth down and shrugged. "Cute."

"Then *you* do it," Beau challenged.

Abby laughed. "Oh, that would be *really* cute."

His blue eyes warmed to the prospect of a dare. "I'll do it if you'll do it."

"What?" Abby's eyes shared none of the warmth of his. "Don't be ridiculous."

"Pajamas are ridiculous. Getting my picture taken in pajamas is downright humiliating. But sharing pajamas with just any woman is indecent. Isn't that right, Aunt Kate?" Kate's jaw dropped, but before she was able to comment, Beau gestured conclusively. "See, that's how I was raised."

"They're not talking about putting you in bed together," Abby insisted, even though she knew she ought to put a stop to the whole thing right now. There were too many people standing around looking suspiciously as though they were on the verge of having a good laugh.

Jackie, for one, who said, "Actually, we wondered if the bedroom might be—"

"See? It keeps gettin' worse." Beau stepped away from the fireplace, approaching Abby with a beseeching gesture, a confidential tone. "Putting me in bed with another woman. Is that what you want, Abby?" He sounded almost serious.

"I don't think we need—"

"I'll do it if you will. That's it. I'm not doin' it with anybody else." One brawny hand signaled the end of the discussion.

"It would be so cute, Abby," Jackie cajoled from the sidelines. "You'd be perfect."

"Like I was just saying," Kate put in, "you could be a model yourself."

"Oh, all right!"

All eyes widened. The crackling fire made the only sound in the room.

"It's no big deal," Abby asserted as she scanned their faces, ignoring knowing eyes and smirky lips. She stuck out her hand. "The pictures will be absolutely unusable, but give me the top."

In his moment of triumph Beau had no trouble baring his beautiful chest.

"*Cute* is not the word that leaps to mind," Gayle muttered appreciatively.

Abby held the voluminous shirt up to her shoulders. "Is this a large? I'm not sure it'll be long enough."

"It'll be long enough," Beau assured her. "Kate, would you show her, uh . . ."

"Your bathroom," Kate decided, signaling Abby to follow her. "Gayle's got mine all full of face paint."

"You might want to try a little of that, Abby," Gayle called out.

Abby preferred to use her own. She did borrow the hairbrush in the bathroom, thinking Beau wouldn't mind, since they'd shared some pretty intimate moments lately. And now she was using his bathroom, breathing the faint, spicy scent of his soap, his aftershave lotion, surrounded by tile still damp from his shower, and it all felt deliciously intimate, just like the notion of wearing half of his pajamas, even though he would probably never put them on again.

"Oh, this is so silly," she muttered as she rolled up the sleeves. But admitting it to herself didn't help much, so she tried again when she returned to the living room. Just so they all knew that she knew. "This really is ridiculous."

"I already said that," Beau reminded her. But he was enjoying it. She could see it in his eyes.

"We'll get some interesting effects from the fire if we close that curtain," Tom Banks told Jackie, who took care of the curtain immediately. "After this, what kind of a bed do we have to work with?"

"Beau has a nice big one," Kate said. "I'll go straighten things up in there a little bit."

"Just leave it, Kate. It's straight." Beau's smile took the edge off the foolishness for Abby as she joined him beside the fireplace. "You look real cute. You could change my mind about owning a pair of pajamas."

"This is part of your bonus," she muttered.

"Okay, now, let's do some fun stuff and some serious stuff." Tom was circling the couple like a predator, looking for an interesting angle. "I mean, like, 'Oh, I just came over to borrow the pajama top,' and then, like, 'With this pajama top, I pledge my undying devotion.' You know what I mean? A commercial with a story.'' He took each of them by the shoulder and arranged them face to face. "Like people might really do this scene."

"I'm the second guy. Seriously committed." Beau propped his elbow on the fireplace and looked into Abby's eyes. His were bright with mischief. "Either that, or I seriously *ought* to be committed for getting my picture taken like this."

"Gayle's right," Abby said. "*Cute* isn't the right word."

"By the fire, we're serious. That's the mood." Tom climbed on the seat of a kitchen step stool. "I want to shoot down on this, get him from behind, her from the front." He lined up his shot over Beau's shoulder. "This is good. I'm getting the monogram on the pocket. Look into his eyes now, Abby. Obviously you've agreed to go to bed with him. Show us what you see in him. That's good. Oh, yeah, he's a prince, all right."

"He's a cowboy," Abby asserted, her gaze locked with Beau's. She wouldn't be able to hold this pose long. The fire was hot. The look in Beau's eyes was hotter.

"Whatever. The man of your dreams. Beautiful, sweetheart." After a few clicks and whirs of the camera, Tom jumped down and grabbed his models' arms. "You know what would be great? Kitchen. Coffee time. The morning after."

Beau laughed.

Abby groaned.

The entourage moved to the kitchen. Tom lined Abby and Beau up near the window, assessed the light, fussed with their hair, which was "too neat, much too neat," shoved a coffee mug between them and lined up his shot. "Okay, playful. One cup between you. You guys share everything."

Abby giggled.

"Niiiice." Click, whirr, click. "Come on, Beau, she makes the best coffee in the world."

"How do you know?"

"I want to see it in your eyes. Nice. Nice." A few more clicks, and Tom was ready for another setting. "Last stop, the master bedroom."

"Oh, Tom, I really think . . ."

"These are bed clothes," Tom said as he herded his flock toward the back of the house. "We're going to wear them—" he brandished his camera like a sword "—to bed! Charge!"

"Tom's really gettin' into this," Beau muttered.

"He's a frustrated artist," Abby returned.

"Frustrated, huh?"

"Okay, he sits, she stands, and everybody else stays in the hallway," Tom instructed, still guiding his models around by the shoulders. "I need plenty of room to work."

Beau sat on the edge of the bed, as ordered, then looked at Abby. "Yeah, this is real natural."

"Okay, she sits on his knee."

"On his *knee?*"

"She sits—" Beau slapped his thigh with one hand, dragged her down with the other "—on his knee, and the damn camera starts rolling."

"As soon as they relax and give the camera what it wants, which is playful, playful."

"Where did you get this guy?"

"I told you, he's an artist." She put her arm on Beau's shoulder, experimenting, looking to Tom for approval as Beau's arms encircled her hips. "He's the very best there is."

"Only the best for Miss Abigail. Hmm, what can we play?" Beau bounced her on his knee. "What would you like for Christmas, little girl? The very best *what* this year?"

"Horse," she said. "But that's what I always ask for, and I never get one."

"Little girls who always ask for horses for Christmas will be the death of a perfectly good children's fantasy. How about a pretty nightgown or—" his gaze swept down, then up with a smile "—some men's jammies."

"I'd want my own whole complete set."

He was still bouncing her. The camera was still clicking.

"Oh, I'd give you the full set. All for you. Even though that's not the way they show them in the catalog. Scoot up here on my lap, little girl, or you're liable to get—" he jerked his thighs apart, and she slipped, silk over silk, until he caught her "—bucked off."

"Tricky," she allowed as she recovered her seat. She was losing herself in the moment, in the game, in the love light in Beau's eyes.

"Just playful," he said, which was the way he hugged her, while something beyond the circle of his arms clicked, whirred and went silent. "Horses are like that, too. Gotta be ready for anything."

"Are you?"

"You know I am." He leaned close to her ear and whispered, "You stand up too soon, everybody else is gonna know, too."

Tom cleared his throat, then announced quietly, "All out of film, but I can reload."

Abby offered Beau an impish smile. "I'm sure we have all we need, Tom." She made a halfhearted attempt to stand, but Beau responded with a whole-hearted hip lock. He was, indeed, ready, and she wasn't going anywhere.

"That's it for today, then?" The floorboards creaked under Tom's gradual retreat. "Nice work, you guys. You wait till you see these shots, Abby. You might want to start a whole new career."

"I don't think so. Beau's right." Her hand stirred on the back of his neck. Her voice dropped almost to a whisper. "You can't share pajamas with just anybody."

"I'll, uh—" the door hinges squeaked "—clear the set."

"Smart man," Beau said. The door clicked shut. "So here we are in our pajamas."

She nodded. "And so...you sleep in the master bedroom." He groaned and turned his head away. "Why didn't you tell me, Beau? What's the big deal?"

He shook his head. "It's no big deal. It's—" He risked a sheepish glance her way. She slipped off his lap and sat beside him on the chenille bedspread. He took her hand in both of his, rubbed one thumb over her knuckles, released a long, slow breath and repeated, "No big deal."

"You're a rancher now."

He nodded once, as though he was owning up to some fatal deficiency in his character.

"Why pretend you're still an itinerant cowboy?"

He looked puzzled, even wounded. "Nothing wrong with that, either, is there?"

"There's nothing *wrong* either way."

"You assumed I was working for someone else. I just let you think I was working for..." He shrugged. "It is my place."

"It's lovely," she said. She didn't quite know what to do with the niggling hurt his deception caused her. Pride, Kate had said, but that explanation didn't make a lot of sense. "What I've seen of it is absolutely beautiful."

"Thanks. I've done some remodeling on it. It still needs work. I mean, it's not quite up to..." He surveyed the white walls, the simple decor of his bedroom. "It's a business, you know, not just a place to live. And it's risky. Riskier than rodeo ever was."

"I wouldn't say that." She turned her hand within the confines of his, pressing palm to palm. "I hold my breath every time I watch you ride. Eight seconds feels like forever.''

''Yeah, well, a bad spring blizzard can feel like forever, too. But this is what I want to do with my life, Abby. It's what I've always wanted to do.''

''Then I'm glad it's what you're doing.'' She stared at their hands. ''I'll be leaving at the end of the week.''

''So soon?''

''I'll have finished what I came to do by then.''

''So just . . . three more days.''

''That's right. Three more days.'' Reluctantly, she rose to her feet. ''I left my clothes in the bathroom.''

''Need any help?''

She laughed mirthlessly. ''I think I can manage. You?''

''My knee's kinda bothering me.'' He rubbed it, looking to her for sympathy.

''Oh, no. That's the one I sat on. Should I get you some . . .''

He shook his head. The look in his eyes became an invitation as he claimed her hands, lacing his fingers through hers and using those bonds to draw her to him. When her lips were within reach, he kissed her, forming another bond. And he would have more. He moved back on the bed, blanketing himself with her body, kissing her hungrily.

He kept her hands tied, her mouth occupied with his, while their bodies greeted each other, hip to hip, soft silk separating them. He was hard and ready, and she, undulating against him, as needy as she'd ever been, wanted to keep him that way. They tormented each other with kisses, but he was the first to give in to a deep groan that said something had to give.

Or someone. He reversed their positions and unbuttoned the shirt she'd designed for him, loving every inch of her as he discovered her anew, in his bed for the first time. Loving her was something else he wanted to do with his life, loving her this way, every way. He couldn't bring himself to tell her in words, risk-laden words likely to spawn words he never wanted to hear again, words like *I can't live like this, Beau.*

But he could show her his loving. He could give her loving hands, loving lips, his loving tongue. He could strip himself of all cover and give her all he had to love her with, so that when she left him, as she was bound to do, at least she would know and remember.

But she didn't leave him. Not right away. As late afternoon shadows stretched from wall to wall she lingered to hold him, to let him hold her. The longer he held her, the better he understood what it meant for a man to love a woman not meant for him. It hurt. It hurt bad. But he wouldn't trade it for a hundred trophy buckles or a thousand acres.

"How's your knee?" she asked, trailing her fingertips over his thigh. "Is it better now?"

"I'm all better." It was a response that sounded good, if nothing else. He nuzzled her temple, smiled into her hair. "All of me feels better. You're good medicine."

"Is that so?" Her fingertips skimmed his hipbone and blazed a ticklish trail along his side. "I'm glad, I guess. If I could bottle it, I'd leave some for you."

"You're still part owner of the All-Around Cowboy Blues store in Rapid City, right?" He closed his eyes as her hand came to rest on his abdomen. He was going to take what he could get, he decided, and an occasional visit would be better than nothing. "So you'll be coming back from time to time?"

"If I have reason to. It was Jackie's idea to open up shop here, since this was her hometown, so..." She sighed. "She probably won't be needing me very often."

He would. "You'll be sure and call me whenever you're in town?"

"Sure."

"I don't get to Denver very often anymore. Don't go much of anywhere anymore, but I don't miss it much." He drew back and tipped her chin up with the edge of his hand so she could see the truth in his eyes. "I'll miss you, though. I *have* missed you."

"I could have sworn you loved me once."

"Thought I did," he said, echoing the claim she'd made to him weeks ago. She lowered her lashes, acknowledging the understatement.

"Okay, so I wasn't very good at it then," he admitted as he traced his finger over the fine curves of her face. "Think I'm better at it now. I'd like to be good medicine for you, too, somehow."

"I'm pretty healthy. Usually pretty careful. No accidents, hardly any unexpected mishaps. Very few bumps and—" her eyes drifted closed "—bruises."

"Have I hurt you, Princess? I didn't mean to—"

"I am not a *princess.*" She bit the word out like an insult. Suddenly wide-eyed, she drew herself up, bracing herself on her elbow. "I'm not like your mother, Beau."

He blinked, confounded, wondering where that notion had come from. "I didn't say you were. Hell, I don't even know what my mother was like."

"You don't know what I'm like, either," she claimed, drawing farther away. "And you won't, unless you're willing to risk some of that cowboy pride you cherish so dearly."

"You want me to chase after you when you go?" He sat up, too. "I just might. I came damn close the last time. This time..." He wasn't ready. She was leaving him right now, inch by inch, and he wasn't ready. "Hell, I just might."

"Do it now."

"You haven't left yet."

"That's right. I haven't. Which means you might just have a chance of catching me." She snatched the pajama top off the foot of the bed and covered herself with it as she sat up, taking herself away.

He reached for her, but he wanted her to meet him halfway, to put her hand in his and let him draw her back.

She ignored his gesture. "Does that scare you?" she asked. "Being so close. Does that...? What would you do if you actually caught me, Beau?"

"I'd keep you." He lay back on the pillow. "In my dreams," he admitted, avoiding her eyes. "In the real world, that's not the way it works, and I don't wish for anything unless I know I can make it happen."

"It's all up to you, then?"

"I made that championship happen." On that note he could look at her. He could sit up and face her with concrete challenges and undeniable accomplishments. "I made this place happen. But you..."

"But I *what?* I'm not for real? I only loved you *once upon a time?*" She jammed her arm into the sleeve of the pajama top. " 'The Princess and the Cowboy.' What a nice bedtime story that would make, Beau. It's one you've heard before, isn't it? Do you ever plan to have children?"

"I hope to, yeah. Someday."

"Some happily-ever-after day?" The other arm shot through the other sleeve. "I hope to have children, too. What do you think about that?" She jerked the silk shirt closed and turned to him, trembling hands full of earth-colored silk, protecting herself from his eyes and whatever his thoughts might be. "You've never asked me, but I just thought I'd tell you. That's one of my dreams."

"Mine, too. Soon as I have this cattle operation up and running to where it can support a family."

"I love you *now*," she insisted, her body rigid, her voice tight. "Right now, today, I'm in love with you, Beau."

"Then love me now," he said quietly, "and keep loving me as long as you can."

"That's little enough to ask, I suppose. And if you ask for something little . . ." She stood, smiling at him wistfully. "Why ask for a doll when what you really want is a horse?"

"When you have no place to keep a horse—"

"You're right," she admitted with a sigh. "I'm wishing for something I can't *make* happen. Not by myself."

The day she was packing to leave, he appeared on her doorstep. Through the open door he saw the luggage sitting by the sofa, saw the boxes on the table, saw that she was really leaving, so he got right to the point.

"I wanted to tell you, just in case you hadn't noticed, I'm in love with you, too. Have been for a long time." He shrugged, smiled, tugged at the brim of his hat. "Most of my life, feels like."

For a moment there she looked happy, but she caught herself, glanced away and stepped away from the doorway. "Come on in."

He glanced across the room, took in the little efficiency kitchen, the door standing open to the bedroom, the corner of a mattress stripped of bedding.

"Nice place."

"It was a lucky find." She padded across the wood floor on bare feet and started fussing with one of the boxes on the little table, pressing the flaps closed first one way, then another. "You know, a short-term lease on a furnished apartment. I wonder if I should hang on to it for a while."

"You're welcome to stay with me anytime."

"Thank you."

"Abby, there's something I want to explain." He approached her hesitantly.

She looked up, equally hesitant. She was wearing a T-shirt and cutoffs, her hair clipped in a wispy ponytail, reminding him achingly of the ingenue he'd met ten years ago.

But she was more, and he knew it, and he ached for that, too. He ached for the woman he'd come to know in the last few weeks, the woman who could surely get along without him any time she wanted to. Like tomorrow and the next day, which scared the hell out of him.

He swallowed hard and pressed on.

"Well, I don't really *want* to, but I should. I know you're doing well with your business, your career, and I'm glad. I always knew you would. You're smart, you're talented, you're..." He stood close to her now. He could hear all the things she was in her every breath, feel it in the warmth of her proximity.

He cleared his throat, shifted his boots, stared at the scuffed toes. "I've done okay, too, up until recently. I told you, I had a bad winter. Lost too many calves, lost a few cows. I'm a small operator, and I don't have too much slack for losses. I took this job with you and Jackie because I needed the money." He lifted his face to hers, offered a thin smile. "I needed it pretty bad."

"How bad? Are you looking at bankruptcy?"

"Not now." He glanced away. "Ten years ago, I'd have given my right arm to be able to ask you to marry me. 'Cept without my right arm, I'd have had a hell of a time supporting you."

"I don't need a man to sup—"

"I know you don't. But I need to be able to think I could." He tucked a thumb into his back pocket. *Damn,* this was hard. "I know it's stupid macho thinking, but there's no point in trying to argue me out of it. I made my living on the rodeo circuit back then, and, like you said, you couldn't have lived that way. You're no gypsy."

"Who knows what I could be if I put my mind to it?" She waited until he looked into her eyes, hoping that he would see her now, see only her. "The one thing I can't be is a princess. Not without being born to the title, or marrying into it."

She shook her head, smiling as she remembered Jackie describing Beau as the king of the cowboys. And she had been right. Standing there, dressed in his own jeans, rubbed soft by his saddle and faded by the sun, he surely had all the requirements. She glanced at the hat firmly planted on his head and smiled. "I don't seem to be in line for a crown."

"I only meant to show you—" smiling, too, he doffed the hat as he cupped his big, callused hand carefully around her face "—how fine I think you are."

She closed her eyes, cherishing the words he'd uttered with unexpected reverence.

"And you're right." His hand dropped to her shoulder, gave her a little squeeze, as though congratulating her for her insight, then slid away. "It was the way my dad referred to my mother, but he was never sarcastic about it. He really believed . . ."

He looked at her, pleading his father's case as much as his own. "He never stopped loving her. I don't know why she left, exactly, except that it just didn't work out for them." He shrugged. "Well, maybe it worked out good for her, but not for him."

"How do you feel about her?"

"I don't feel much of anything. Didn't know the woman."

She gave him a dubious look.

"Aunt Kate said that my mother wanted to give me up for adoption, but my dad . . ." The memories came hard as he fingered the crease in the crown of his hat. "Kate said I was the only thing my dad ever begged anyone for. In his whole life, that was the only time. Not for her to stay, but for her to let him raise his son."

"I wish I'd known him." She laid her hand on his arm, encouraged him with her smile when he looked into her eyes. "I guess I do know part of him."

"I guess you do."

"The kind of father I'd want for my children would set aside his pride for them just the way you described."

"You're not trying to tell me..." His Adam's apple bobbed quickly as he stared. "You're not pregnant, are you?"

She glanced away.

"Are you, Abby?"

"No, I'm not." She sighed. "That would make it too easy, Beau."

"I wouldn't let you go."

"What would you do? Lock me up and throw away the key?" Her hand latched onto his forearm. She wanted to shake him. "You don't have to do that."

"What would I have to do?" He gripped her elbow. His voice dropped to just above a whisper. "What would it take?"

"What do you *want?*"

"What I said before. I want you to be with me."

"I've *been* with you."

"Forever!" His hat hit the floor as he gripped her shoulders, clearly wishing he could shake her, too. "I don't want you to leave me, ever. Don't you understand that?"

"Then ask me, Beau. Put aside your pride and take the risk."

"I don't see how it can work, with me..." He glanced away, fastening his gaze on the suitcase by the sofa, waiting to be carried out the door. "And you...with your..."

"I think we can find a way if the love is there. I promise you this, Beau, there's plenty of love here." She moved his hand, placing it over her heart. "Right here, there's love for you that won't quit. It will never, never—"

He pulled her into his arms and hugged her desperately.

"Oh, Beau, I would love you anywhere. I would live with you anywhere. All you have to do is—"

"Marry me, Abby." He drew back, held her at arm's length and let her see the desperation of a man wishing for something he couldn't *make* happen. "You wanna see all-around cowboy blues? Try turnin' me down. I'm hanging way out on a limb here. You take out your royal saw, and you'll see—"

"Not a chance. Not if you're serious. And you try taking that proposal back, and you'll see—"

"Not a chance. All I have to do is what?"

"Ask."

"Damn, I—" He swept his hat off the floor and clutched it to his chest as he went down on one knee. "I'm askin', as humble as you'll ever see me. Will you please marry me, Miss Abigail?"

"Yes, Beau Lassiter, I believe I will."

"For richer, for poorer?"

"In sickness and in health," she assured him, her heart singing to the tune his beautiful blue eyes were playing for her.

"Hot damn, that's just what I need." He grinned. "Now will you please help me up, Miss Abigail?"

* * *

Within a few months, Abby had the horse she'd always wanted, along with the place to keep it. Within a year she had a new ring on her finger. Within another year, she was expanding her catalog to include "togs for the little buckaroos."

Beau Jr. was her first model.

* * * * *

Dear Reader,

My heroes have always been cowboys. Yes, ma'am, from the first moment I saw that handsome wrangler in the straw cowboy hat, red Western shirt, boots and jeans breaking a horse under the hot summer South Dakota sun, I was a goner. So was he. We've been married twenty-five years now, and my hero still has a cowboy heart, even though he makes his living as a teacher.

Naturally my very first book, *Someday Soon* (Silhouette Special Edition), had to be about a cowboy. There have been quite a few books and quite a few heroes between Sean Brannigan and Beau Lassiter. My hero may "love his damned ol' rodeo," but in the end he always rides into the sunset with the right lady by his side.

The cowboy and the lady—one of my favorite matchups. Beau's a little older and a whole lot wiser than he was when he first met Abby, but he's still a dreamer—all cowboys are—and still her dream man. All he has to do is convince her of that. He's been a lonesome cowboy long enough. Let's remedy that, shall we?

Happy trails!

Kathleen Eagle

GONE FISHING

Joan Hohl

Chapter One

"I'm going fishing."

"What did you say?"

Alexander Forester suppressed a laugh at the incredulous expression on his assistant's face. "I'm going fishing," he repeated.

"That's what I thought you said. But, at the same time, I felt certain I misheard you."

Alex could no longer contain his amusement; he expressed it with a low chuckle. "You didn't mishear or misunderstand, Josh. I said I'm going fishing, and that is precisely what I'm planning on doing."

"But—but—" Josh gave his employer a helpless look. "I had no idea you enjoyed the sport."

Alex could understand the man's obvious confusion for, not only had he not been fishing in a very long time, he had not taken a vacation, other than the rare extended weekend, for over fourteen years. Josh's puzzlement was fully understandable, since he had been with Alex for more than half of those years.

"It's been a while," Alex admitted. "But, yes, I do enjoy the sport...primarily deep-sea fishing."

"Ahhh," Josh murmured. "You're going to be heading to warmer climes?"

"No." Alex smiled, conceding that his assistant's assumption was also understandable. Although it was early June, a cold wave made the air feel more like early spring, hardly the ideal weather for a vacation of fishing in the cold waters of the Atlantic Ocean.

"But," Josh began, shaking his head, "I don't get it. Why would you—"

"Because there's a certain place here on the East Coast, in South Jersey that I want to visit," Alex interrupted. "A place I haven't been to in a long time."

"I see." Josh frowned. "I think."

Alex smiled. Josh was probably wondering why Alex didn't just postpone his vacation until next week, when the temperatures were supposed to rise into the seventies. To go fishing during a cold wave wouldn't enter into consideration for most people.

Except Alex. But then, he had no desire to lie on a beach, baking in the summer sun.

"I have my reasons." His brisk tone, along with his abrupt movement to draw his chair up to his desk, was a clear indication that the subject was now closed. "Since I'll be leaving at the end of this week," he continued, his tone all business, "I have a few things to go over with you."

On Saturday morning, once he was through the worst of the Philadelphia traffic, and across the Ben Franklin Bridge, Alex felt he could relax a bit, to reflect upon his motivation for deciding to take his first real vacation in fourteen years, away from the office and his work.

In a nutshell, Alex was tired, bone-tired. But that particular nutshell went deeper than mere weariness. In this instance, the most pressing motive driving Alex was the very real fear that he was burning out.

Alex didn't deal well with fear, nor did he accept it as part and parcel of life. He lived by the concept that, on the occasions when fear reared its debilitating head, an intelligent person confronted it, conquered it and went on.

And so, even though he had pressing business matters on his desk that needed his personal attention, Alex had decided to comply with his philosophy by driving to the Coast, to confront and conquer, not only his fear of burnout, but a host of other, older, deeper and more personal concerns he couldn't repress any longer.

A wry smile flickered on his lips as Alex acknowledged that his choice of location for his retreat had little to do with fishing.

Alex did enjoy fishing, at least he used to, and he fully intended to get some fishing in, cold Atlantic waters or no. But his primary objective during the jaunt was to revisit the past, a particular period of his past, and hopefully exorcise the memory ghosts haunting him.

Alex had decided that it was time, probably long past time, for him to return to Cape May, New Jersey.

He had visited Cape May many times before, during his formative and college years. Yet one trip in particular had altered his life.

Alex's lips tightened into a straight line. In truth, that trip fourteen years ago had not been volitional, but had come about as a result of outside influences. He had reluctantly driven to the seaside resort at the request of his best friend, Mike Peterson.

At the time, Alex had already made advances along the fast track toward his single-minded goal of business success. He had had little time or patience to spend on what he had considered the self-indulgence of a vacation. Business competition was keen, and he hadn't wanted to dull the edge on his business skills he had so carefully honed.

But then, by the same token, Alex had felt he could neither ignore nor deny his friend's request. Mike was getting married, and he wanted Alex to stand beside him as his best man.

Alex and Mike had been buddies for what seemed like forever. They had grown up together, played sports together, attended the same college, double-dated. Their parents were close friends, as well. Their families had spent winter holidays in Philadelphia, at the spacious home of Alex's parents, and summer vacations together in the large Victorian house the Petersons owned in Cape May.

Alex had always cherished fond memories of those halcyon days of family gatherings and youthful high jinks. And so, of course, he had honored Mike's request, not only to be in attendance for the wedding, but to spend the entire week prior to the event at the Petersons' summer house.

As it turned out, he had spent more than a week away from the office and his work. In total, his vacation had stretched to two weeks—but not all of it in Cape May. That second week was the part he had tried so hard to forget.

Alex's eyes flickered as he caught sight of the large green and white sign indicating the exit off the Atlantic City Expressway and onto the Garden State Parkway to points south.

It won't be long now, he mused, stomach muscles clenching as he drove up the slight incline of the entrance ramp. The parkway ended at Cape May, a mere few miles away from the well-remembered summer home of his friend.

With each succeeding mile and exit sign he passed, marking Ventnor, Margate, Ocean City, the Wildwoods, Alex felt his nerves tightening, suppressed memories bubbling to the surface of his consciousness. The pleasant remembrances of family fun and lighthearted camaraderie with friends were swamped by the wave of buried memories of his last fateful visit to the quaint Victorian town and house.

The knuckles on his fingers turned shiny white from the strength of his grip on the steering wheel. A fine film of moisture slicked his forehead. Tension coiled and writhed like a deadly serpent inside him. His eyes narrowed to slits as he stared at the last exit sign.

Dammit! Alex railed in silent protest, continuing, while every self-protective instinct urged him to turn around, go back, forget.

Forget. Good advice, easy to give to oneself, he thought ruefully, making a right turn onto the familiar tree-lined street. He had tried, with all the considerable inner strength he possessed, to wipe that chapter of his life from his mind. But how did one succeed in totally forgetting the most significant, emotionally devastating event of one's life?

His throat dry, his palms wet, Alex skimmed a narrowed glance along the houses facing the street. His gaze touched on a wrought-iron–fenced yard, then lifted to the gabled house set back, away from the street.

On sight of the house, the flood of memories crested the barriers he had so carefully erected inside his mind, spilling over into his consciousness.

Her name was Carolyn Cole.

In that instant, Alex could hear her soft laughter, see the teasing light dancing in her green eyes, smell her distinctive scent of spicy perfume and enticing woman, taste the heady flavor of her full and luscious mouth.

Only she wasn't a woman fourteen years ago. She was an immature child, disguised by a woman's body.

Gritting his teeth, Alex steered the car into a parking space along the curb. Switching off the engine, he sat still, drawing in deep, calming breaths, fighting a drowning sensation as he stared intently at the house in which he had met his near destruction.

The memory flood swept Alex back in time to the day, fourteen years ago, when he had first met her.

Alex had arrived at the Victorian house feeling edgy and disgruntled. Not only had he had to leave unfinished work on his desk, he would be missing some crucial business meetings . . . a heretofore unthinkable situation.

Mike's wedding could not have come at a less convenient time for Alex—although, considering the schedule he maintained, there really was no convenient time for personal indulgences.

Nevertheless, Alex had agreed to act as Mike's best man, and spend the entire week at the Cape May house in the bargain. But that didn't mean he had to enjoy it.

Alex was in a foul mood, and deeply entrenched in his determination not to enjoy himself when he arrived on the scene early that Saturday morning in June, exactly one week before the wedding. His determination was tested by the very first person he encountered.

She was seated, bare legs curled beneath her, on a padded wicker chair on the veranda. Shaded by the porch roof, Alex could not discern the color of her eyes, but he felt her steady regard as he traversed the walkway from the fence gate to the veranda steps.

"You're Alexander."

He stopped dead in his tracks, right foot planted on the first step, struck by the enchanting sound of her soft voice, and the conviction in her tone.

"Yes." Alex was somewhat amazed by the firm coolness of his own voice, considering the leap of excitement inside him that set his pulse racing and his heartbeat hammering.

All this from the sound of her voice?

Ridiculous.

Intent on proving his immediate conclusion to himself, he mounted the steps to get a better, closer look at her.

"I'm afraid you have the advantage," he said, gliding a quick but comprehensive glance over her.

He noted a shoulder-length mass of dark hair, gleaming with red highlights; clear green eyes the exact shade of flawless emeralds; a trim body curved in all the right places and, while he couldn't judge the length of her legs curled under her neatly rounded tush, the area exposed from the edge of her shorts to her knees revealed slim creamy thighs.

The picture she presented dried all the moisture in his mouth and throat. Fortunately, he was spared the effort of enlarging upon his remark for, giving him a rakish grin, she tossed part of it back at him.

"Afraid?" She raised exquisitely arched eyebrows. "I can't believe you're afraid of anything."

"Not much of anything," he confessed with unaffected self-confidence. He lifted his own dark eyebrows in a mirroring arch. "But I do feel at a disadvantage at the moment."

"How so?" Though her tone was serious, her sparkling eyes continued to laugh at him.

"You obviously know who I am, since you know my name," he replied, leaning back against the porch pillar in a deceptively lazy-looking pose. "While I haven't a clue about either your name or who you might be."

She appeared to ponder his response for a few seconds. Then she flashed her white teeth in another grin. "I might be the best friend of and designated maid of honor to the bride," she said. "My name is Carolyn Cole...my friends call me C.C."

"For obvious reasons," he murmured, dry-voiced. "But I prefer Carolyn or, better yet, Caro," he went on, mildly surprised at himself for feeling interested enough to bother. "If you don't mind?"

"Whatever floats your boat," she returned, lifting her shoulders in a light shrug. "For myself, even though I know your friends call you Alex, I prefer Alexander."

"Why?" While he assured himself that he was simply curious, and really didn't care, Alex knew he was lying to himself, and that for some strange, incomprehensible reason, her answer mattered.

She shrugged again. "Because Alexander fits, first the impression your friends gave me of you, and now, the overall look of you."

In an inexplicable way, he felt complimented, even though he wasn't sure she had meant to compliment him.

"My friends have been discussing me?" he asked, choosing not to demand clarification from her concerning the "overall look" of him.

"Yes," she admitted without hesitation. "They seem to be somewhat in awe of you."

"Sure they are," he drawled in a tone of patent disbelief. "But you're not?"

"Oh, but I am!" She opened her eyes wide, in what he was certain was feigned admiration. "Stunned might be an even better description."

Alex blinked, propelling himself out of the past and into the present, and the painful reality that, back then, Caro had been living in an immature world of imagination.

Shaking himself free of memory's grip, he suddenly noticed the sign posted on the gate in front of the Petersons' house.

Leaning across the seat, he peered through the window to read the words on the white sign. The startling information imparted was that the house was now a bed and breakfast.

When had the Petersons converted the house into a bed and breakfast, open to the public? Did they still own the place, or had they sold it at some point over the past fourteen years?

Alex grimaced at the realization of how long it had been since he'd had any form of contact with either Mike or his family. To his chagrin, he acknowledged that his contact with Mike had dwindled from sporadic to nothing within a year of Mike's wedding.

Deciding to investigate the house situation, he stepped out of the car.

Up close, the sign appeared weathered, as if it had been in place for some time. Frowning, Alex swung open the gate, and strode to the porch. The place looked deserted. Still, shrugging, he mounted the steps, crossed the porch and jabbed his finger against the lighted doorbell button.

Within moments, the door was pulled open, and Alex found himself staring into the face of a green-eyed pixie of approximately ten or eleven years of age.

"Hey, Mom!" the girl yelled on sight of him. "Come quick, I think we've got a live one!"

Chapter Two

Alex couldn't suppress the roar of laughter that burst from his throat; the kid was so damned cute.

"Hi," she said, gazing up at him, her eyes alight with the sheer joy of life.

"Hi, yourself," he returned in warm appreciation of her exuberance. Lately, it had seemed to him that so many youngsters appeared not only sullen but jaded long before they attained their teenage years.

Staring down into the child's refreshingly open, untroubled face, Alex was only vaguely aware of another person coming to a stop behind the girl. But he clearly heard the sound of a sharply indrawn breath.

Frowning, he raised his eyes, then felt his own breath lodge painfully in his throat at the sight of the woman standing behind the girl, her eyes wide, staring at him in stark disbelief.

And she was now a woman, mature, and even more beautiful than the eighteen-year-old of fourteen years ago.

"Caro?" Alex barely recognized the raspy sound of his own voice saying the name he had refused to allow himself to think, let alone speak, for years.

"Alexander." Carolyn's voice was faint, and as strained as his.

Alex wondered if his face was as devoid of color as hers. As if mutually stunned, they stared, his clouded gray eyes into her shadowed emerald for an endless moment.

"Hey, you guys know each other?"

While not at all loud, the girl's pertly piped question hit Alex like the roar of cannon shot; he flinched as if struck by the fire...as did Carolyn.

"Uh...yes...er...I..."

"A long time ago," Alex inserted, saving Carolyn from her stuttering attempt.

"Gee..." The girl shifted a grin between the woman behind her and the man she faced. "Neat."

Yeah. Neat. With effort, Alex managed to return the innocent one's smile.

"You lookin' for a room?"

The kid's question not only startled Alex, but animated the seemingly frozen woman behind her, and thawed her tongue, as well.

"I don't..." She faltered, shifting her gaze from him to the girl.

"Er...yes, I am, but..." Alex shook his head, too stunned by the shock of seeing Caro to respond intelligently.

"Uh...Jess, honey, I think I hear the stove timer ringing," Carolyn said in an awkward rush. "Will you please run and turn it and the oven off?"

"Aw, geez, Mom," the girl groused, scuffing one small, sneakered foot on the foyer carpet. "Must I?"

"Yes."

"Oh...okay," Jess muttered, staring with open interest at Alex before turning away. "But I'm coming right back."

Alex barely heard the girl's parting promise; his mind was still grappling with the startling realization that the child was apparently Carolyn's daughter.

"I'm sorry, but I can't offer you a room."

Her unapologetic tone snared his attention and sparked irritation. "I don't recall asking for a room," he retorted. Then, out of sheer annoyance, he flicked his hand to indicate the posted sign. "But why can't you? If you're open for business?"

"But I'm not," she said too quickly. "I'm... ah...still in the process of getting the rooms ready. I won't be ready to open until the official first day of summer."

"I see," he murmured, certain that he did in fact see—or rather, hear the underlying rejection in her breathless, stumbling explanation. Alex felt positive he'd have been turned away even if the place was open for business and every one of her rental units was vacant.

"All of the hotels and motels are open now," she said helpfully while inching back from the door.

"Thanks, I'll find something."

"I'm sure." Carolyn moistened her lips, and inched back another step. "Goodbye, Alexander."

"Goodbye, Carolyn." He gave her a tight smile, then turned away. He was at the gate, and halted momentarily, when a young voice called out to him.

"Hey, mister! Where're ya goin'?"

Glancing back over his shoulder at the girl, he smiled and mentioned the name of a nearby large, well-known hotel facing the ocean.

"Oh...but—" The girl broke off as her mother murmured something to her.

Alex saw Carolyn frown, saw the strained expression on her face as she spoke to the girl. Lifting the latch on the gate, he swung it open and stepped onto the sidewalk.

"See ya," the girl called out after him.

"Yeah, see ya," Alex called back, his face grim as he walked to his car.

"But why didn't he want to stay here?" Jess demanded, her pixie face puckered in a scowl as she stared at her mother. "We've got plenty of room." She made a snorting sound. "All our rooms are empty."

"Maybe he wanted a view of the ocean," Carolyn prevaricated, latching on to Alexander's reply to the girl.

"But that don't make sense," Jess persisted. "If he didn't want to stay here, why did he ring the bell in the first place, anyway?"

"Doesn't," Carolyn automatically corrected the child while raking her rattled mind for a way to end the discussion.

"Huh?"

Carolyn sighed. "That *doesn't* make sense," she explained. "You said, it *don't* make sense."

"Well, it don't," Jess said mulishly.

Carolyn raised an eyebrow.

"Okay, it doesn't," Jess gave in with obvious reluctance. "But either way," she went on doggedly, "I don't see why he bothered to ring, if he wasn't looking for a room."

This time, Carolyn's sigh was heavier, louder. "Jess, let it drop, it's not important."

"But—"

"What is important," Carolyn went on as if the girl hadn't uttered a sound, "is the mess on the dining-room table. Will you please stop arguing and go clean it up?"

"Mess!" Jess cried indignantly. "That's not a mess, that's my shell collection!"

"Well, at the moment, your collection is scattered all over the dining room." She leveled a stern maternal look on the girl. "And I'd appreciate it if you'd get busy gathering it up. I'd feel embarrassed to show anyone around, in the event a real prospective guest rang the bell."

"Oh, all right," Jess gave in, turning and marching back along the central hallway. "But, *I'd* appreciate it a lot if you wouldn't call my collection a mess," she muttered, scuffing her sneakers against the floor.

A fleeting smile softened Carolyn's lips, but faded as the girl disappeared into the dining room.

Alexander.

A bone-deep shudder ran through her as her mind flashed an image of him, standing bold as sin on her veranda.

How old was he now? Carolyn grimaced at herself; she knew exactly to the day how old he was. Alexander would reach the milestone of forty on July the twelfth.

Tall, muscularly slender, his light brown hair full, wavy, vital-looking, his blue gray eyes sharp with intelligence and wit, he certainly didn't look like the concept of a middle-aged man. But then, with the current craze to remain fit and youthful for as long as possible, not many men of that age did. Even so, Alexander looked better than most other men, except for the lines of strain scoring his forehead and bracketing his mouth.

Alexander's mouth.

Dear Lord, she thought, clasping her arms around her midriff, he's more handsome, compelling, attractive and intimidating than he was fourteen years ago.

Fourteen years ago, so long a time, and yet . . .

Standing stock-still in the foyer, Carolyn stared into space, looking back, feeling anew the sense of thrilling excitement she'd experienced the first time she had ever seen Alexander Forester.

He literally took her breath away.

A delicious chill raised the short hairs on Carolyn's arms and at her nape, a shiver unrelated to the deeply shaded veranda, where she sat curled on a cushioned rocking chair. Only moments before, she had come onto the veranda, seeking a breath of cool air in relief of the stuffy un–air-conditioned interior of the Peterson house.

Trembling in response to the tingling sensations rippling through her, Carolyn watched the newcomer enter the gate and saunter up to the porch.

She knew who he was, of course. She could hardly not have known, after hearing praises sung about his looks and character by the Peterson family and their assembled friends since her arrival at the house early that morning.

And he lived up to every one of their assertions.

Barely able to catch a decent breath, Carolyn was slightly amazed, and rather proud of herself, when she managed to articulate an opening statement to him.

"You're Alexander."

"Yes."

The soft, masculine sound of his voice intensified the shiver feathering her arms.

"I'm afraid you have the advantage."

She had the advantage? Ha! Carolyn thought, feeling hot, then cold from the quick glance he swept over her body. Sudden keen awareness of herself as a woman, and him as a man, ignited a spark of an ache in her stomach, and a flicker of heat lightning in the core of her femininity.

His eyes . . . oh, heavens, his eyes! Were they blue? Were they gray? A combination of both cool colors?

Did it matter?

Not at that moment.

All that mattered was the feelings those eyes were evoking inside her, feelings unlike anything she had ever before experienced or even dreamed about.

In that instant, on the spot, Carolyn wondered if what she was feeling could in any way be related to what she had heard described as love at first sight.

Could it really happen so very suddenly, so unexpectedly, so devastatingly?

Or, more realistically, was she too young at eighteen to discern the fine shade of difference between love and the romantic illusion of the condition?

He spoke.

She responded, even though she was only vaguely aware of what she said. But she was aware of confessing to him that she was feeling stunned by his presence.

And that was the exact truth. His appearance, so soon after hearing his friends rave about him, had a stupifying effect on her.

Alexander laughed.

The sound of his laughter, while carrying a thread of mockery, wove a vibrant and rich tapestry of the fulfillment of secret dreams and forbidden pleasures through her imagination.

The never-forgotten echo of his laughter resounded in Carolyn's mind, jarring her out of the then, and into the fearful uncertainty of the now.

Jess!

Anxiety crawled on a thousand tiny legs along Carolyn's nerve endings.

She had to protect Jess.

"Okay, Mom," that most precious of children called from the dining room. "I got all my shells away," Jess went on, her voice growing stronger as she came through the dining-room doorway and along the hall. "Can I go down to the beach and look for more?"

Carolyn swallowed the coppery taste at the back of her throat, and worked her lips into a gentle smile. Only the Lord knew how very much she loved this child, more than her own life.

"Did you make your bed and straighten your room, as I asked you to do at breakfast?" And only the Lord knew how much it cost Carolyn to keep her voice even and natural, to keep herself from drawing the girl into her arms in a tight, protective embrace.

"Yeah, I did all that." Jess frowned. "I told you already. Don't you remember?"

Pull it together, Carolyn, she rebuked herself silently, dredging up a creditable, if short, laugh from somewhere.

"Oh, yes, of course you told me." She lifted her shoulders in a helpless shrug. "It slipped my mind."

"I even loaded the dishes into the dishwasher."

The girl's self-satisfied, boastful tone drew a genuine spurt of laughter from Carolyn.

"You did all that, and before lunch?" she chided teasingly. "Amazing."

"Yeah, ain't I?" Jess flashed her perfect teeth in a mother-melting grin. "Can I go?"

"I don't know. Can you?"

Jess heaved a sigh. "*May* I go?"

"Yes." Carolyn hid a smile with a stern face. "To the beach, Jess. Not to the ocean."

Jess tossed her a look that only thirteen-year-olds could master. "I'm not stupid, you know. What would I want in the ocean? That water's cold!"

"What about lunch?" Carolyn asked belatedly.

"No big deal." Jess dismissed the worry with a shrug. "I'll eat when I get back."

Carolyn glanced at the serviceable, inexpensive watch strapped to her wrist. "Actually, it's already past lunchtime," she said, surprised at how fast the morning had fled. "It's now twelve-seventeen."

"But after all the pancakes I ate for breakfast, I'm not hungry yet," Jess argued. "Can't we have lunch a little late today, say, one-thirty...please?"

"Okay, run along." Carolyn gave in to a smile. "I suppose I'll survive till then."

She stood staring at the door for some time after Jess banged it shut behind her.

Chapter Three

When had Carolyn remarried?

Alex stood at the wide hotel-room window, staring out over the beach and the breaking waves of the Atlantic Ocean stretching to the horizon beyond.

The persistent question had plagued him ever since he had heard the girl call Carolyn 'Mom,' retreating while he'd gone about the business of registering at the desk, surging back the instant he'd shut himself into the room.

Caro had a daughter, a pixie-faced little imp with a disarming grin and eyes the same beautiful, emerald-green color as her mother's.

Dear God, he felt sick.

Alex closed his eyes, grimacing in reaction to the roiling sensation in his stomach.

A beautiful child of Carolyn's flesh.

A beautiful child of another man's flesh.

Nausea strung a ribbon of sour fire up his chest and into his throat.

Dammit! What in hell was wrong with him? Alex berated himself. His time with Carolyn had ended over thirteen years ago, after less than a year of marriage. He hadn't wanted a child then. He had been too busy pursuing success to spare the time necessary to raising a child.

Caro had wanted a child. She had wept pleading tears for a child to love and care for.

Alex went still at the stabbing pain of memory.

She had wept.

He had been impatient with her immature tears.

A self-derisive smile curled his lips as he reluctantly recalled that the only time he hadn't been impatient with Caro was when they were making love.

While caught up in the silken web of lovemaking, Alex had been enthralled with Caro.

Once again, memory nudged against the barriers he had so ruthlessly erected in his mind. Weakened by his earlier lapse, the barriers gave way with little resistance, releasing a fresh flood of remembrances.

She was enchanting, and Alex fell under her spell within moments of meeting her, right there on the veranda.

Alex had actually banished all thought and consideration of business from his consciousness, so very enchanted was he by her enticing laughter, the dancing sparkle in her unbelievably beautiful eyes. And, as he very quickly learned, her legs were long, shapely, satiny-looking from the top of her thighs to her narrow ankles.

Alex immediately was, in a word, besotted.

He longed to protect her fragility, cherish her intrinsic sweetness, possess and own her innocently sensual body. And he set out with intent to satisfy his longing.

Throughout that prenuptial week, Alex played the courting game with lighthearted abandon. He teased her mercilessly, laughed with her delightedly, touched her in ever-growing intimacy.

Guileless, a novice to the game of seduction, Caro was his for the taking by the end of that week.

The day of the wedding dawned sunny and hot.

Fortunately, the church was air-conditioned.

Cool, while his friend, Mike, and his groomsmen appeared to be falling apart around him, Alex quietly and efficiently went about keeping them in line, and on target.

Finally, the ceremony was over.

The bride's mother cried.

The bride cried.

Mike cried . . . for heaven's sake.

Caro cried.

Alex had to restrain himself from kissing the tears from her flushed cheeks and moisture-spiked lashes.

After giving the requisite toast at the reception, Alex stared over his champagne flute at the beautiful, laughing young woman he had decided to make his own.

Caro presented a delicious picture in the frothy lace and chiffon confection of her maid-of-honor dress. The variegated shadings of green enhanced the purity of her pale skin, and heightened the color of her eyes.

The wispy chiffon caressed her tip-tilted breasts, and swirled lovingly around her slender hips and long legs.

In a strange but interesting way, Alex found seeing Caro in the gown more exciting and sensual than seeing her revealed in a bikini constructed of little more than the two swatches of cloth.

In a fruitless attempt to quench the fire building inside him, Alex took a long swallow of the chilled champagne, emptying the contents of his glass in a gulp.

He was immediately sorry, for at that instant, Caro glanced at him, her eyes widening in understanding of the message being sent to her from his heated gaze.

His mouth and throat felt parched and tight, reflecting the painful tightening in his loins.

From across half the width of the reception ballroom, he saw her lips form silent words of invitation.

Come, dance with me.

Setting the glass aside, he slowly moved toward her.

Caro came into his arms with a smile on her lips . . . and a promise in her emotion-shadowed eyes.

Dancing with her lithe form pressed intimately to his hardening body was exquisite torture.

"How soon do you think we can escape this crush?" he whispered into her ear, his excitement flaring at her responsive shiver.

"Not before the bride and groom," she whispered back, caressing the curve of his neck with her breath.

Alex suppressed a groan born of frustration and heightened arousal. He muttered a curse instead.

"Why do you ask?"

At once, Alex decided to stop playing games and get down to serious seduction.

"Because I want to kiss you . . . in private."

"I want to kiss you, too."

That did it. Impatience clawed at his nervous system. "Do you honestly believe anyone in this mob would miss us if we quietly slipped away?" he demanded softly, more than willing to forgo protocol.

Caro raised her face from the cradle of his shoulder to gaze at him with dreamy eyes.

"Would you dare?"

"To be alone with you?" He smiled, danced her around the crowd to the ballroom entrance, and into the lobby of the old, prestigious hotel. "I'd dare the devil."

Moments later, they were free, laughing together as they ran, hand-in-hand, from the hotel to his car.

But where could he and Caro go to be together in private?

Even though he knew the Petersons' house was empty, with everyone at the wedding reception, there was no way he would use Mike's parents' home for the purpose of seduction.

That left Alex with two options, the car or a motel room.

Neither option appealed to Alex. The first struck him as juvenile, the second as sleazy, and neither nearly good enough for Caro.

"Alexander?" Caro's soft inquiry pierced his concentration on the dilemma.

Focusing on her questioning gaze, he sighed. "I'd dare the devil to be with you," he said. "But damned if I'll dare offering you less than you deserve."

"I don't understand."

The sharp blast of a car horn on the street in front of the hotel shattered Alex's reverie.

Disoriented, he glanced around the room. The memory moment had been so fresh, so vibrant, he was slightly surprised at not finding himself standing in the parking lot of a different hotel, located a few blocks away.

Expelling a half laugh, half sigh, Alex raked a hand through his hair. This revisiting-the-past business was getting a little weird, he chided himself, even as an echo of Caro's young voice whispered through his mind.

I don't understand.

Of course, that had been the major cause of contention between them; the immature Carolyn had never understood the demands of being an adult.

Had she changed, grown up? Had the intervening years imposed . . .

Another car-horn blast scattered his thoughts. Frowning, and wondering if his request for an ocean-front room had been a mistake, Alex leaned forward and peered through the window. Traffic moved smoothly along the broad street; apparently, whatever had impelled the drivers to hit the horn had been of little importance.

Dismissing all horn-happy drivers with a shrug, Alex momentarily stared at the ocean, then directed a leisurely glance along the beach. His roving gaze passed by, hesitated, then backtracked to home in on a small figure.

Jess? The youngster strolling along, small sand pail in one hand, pausing to prod at the sand with a sneakered toe, sure as hell looked like Jess. Shell hunting? Alex smiled. As a boy, he had spent many contented hours on the beach, seeking interesting shells.

A sudden whim had him turning abruptly to stride from the room. Moments later, Alex took advantage of a lull in the stream of traffic to dash across the street. And a few moments after that, he was on the beach, trudging through the sand to the girl, now kneeling to dig into the sand with a child's small sand shovel.

"Hi. Digging for buried treasure?" Alex asked, hunching down next to the girl.

She cocked her head to glance at him, a suspicious expression on her face, telling Alex she had been well and rightly trained in being cautious about strangers, most especially men, he suspected.

"Oh, hi, Mr. . . ." Jess recognized him at once, but hesitated over his proper name.

"Alex," he offered, smiling.

"Okay, Alex." Her tight expression dissolved into a cheeky grin. "No, I'm not hunting for treasure, I'm looking for shells. But they say there is treasure buried here, somewhere along the beach."

"Yeah, I'd heard that, too." Alex returned her grin. "When I was a kid, I used to hope I'd find a fortune while I was digging for shells."

Jess left off digging to flop her denim-covered bottom onto the sand. "You dug for shells . . . here?"

"Sure, all the time." Alex dropped onto the sand beside her. "It was one of my favorite pastimes."

"Did you come here a lot when you were a kid?"

"Yes, every summer." Alex stretched out his legs, unmindful of the scrape of sand against his expensive pants. "Matter of fact, my family spent nearly every summer here in Cape May, in the house you're living in now."

Her face lit up. "You know the Petersons?"

Alex nodded. "Mike Peterson and I grew up together."

"Uncle Mike!"

Uncle Mike? Alex frowned. "Mike Peterson is your uncle?" he asked, trying to figure out the familial connection.

Jess shook her head. "No, not really my uncle," she explained. "I just call him that."

"Oh, I see," he said, recalling that Mike's wife had been, and apparently still was, Carolyn's best friend.

"Did you ever find any really neat shells?" Jess asked, recapturing his attention.

"Plenty," Alex assured her, suddenly wondering what had become of his extensive collection. Very likely, his mother had thrown it out when she'd redecorated the house after he moved from his parents' home into a place of his own. "Have you?"

"Lots." She treated him to her pixie grin. "Mom's forever nagging me to clean 'em up."

Alex chuckled. "So was my mom."

"I paint mine sometimes."

"So did I." Alex smiled, remembering the hours he and Mike and Mike's two younger sisters had spent brushing water paints onto the shells.

"Cool." Jess smiled back at him. "What else did you like to do when you were here?"

"The usual stuff kids do at the shore in summer." Alex shrugged. "Fool around on the beach, try to surf..." He grinned. "We weren't too good at it."

"Waves aren't high enough," Jess opined.

"Yeah," he agreed. "When we weren't on the beach, we sometimes rode our bikes down to the point, to look for Cape May diamonds. Never did find any."

"Neither did I." Jess laughed. "But the fun's in the searching, not the finding."

Pretty bright for a kid, Alex mused, laughing with her. "But we did catch fish."

Her little face became even more animated. "You like to fish, too?"

"Well, I haven't done any for a long time, but I used to love it." He gazed at her in wonder, surprised at the number of things they had in common; or did all kids have similar interests? "You like to fish?"

"I'll say!" she said enthusiastically. Then she made a face. "But Mom hates it."

Obviously not *all* kids have similar interests, Alex revised his thinking. "What about your dad?"

Jess gave a careless shrug that didn't come off looking at all careless. "I don't have one."

"I . . . er, see," Alex murmured, tamping down an urge to question her about things that were none of his business. "I'm sorry to hear that."

"He died." Jess sighed. "When I was a baby. I don't remember him, but I know what he looked like. Mom had a snapshot of him enlarged and put it in a neat frame for me. I keep it on my desk in my room."

"So it's just you and your mother, huh?" he asked, probing despite his distaste of meddling. But he had to know, had to find out if there was a man—or yet another man—in Carolyn's life. Even while he told himself it didn't matter, Alex called himself a liar.

"Yeah," Jess answered. "But that's okay, Mom's great. We do just fine together."

"Good." Alex smiled at the girl, vaguely surprised at the feeling of elation soaring through him.

A movement beside him caught his notice; Jess was fingering the sand, making tiny mounds, then flattening them with her palm. He shifted his glance to her face; she was frowning. Her white teeth gnawed at her bottom lip.

"Something bothering you?" he asked bluntly.

"Uh..." She shot a quick look at him.

"Spit it out, kid," he ordered kindly.

"I was... well, just wondering how long you'll be staying," she muttered, sliding another quick look at him. "Here in Cape May, I mean."

Intrigued at what she was getting at, Alex answered, "Oh, a week or so. Why?"

Jess slid a hesitant glance at him. "I guess you wouldn't want to... uh... go fishing with me?"

Remembering the girl had no father, or apparently not even a father figure, Alex smiled and gently covered her restless small fingers with his much broader hand. "You guessed wrong," he said softly.

Her head snapped up and her green eyes grew wide. "You would like to go... really?"

"Really."

"Terrific!" Jess cried, her jubilant voice startling a nearby gull. "Do you want to help look for shells?" She noted his pants with a swift, appraising look. "I mean, not now, but someday when you're not dressed up?"

Alex's burst of laughter sent the gull flapping away. "Tomorrow?" he asked when his laugh subsided.

"You mean it?"

"Sure." He paused, then qualified, "Unless it's raining, of course."

"Oh, of course." Jess dismissed the very idea of rain with a flick of her small hand. "But they said on the weather report this morning that it's gonna be clear and warmer tomorrow. Not a sign of rain in sight."

"Then you've got yourself a date." Again he paused, wondering how Carolyn would feel about it. "Your mother won't object?"

This time, Jess successfully pulled off a careless shrug. "Why should she? It's not like she don't know you."

"Doesn't," Alex absently corrected her grammar, while thinking Carolyn's knowledge of him was precisely what worried him.

"You sound just like Mom, she's always—" Jess broke off, consternation vivid in her face. "Oh, yikes, Mom! Do you have the time?"

Alex glanced at his slim gold watch. "It's ten after two," he said, frowning as she scrambled up and swiped her bottom to scatter the loose sand. "Why?"

"I was supposed to be home by one-thirty, that's why." She gave him a look of mock horror. "I gotta run." She started away, only to glance back at him, while continuing to move forward. "What time tomorrow?"

"What time do you usually eat breakfast?"

"'Round eight."

"Eight-thirty, nine?"

"Better make it nine." She grinned her impish grin. "I'll offer to clean up the breakfast dishes to make up for being late back today."

"Good thinking," he said in a conspiratorial tone. "See you then."

The girl took off at a run, then spun around, kicking up a spray of sand, and dashed back to him.

"Would you like to come for dinner tonight?" she asked in a hopeful rush.

Instinct urged him to decline, but the kid's eager expression weakened his defenses. Besides, there was something about the girl that puzzled him, not Jess personally, but the very fact of her.

Something didn't fit right, Alex mused, reading the excited anxiety mirrored on her face.

"Alex?"

There was nothing else for it. There was no way he could withstand her young, hopeful look. Alex surrendered with a soft smile.

"I'd be honored to have dinner with you."

"Awright!" Jess hooted, doing a little sand-stirring dance. "Gotta go!" she yelped, turning.

"Wait, wait, Jess!" Alex called, bringing the girl to a hovering halt, and laughing as she paused, teetering in place. "You didn't tell me what time."

"Oh! What a nerd," Jess groaned, smacking her forehead with the heel of one hand. "We usually eat dinner around six. Is that okay with you?"

"Six is fine," he assured her. "Now, you'd better get moving or you're going to be in trouble."

"Right. I'm outta here." Flipping him a wave, she took off at a sprint.

Alex watched her small retreating form in bemusement until she was out of sight, wondering at the sense of empathy he felt for the girl, and asking himself if he was going soft in the heart or in the head.

Chapter Four

Carolyn had lost all sense of the passage of time soon after Jess slammed out of the house.

Due to a sudden and unexpected necessity to replace some plumbing pipes in early spring, there was now so much to do to get the house ready for her delayed opening day. So many of the hotels and bed and breakfasts were booked, Carolyn knew she'd attract impulsive vacationers when she opened for business. Mentally ticking off the chores to be done, she squashed her tendency of overprotectiveness toward Jess. Telling herself the girl would be perfectly safe on the beach, and sending out a fervent, if silent, prayer she was right, she got busy.

Since the work was routine, and didn't require her undivided attention, Carolyn's mind drifted. Unfortunately for her peace of mind, it drifted back in time, to that incredible night fourteen years ago.

After one short week of being in his company, Carolyn was utterly infatuated with Alexander Forester.

He was the personification of every fantasy she had ever dreamed of the ideal man; he was handsome, self-confident, assured and he possessed a keen wit and humor.

Carolyn had observed—as indeed had everyone else—that out of all the men in attendance for the wedding, younger and older, Alexander had been the one to remain cool, controlled, thus able to keep everyone else on track and on schedule.

Thanks primarily to Alexander, the ceremony, the entire day, had gone smoothly, with only minor hitches. His performance gave ample proof that he was a born leader, a natural organizer, a man to be reckoned with.

Carolyn found herself in the position of reckoning with Alexander during the wedding reception. She invited the test by issuing a silently mouthed plea for him to dance with her. And she failed the test, conceded victory from the instant he drew her into his arms.

For Carolyn, dancing with Alexander, being held close to the warmth and strength of his slim, muscular body, hearing his soft voice at her ear, feeling the moist brush of his breath against her sensitized skin, was sheer heaven and abject torture. She wanted more; she wanted everything.

And, within moments of their dancing together, he made a murmured suggestion of offering her everything.

He said forcefully that he would dare the devil to be alone with her.

Thrilling stuff for any infatuated woman; even more so for a dreamy-eyed eighteen-year-old.

Do you honestly believe anyone in this mob would miss us if we quietly slipped away?

His suggestion to slip away, desert the reception before the bride and groom departed, to be alone together, both excited and shocked Carolyn.

Excitement won, and she went not only willingly but eagerly when he danced her through the entranceway to the reception ballroom. Anticipation bubbled through Carolyn as they ran hand-in-hand from the hotel to the parking lot.

Uncertainty dimmed her expectations when, after reaching his car, Alexander hesitated, a frown scoring his forehead.

"Alexander?" she queried timidly.

"I'd dare the devil to be with you," he said. "But damned if I'll offer you less than you deserve."

While his assurance restored her shimmering expectation, it did little for her comprehension.

"I don't understand," she admitted, certain he had changed his mind, and already hurt because of it.

"I don't know where we can go to be alone," Alexander explained, his frown turning into an impatient scowl. "I won't insult you by suggesting a motel room, and I wouldn't even consider making love to you in the back seat of my car—like some wet-behind-the-ears teenager."

Flattered by his concern, and thrilled by hearing him confess to wanting to make love to her, Carolyn innocently, yet knowingly, consigned her youth, virtue and reputation to his disposal.

"I wouldn't mind."

Alexander blessed her with a smile that made the risk she was willing to take worthwhile.

"Ah . . . Caro," he murmured, raising their clasped hands to brush her fingers with his lips. "Your trust makes me feel like a giant." He raised his head from her fingers, his lips twisting in a grimace. "But if I accepted your offer, I know, by tomorrow, or even sooner, I would feel lower, smaller than the tiniest insect for having taken advantage of it."

"But," she began in protest, fearing he had decided to return to the reception, after all.

"There's nothing else for it," he interrupted her in a thoughtful tone. "We'll have to get married."

"Married!" Carolyn's voice came out in a dry croak that belied the leap of joy she felt inside.

"Yes." His voice was firm, his stare direct. "Will you marry me?"

"Yes. Oh, yes!" she cried, dismissing the fact that they had known each other one week. She paused to moisten her excitement-parched lips. "When?"

"As soon as legally possible," he answered decisively, swinging open the passenger-side door of his car and ushering her onto the seat. "Let's go."

Her mind whirling, Carolyn sat numb, watching him circle around to the driver's side and slide behind the wheel. She found her voice when he pulled the door shut after him. "Go where?" she asked as he fired the engine.

"Back to the Petersons'," he said, calmly setting the car into motion. "To pack."

"Pack?" She blinked and shook her head again, trying to clear her swirling thoughts. "Where are we going?"

"Where else?" He laughed. "To Maryland. Isn't that where everyone goes to elope?"

"We're eloping?" she exclaimed, suddenly so excited she could barely contain herself.

"Yes, if you're game." Alexander slanted a smoldering, challenging look at her. "Are you?"

Was she? Oh, heavens, was she ever!

"Yes," she answered in between gulps of breath. Her hands were trembling, her lips were trembling, her insides were trembling; it showed in her voice. "That is . . . if you're sure it's what you want?"

Alexander pulled the car to a screeching stop in front of the Peterson house, switched off the engine, then turned in his seat to singe her with a fiery look.

"Oh, Caro, I'm very sure," he said, reaching across the seat to stroke his fingers along her flushed cheek. "I want you for myself . . . for always."

Carolyn startled herself into the present with her own choking sob. Blinking against a sting to her eyes, she glanced around through a veil of tears, surprised to find herself sitting on the bed in the guest room she had been in the process of getting ready for occupancy.

For always.

A long sigh broke the stillness of the room.

Sadly, for her, Alexander's *always* didn't last very long; less than a year in actual count of months, and even less than that in the count of a real relationship.

In truth, their marriage had failed very soon after they had exchanged vows. Alexander had killed it, and the weapon which he had used to do it was neglect. Like any other living thing, their love had withered from lack of nourishment.

A flash of resentment mixed with fear propelled Carolyn off the bed, resentment against Alexander's sudden appearance, which had caused the resurgence of all the painful memories she had worked so hard to suppress, and fear of him learning secrets she absolutely could not have revealed.

Motivated by a shot of anger-aroused adrenaline, Carolyn grabbed the dust cloth she had discarded while woolgathering, and attacked the bedside table with it. Her gaze skimmed the face of the turn-of-the-century windup clock, then sliced back when her brain registered the position of the hands.

Two-fifteen! Carolyn stared at the clock in disbelief, and raised it to her ear. The sound of a steady ticktock assured her the clock had not stopped running.

But how could that be?

Jess had promised to be home by one-thirty.

Jess. Uneasiness crawled into Carolyn's throat. Had something happened to Jess? Where was—

"I'm home, Mom," Jess called up the stairs to her from the foyer. "Sorry I'm late. I lost track of time."

Carolyn reacted like most mothers gripped by fear for a child, only to find the fear was pointless; her fear immediately changed to angry impatience. Clutching the dust cloth in her trembling fingers, she ran from the room to the top of the stairs.

Her daughter was nowhere in sight.

"Jessica," she called sharply, descending the stairs at a near run. "Where are you?"

"I'm right here," Jess answered, appearing in the kitchen doorway at the end of the central hall. "And I'm all right," she said, clearly anticipating her mother's next question.

Composing herself with some effort, Carolyn walked at a more sedate pace to the kitchen. "I'm very annoyed, Jess," she said in a stern but calm voice. "You know my feelings. You're a pretty girl, and with all the awful things you read and hear about today, you know I worry about your safety."

"I know, and I am sorry." Jess hung her head abjectly. "I forgot to wear my watch and—"

"But you had to realize the passage of time," Carolyn interrupted her to scold.

"Yeah, I probably would have, but—"

"But you lost all track of time searching for shells," Carolyn interrupted again, her voice shaded by a tinge of knowing indulgence.

"No." Jess shook her breeze-tousled head. "I lost track of time while I was talking."

"Talking?" Carolyn frowned. "Did you run into one of your friends?"

"No." The girl's contrite expression fled before a bright smile. "I was talking to Alex."

Fear slammed back into Carolyn, for an instant robbing her of breath and thought. "Alex?" she repeated starkly when her breath and senses returned.

"Yeah, you know, the man who was here earlier. The man you called Alexander." Knowing full well her mother's strictures about addressing an adult by their first name, Jess quickly explained. "I didn't know his last name, and anyway, he said right off that I should call him Alex."

Thank heaven for small mercies, Carolyn thought, swallowing to dislodge the tightness blocking her throat.

"I see," she said inanely, clearing her throat, and working her stiff lips into a faint semblance of a smile. "*That* Alex."

Jess nodded, then gave her a wary look. "I . . . er . . . hope you don't mind, Mom," she said slowly, looking guilty as she scraped one sandy sneaker over the tiled floor.

"Mind?" Carolyn injected when the girl hesitated, gnawing her lower lip. She had a queasy feeling that she wasn't going to like what she was about to hear. "Mind what?"

Jess hesitated an instant longer, then went on in a verbal gallop, "I invited him to dinner tonight."

Chapter Five

"Dinner?" Carolyn's voice was barely there, and had a definite squeaky sound.

"Yeah, dinner." Jess gazed at her with pleading, soulful green eyes. "It's okay, isn't it?"

"But you hardly know the man," Carolyn said, deliberately saying "you" instead of "we."

"But he's really nice, Mom," Jess wheedled. "We had a long talk on the beach."

"He was on the beach?" Disbelief widened Carolyn's eyes; it certainly didn't fit with the Alexander she had come to know during their brief union...other than during that first week. But then, of course, he'd been set on enchanting her for the purpose of seduction.

"Uh-huh." Jess nodded. "He didn't even mind the sand getting all over his pants and shoes. He told me he used to collect shells, too, when he was a kid."

"Really?" Carolyn raised her eyebrows; he had never told her he had collected shells as a kid.

"Really," Jess echoed. "And not only that. He said he likes fishing!" she exclaimed, as if that fact alone made him a special case.

"No kidding," Carolyn murmured through gritted teeth. Just another little bit of knowledge about himself Alex had never bothered to share with her.

"You don't really mind if he comes for dinner, do you, Mom?" Jess asked anxiously.

Of course Carolyn minded, she minded like hell. There were circumstances surrounding Jess's parentage the girl didn't know, circumstances that, even more unnerving, Alexander didn't know. And, because he held a position of power, Alexander could be dangerous, not merely to her peace of mind, but to the most important elements of her life.

Alexander could hurt her, badly, and should he learn certain facts, Carolyn felt positive, to his way of thinking, he would feel she deserved every punishment he meted out to her.

No. She couldn't, Carolyn thought wildly, hanging on to her surface composure, while inwardly seeing her future, her very existence, threatened by her former husband. She couldn't have Alexander in the house, spending time with Jess, perhaps discerning the truth... getting too close to her.

She couldn't afford to have him around for another, even more humiliating, soul-wrenching reason because...

Damn Alexander to hell... she still loved him.

"Mom?" Jess's plaintive voice reached Carolyn, reached the very center of the burgeoning panic paralyzing her.

"Jess, I—" Carolyn broke off, raking her mind for an excuse, any excuse to deny her daughter's plea. Her mind betrayed her; she couldn't think of a plausible reason to refuse Jess without crushing the girl's buoyant spirits. Besides, Jess had already invited him. How would she go about canceling the invitation?

"I guess not," she finally said, sighing in defeat. "But I wasn't planning anything fancy for dinner. I was just going to toss some burgers and dogs onto the gas grill, throw together a salad and open a can of baked beans."

"I'm sure that will be fine with Alex." Jess licked her lips. "It sounds great to me."

Yeah. Great.

Carolyn beat back a cry born of sheer hysteria.

She had to get control of herself, her emotions, she thought, turning away to hide whatever betraying expressions shaded her face.

Knowing she needed time alone, if only a few minutes, to pull herself together to face the evening ahead, Carolyn grasped at the first idea to come to mind.

"Ah . . . honey, we're going to need more rolls if we're having company for dinner," she said, careful to keep her voice steady and free of inflection. "Will you run to the store, please? And, oh, yes, there's nothing for dessert."

"Okay," Jess said, sounding eager to comply. "Can I pick whatever dessert I want—like chocolate cheesecake, maybe?"

"Yes, you *may*," Carolyn answered, emphasizing her last word, and smiling despite her misgivings about the entire situation; chocolate cheesecake was Jess's current passion and favorite dessert.

Kids! Carolyn grumbled to herself after Jess tore from the house heading for the store.

How would she ever get through the evening? She shuddered in anticipatory dread. What could she say to Alexander? She had difficulty making small talk with men, any man . . . let alone this particular man.

It would be like tiptoeing through a field loaded with hidden obstacles and land mines. One verbal misstep and—*boom*—her serene life would be history. Instinct and past experience assured Carolyn that, should Alexander learn what she had done, the liberties she had taken, he would not be thrilled. Justifiably angry came closer to the mark.

Her shoulders slumped in unison with her sinking spirits, in foregone conclusion of impending doom, and Carolyn glanced around, as if seeking escape. All her search produced was the realization of the untidiness of her surroundings. The kitchen was a cluttered mess of cleaning utensils; mop, bucket, cloths, solvents and polishes.

She couldn't have Alexander to dinner with the place looking like this! Carolyn thought, her shoulders and spirits rising to the challenge.

Galvanized into action, she got to work, determined to have her home in spotless condition by the appointed time of arrival of her most unwelcome guest.

Alexander would have wagered a sizable sum that Carolyn would hate the very idea of having him in the house . . . never mind seated at her table.

He scowled at his reflection in the bathroom mirror as he carefully drew the razor over his right cheek. Upon inner reflection, he likewise was having second thoughts about the arrangement.

But Jess was such a cute, appealing kid, and Alexander had found it hard to refuse her spontaneous invitation.

Still, Carolyn had been less than enthusiastic when he'd appeared at her door that morning.

Had it only been that morning?

His face cleanly shaved, Alexander stepped into the shower, to stand absently beneath the hot spray, the water beating against his skull, while his thoughts beat inside his head.

They had never—or hardly ever—found a common ground of conversation after a month of marriage fourteen years ago, so what could they possibly find to talk about now?

She apparently was managing the bed-and-breakfast establishment for the Petersons. He had risen to the position of CEO of his firm.

Hardly common ground.

But then, the only common ground they had ever shared was within the perimeters of their bedroom.

There, within the boundaries of their king-size bed, he and Carolyn had communicated very well.

Alexander shivered in response to remembered sensual delights and erotic explorations.

Heaving a sigh of regret, he lathered from head to toe, rinsed, then turned off the water and stepped from the shower into the steam-clouded room.

While toweling off, he pondered the advisability of bringing Carolyn a hostess gift.

Should he take her flowers?

Hell, he thought, tossing aside the towel and striding into the bedroom. He had never taken her flowers either before or after they were married, she'd probably...

Alexander's thoughts frayed like the edge of a much-laundered blanket.

He had never taken her flowers.

He had never taken her shopping.

He had never taken her on vacation.

He had been too busy pursuing his career to pursue Carolyn after she had become his wife.

Standing still, and buck-naked, Alexander came face-to-face for the first time in his life with his monumental and overbearing arrogance.

What a jerk he was then, he ruefully acknowledged.

He couldn't blame Carolyn if she not only didn't want him in the house, but didn't want him on the same planet.

His somber gaze homed in on the bedside phone. Should he call and beg off?

Alexander took two steps, then hesitated, stopped in his tracks by the image of Jess that filled his mind. She had been so animated, so eager. Could he in good conscience so much as consider dashing her youthful exuberance?

He ruefully acknowledged that he could not. Barring the unlikely event of a sudden hurricane, or his own demise, Alexander accepted as fact that he would arrive at the Peterson house at precisely six o'clock. Playing the genial guest for the effervescent Jess was not going to be easy, but he would do it if it killed him.

A wry smile twitched at Alexander's lips as he pivoted and walked to the closet. A smile caused by the reflection that if *it* did not kill him, Carolyn might.

A little over an hour later, Alexander jabbed his finger into the lighted doorbell button of the bed and breakfast.

He felt like a fool for, in addition to the bunch of white daisies he clutched in his right hand, the fingers of his left hand were curled around the handle of a brightly colored plastic sand pail, at least one and a half sizes larger than the one Jess had been carrying earlier on the beach.

Chapter Six

"He's here!"

"Obviously." Carolyn pushed the muttered word through teeth that had clenched at the sound of the doorbell. It didn't matter that her voice had a strained edge; Jess didn't hear it. She had taken off like a shot for the door.

"Hi, Alex."

Carolyn heard Jess greet their guest as she exited the kitchen, reluctantly following the girl to the door. She was midway along the central hall when she heard her daughter exclaim in surprise.

"For me? Thanks!"

Had Alex brought Jess a gift? Carolyn wondered, narrowing her gaze on the silhouettes standing just inside the shadowed doorway. Alexander Forester bringing gifts? It certainly didn't fit with the memory she had of him; so far as she could recall, and she unwillingly recalled every minute of their time together, Alexander had never brought gifts, not for her, not for anyone.

"Mom, look what Alex brought for me!" Jess's voice held laughter and excitement. She proudly held aloft a large hot-pink and orange–colored plastic sand pail. "It's for when I go shell-hunting. Isn't it radical?"

"Mmm," Carolyn murmured, dredging up a smile for the girl. "Bright, too."

"Hello, Carolyn," Alex said with quiet dignity, drawing her attention, and her averted gaze to him. He extended a hand, in which his fingers curled around the white paper-wrapped stems of a bunch of daisies. "These are for you." He smiled, then added, "I figured you didn't need a sand pail."

"Why...thank you, they're lovely," she responded, feeling suddenly shy as she accepted the flowers. "Ah—er—" She cleared her throat, and remembered her manners. "Come in." She motioned at the doorway into the living room. "Jess, entertain Mr....er, Alex, while I put these in water."

"Sure." Jess grinned at him. "You want to see my shell collection?"

"Sure," Alex echoed, grinning back at her.

Carolyn fled to the kitchen, stricken by the quivering inside her from the effects of his rakish grin. Dear heavens, she thought, pausing next to the sink to gather her wits. She had believed that by now, after all these years, that megawatt grin would have lost its power.

Drawing deep breaths, she retrieved a vase from the back of the cabinet beneath the sink. While rinsing the accumulated dust from the cut-glass vase, she let the cold water splash over her wrists, in an attempt to cool her heated and racing pulse.

"Hey, Mom," Jess sang out, startling Carolyn so much she nearly dropped the vase. "Alex asked if he could help with dinner," the girl went on, sauntering into the kitchen, their guest in tow. "He says he flips a mean burger."

Alexander? Carolyn turned to stare at him in patent disbelief. First gifts, and now an offer to actually help prepare dinner? Too much.

She frowned.

He smiled and shrugged.

"You make a mean hamburger?" Being discreet because of Jess, she refrained from reminding him that he couldn't boil water, and had never offered to so much as set the table during the brief tenure of their marriage. She merely arched her eyebrows. "Really?"

"Really," he repeated wryly. "When you live alone, you either eat out all the time, or you learn to do for yourself. I got tired of eating out all the time years ago." He shrugged again. "So I learned to cook."

"Utterly amazing," Carolyn murmured.

"You live alone?" Jess piped in with teenage artlessness. "You don't have a wife... or anyone?"

"No, I don't have a wife... or anyone," Alex said in a droll tone, the look he sent Carolyn telling her he hadn't missed her murmured comment.

"Must be pretty awful," Jess commiserated. "Living all alone, I mean."

Not if all you live for is your work, Carolyn thought, prudently keeping the observation to herself.

"It gets lonesome at times," Alex said, sending Carolyn another look that told her he knew precisely what she was thinking.

"Don't you have any girlfriends?" Jess asked in an innocent, if unsubtle, probe for information. "Or even go out on dates?"

"Jess! That's none of your business," Carolyn chastised the girl—telling herself she couldn't care less, while waiting with bated breath for his response.

Alex laughed.

Chills chased one after another down Carolyn's spine.

"I don't mind her questions," he said to Carolyn before giving his attention to Jess. "And yes, I do have lady friends, and I date occasionally. Do you?"

Although he had directed his question at Jess, Carolyn instinctively knew he had meant it for her. Not about to admit to never dating, she kept her mouth shut. But Jess felt no like containment.

"I'm not allowed to date yet," she said without rancor. "Not until I'm fifteen."

"And how long is that . . . four years, five?"

"No, two," Jess said, looking insulted. "It seems like forever," she went on, heaving a dramatic sigh. "But I guess I don't mind not dating, since Mom never does."

Blabbermouth, Carolyn accused her daughter in fuming agitation. "Jess," she began, suddenly realizing that Alex could become suspicious about the girl's age.

"Never?" Alex smoothly interrupted, shifting his drilling eyes to her. "Indeed?"

Carolyn felt both relief and annoyance; relief because he had zeroed in on the bit about her not dating instead of Jess's age, and annoyance because he had zeroed in on the bit about her not dating.

A cleft stick, for sure.

Nevertheless, with his cool, intense gaze probing her eyes, as if trying to read her mind, Carolyn was left with little choice but to answer. And she couldn't fabricate. It would set a bad example for Jess.

"Never," she admitted with obvious reluctance.

"Why?"

Persistent son of a... Carolyn drew a controlling breath, reminding herself that he always had been persistent. Hadn't he persisted in rushing her to the altar—and directly from there, into his bed?

The errant thought of being in his bed, with him, sent a sizzling bolt of excitement through Carolyn, making her pulse race and her cheeks warm.

Get a grip, she berated herself, maintaining his stare with Herculean effort.

Shaken by her response to him, the strength and intensity of the sensual attraction still crackling between them after all these years, Carolyn concealed herself behind a facade of cool indifference.

"I'm a single mother," she replied in repressive tones. "And I take my responsibilities of parenthood very seriously," she continued, despairing at the superior note in her voice. "I don't like leaving Jess with a sitter."

"So there," Alex retorted dryly.

Jess giggled.

He grinned.

Feeling utterly foolish, Carolyn flushed.

"Well, I don't know about anyone else, but I'm hungry," Alex abruptly announced, drawing attention away from her. "Suppose we get this dinner show on the road?"

Grateful to him for taking the spotlight off her, Carolyn was only too happy to fall into line.

"Yes, dinner." She moved to go to the back door. "Jess, gather the salad makings from the fridge, please, while I light the grill."

Alex caught her by the arm as she drew level with him, bringing her to a halt, and an uncomfortable awareness of him, his seemingly effortless effect on her senses.

Startled by the warmth radiating through her from his light hold on her, the tingling sensations skittering up her arm, and from there to the rest of her body, Carolyn stared at him in speechless wonder.

"I'll take care of the grill."

Such a simple statement, and yet, the softness of his voice, the glow in his eyes, in concert with the gentle touch of his hand on her arm, had the powerful impact of an intimate physical caress.

Carolyn was helpless, floundering in her own backwash of emotions. She could do nothing but agree.

"All right." She moistened her parched lips, and felt lightning strike her at the sudden intentness of his eyes following her motion. Swallowing, she tore her captured gaze from the lure of his eyes. "I'll...er...get the hamburger meat ready."

"You do that." Smiling to melt her insides, and her resistance, he removed his hand and turned away.

"Isn't he radical?" Jess enthused the minute Alex shut the door behind him. "I think I'm in love," she went on, sighing dramatically.

I'm afraid I'm still in love.

Confining her frightening thought inside her rattled mind, Carolyn dredged up a smile and a drawl. "I think there's a bit of an age difference."

"Aw, Mom," Jess groused. "I don't mean that kind of boy-girl mushy stuff."

"I know, honey, I'm teasing you." Her smile genuine and affectionate, Carolyn walked to the fridge to withdraw both the hamburger meat and the package of hot dogs just as Alex reentered the kitchen.

"What mushy stuff?" he demanded, peering suspiciously at the meat in Carolyn's hand. "Is there something wrong with the hamburger?"

Jess hooted with laughter.

Caught off guard, Carolyn blurted out the first lame explanation to come to mind. "No, no, the meat's fine—the mushy stuff was simply girl talk."

"Mmm...I see," Alex murmured, gliding a gleaming glance between the two females. "And males are excluded from simply mushy girl talk?"

"Well, of course," Jess said, executing a very adult toss of her head. "If they weren't, it wouldn't be girl talk, now, would it?"

Carolyn laughed in blatant pride and appreciation for her daughter's logical riposte.

"Okay, I know when I'm outnumbered." Chuckling, Alex raised his hands in surrender. "I'll shut my mouth and get to work." He crossed the room to take the wrapped hamburger from Carolyn. "Now, who wants onion in their burgers?"

All in all, the evening had turned out to be suprisingly pleasant, considering the possible dangers inherent in the situation, Carolyn thought later that night.

In bed, tired, but still wide-eyed and awake, she was conducting a solitary postmortem of the evening's events.

Alex had been a congenial and accommodating guest, for he had not only displayed good spirits, but had made himself useful, as well.

He had made the burgers, and had cooked both them and the hot dogs—which in truth were exceptional. And then, after dinner, he had amused Jess with his antics while helping with the necessary cleanup chores.

The cleanup chores, for heaven's sake! Alexander Forester. Would wonders ever cease?

In a way—no—in a *big* way, his willingness to pitch in and help agitated more than pleased Carolyn.

Could this possibly be the very same Alexander Forester who had never lifted a helping hand during the months of their marriage? The same man who had barely even noticed the spotless condition of their home—the house he had bought a few months after their marriage, the house he had insisted she keep under conditions of their divorce, the very same house that had enabled her to make this home for herself and Jess?

Carolyn grimaced, remembering the isolated instance that Alex had noticed her efforts. At one shocking point, he had noticed enough to compare her housekeeping skills to those of the professionals contracted to clean the corporate offices at his place of employment, the one place he spent the majority of his time, his effort, his life.

Recalling too vividly the many arguments they had had over his single-minded attention to his work, Carolyn relived once again the searing pain of rejection she had endured throughout their brief union.

When the pain had overwhelmed her, Carolyn had ended it, not calmly and intelligently, but emotionally, wildly, with tearful accusations.

She had accused Alexander of having a mistress, not a living, breathing woman, but the much more threatening mistress of ambition and the driving need to succeed.

With the passage of years, Carolyn had accepted the bitter realization that she had reacted immaturely, simply because she had been immature, young and still clinging to the illusion of Alexander as her hero, her perfect mate.

A sad-sounding chuckle of self-understanding whispered in the quiet room, born of insight garnered from maturity.

The insight begged an inner question: Why would a hero, the perfect mate, choose the imaginative girl she had been at eighteen to share his life?

Carolyn knew she was no longer that same starry-eyed girl. She was an adult, realistic, a woman. She had changed.

Had Alexander also changed?

The Alexander she had known and lived with had never lifted a helping hand.

The Alexander of today hadn't hesitated to do so.

The Alexander she had known and lived with had never thought to bring her flowers.

The Alexander of today hadn't hesitated to do so.

The realization sent her mind back, replaying the evening's events.

When the kitchen had been restored to order, Alex had challenged Carolyn and Jess to a friendly game of

Monopoly, and proceeded to bankrupt the two of them.

Oh, yes, Alex had been an exemplary guest, she conceded in consternation. His teasing had had Jess in a near-constant state of the galloping giggles and, Carolyn feared, a state of utter enthrallment.

In fact, so obviously taken was Jess by Alexander, she didn't voice much more than a token protest when the subject of Sunday morning came up.

Alex inadvertently raised the issue by mentioning the plans he and Jess had made for the next morning. The evening was winding down—much to Carolyn's relief—and they were in the process of returning the games pieces to the box, when Alex made his innocent blunder.

"So, we're on for early tomorrow morning," he said, smiling at Jess. "Right?"

"Yes," Jess answered as innocently, dropping her top-hat game piece into the box.

Carolyn's head snapped up. "Tomorrow morning?" She shifted a sharp-eyed glance from Alex to Jess, and arched her eyebrows at the girl. "What about tomorrow morning?"

"We're going shell-hunting," Jess replied, tossing a grin at their guest. "Alex and me."

"Alex and I," Carolyn automatically corrected the girl before squashing the idea. "And, no, you are not going shell-hunting in the morning, young lady. You're going to Sunday school, and then on to church."

"Aw, Mom," Jess whined. "I don't know how long Alex is going to be here, and I gotta go to school Monday. Can't I miss one Sunday?"

Already shaking her head in the negative, Carolyn opened her mouth to refuse the plea, but Alex, mirroring her head motion, beat her into speech.

"Wait a minute, Jess, you never said a word to me about Sunday school and church."

"I'm sorry." Jess sighed, lowering her head in a show of abject repentance. "I was so excited about shell-hunting with you, I guess I forgot that tomorrow was Sunday."

"Well, tomorrow is Sunday, and," Carolyn began sternly, only to have Alex interrupt, and in her opinion, usurp her authority.

"And you'll attend Sunday school and church, as usual," he instructed in a softer, gentler tone. "We can go later, after you get home from church."

"After Sunday dinner," Carolyn inserted, regaining control of her authority.

Alexander's lips twitched, betraying a mocking smile. "Yes, after dinner," he echoed in apparent seriousness.

Carolyn felt hard-pressed not to smack him one, but she held on to her temper, and her itching hand.

"Can Alex come to dinner?"

Jess's request cast Carolyn into an awkward position. She desperately wanted to deny the girl's request, for her own peace of mind. And yet, how could she refuse to have Alex come for the midday meal, when he was planning to spend the rest of the afternoon with Jess? She couldn't, of course, so... Resenting the bland expression on his face, she sighed and relented.

"May Alex come to dinner," she corrected, before giving in to the eager-faced girl. "And, yes, he may." Holding out a feeble hope, she raised her eyebrows at him and added, "That is, unless you have other plans...?"

"No," Alex responded, smiling with aggravating assurance. "I haven't enjoyed a home-cooked Sunday dinner in years. And I'd be delighted to join you. Thank you."

By the time Alex finally said good-night, Jess appeared to be completely gone on the man.

Easy to understand, Carolyn mused, her sigh sounding loud in the quiet room. Hadn't she, herself, fallen under Alexander's spell from the first moment she saw him, spoke with him, fourteen years ago?

Fourteen years ago?

The taunt came from deep within Carolyn's subconscious. How about now, and the recurring attacks of tingles she felt throughout the evening?

Proximity, Carolyn defended herself against the inner voice of truth. It was merely a chemistry thing, a physical pull of the senses.

She moved her head against the pillow dismissively. Out of sight, out of mind.

Yeah, right, the taunting voice drawled. So, explain the present wakefulness, then the continuing tingles and the forever empty feeling in the core of your femininity, an emptiness that only Alexander could ever fill.

The voice, the words, caused a mental flood. Sensations washed over her, drenching her senses, drowning her in the unfettered flow of sensual memories.

Carolyn shivered with the remembered thrill of Alexander's mouth devouring her lips, his tongue inciting her response, his hands inflaming her senses.

For one beautiful moment, she could feel the muscled strength of his slim body demanding all, everything she had to give. She experienced again the glorious freedom she had felt then, the freedom from inhibitions of stroking his warm skin, teasing his seeking mouth, clasping her legs around him in an intimate lovers' embrace.

Her soft moan of need for him, her prolonged emptiness shimmered on the summer-night air.

The taunting voice inside echoed her moan with a murmured mocking laughter.

Oh, Carolyn thought helplessly, shifting her legs in a fruitless effort to ease the longing ache...

Shut up.

Yet, even as the silent plea swirled inside her tired mind, Carolyn knew the taunting voice spoke truth.

Chapter Seven

Sleep eluded Alex.

Grumbling to himself, he threw off the disheveled covers and left the bed to stand at the window, staring moodily at the moon-washed sea.

Damn, Carolyn was still as beautiful and exciting as she had been fourteen years ago.

No. Alex shook his head. She was even more beautiful, more exciting now.

Did she, he wondered, still believe him to be a slave to the mistress of ambition?

Probably, he mused uncomfortably. And why shouldn't she, when, in fact, it was the brutal truth.

At least, Alex amended, he had slavishly pursued his career, selfishly thought of little else, until he'd come face-to-face with a pixie-faced, pert kid.

Carolyn's child.

Alex frowned against the too-vivid memory of Carolyn begging him to give her a child. She adored children, and had told him she would love having at least three. He had refused her, claiming they should have some time to themselves before starting a family, while secretly believing she was too young to take on the responsibilities of motherhood. In all honesty, he was faced with the cold fact that what he had wanted was the freedom to pursue his consuming ambition.

With the truth of his own selfishness pounding inside his brain, Alex had little option but to admit that he had been wrong, on many counts, but most especially about Carolyn being too young to be a good mother.

Having a child had wrought many changes in Carolyn. The thought conjured an image of the differences in her once ultraslender shape; now she was lushly rounded.

His body stirred in memory of past delights.

Alex groaned aloud.

He wanted her, with an even stronger hunger than he had experienced fourteen years ago.

Alex shook his head again, sharply, in denial of the heated thoughts searing his mind.

His defenses down, he admitted in tired surrender that, not only did he want Carolyn in the physical sense, he wanted to be with her, cherish her, love her on a permanent basis.

No doubt about it, Forester, he told himself wryly, you are in big emotional trouble.

Recalling that the first time he had courted her—courted her? Ha!—Carolyn had been an imaginative young girl with fantasy-stars in her eyes.

In fact, for Alex, Caro had been a pushover.

Those days were gone forever.

In the interim, she had accepted another man into her life, into her body.

Alex ground his teeth until his clenched jaw ached. As stupid and unrealistic as he knew it to be, he felt a soul-deep sense of cold betrayal and hot anger at the very idea of Carolyn coupling with another man, any man other than he himself.

Memory flashed, sharp and clear of the nights he had spent in bed with Caro, the sheer, exhilarating joy he had experienced while his lips and tongue plundered her eager mouth, and his throbbing body was buried deeply within hers, celebrating the physical expression of their love.

The mental scene whirled, changing to Caro, giving herself in the same way to another man.

No!

On the fringes of his consciousness, Alex felt, knew, his reaction was irrational. He had certainly not remained celibate all this time—although, in truth, he had not sought physical release, or even companionship with another woman for over a year after he and Carolyn had parted.

But eventually, there had been other women, of course, brief affairs entered into and conducted with mutual understanding of no strings, no commitment.

It would be unrealistic to so much as dream Carolyn had taken no lovers.

No, no, she is mine! Still the protest reverberated inside his head. She has always been mine.

Alex curled his fingers into tight fists, fighting the insidious self-denial of fact.

Because the unpalatable fact of Caro's sharing of herself with another man lived and breathed in the form of the child Caro and this nameless, faceless man had created together.

Jess.

A soft smile smoothed the rigid line of his lips as an image of the girl rose in his mind, silencing the inner protest, comforting the blinding rage.

Jess of the dancing green eyes, the sparkling personality, the endearing pixie-pretty face and the alternate flashes of sensibility and giddiness of a thirteen-year-old.

Thirteen?

Alex frowned as the import of the number crashed through the barrier of his own self-absorption.

Jess had said she was thirteen. And Carolyn had not disputed the girl's claim.

A queasy sensation invaded Alex's stomach and mind. Feeling drained, he stared with blank, unseeing eyes at the path of moonlight skipping across the undulating sea.

When his mind reactivated, his thinking process came back with a force strong enough to rock his carefully planned, so meticulously organized world.

It was now fourteen years since he and Caro had rushed blindly into marriage. And it was now over thirteen years since their divorce.

Alex's mental wheels went into overdrive.

Either Carolyn had been unfaithful to him with Jess's father before the divorce . . . or . . .

Alex blinked.

Either Carolyn had been unfaithful . . . or . . .

He had fathered Jess!

For several long seconds, Alex couldn't move, or breathe, or think. He felt sick. The nasty taste of bile rose in his throat, choking him.

"Damn her to hell."

The harsh and vicious sound of his own voice startled Alex. The content of his words shook him.

He was cursing Carolyn, the only woman he had ever loved. Cursing her, and yet, he didn't have any concrete facts, couldn't be certain that she had either cuckolded him or deceived him.

Cuckolding would be enough to warrant his ire. But if she had deceived him by not telling him he was going to be a father . . . then she deserved much stronger punishment than a snarled curse.

If she had deceived him, Carolyn had robbed him of not only the thrill of holding in his arms his first-born infant, but of the joys of watching the child grow, cut her first teeth, take her first unsteady step, say her first words.

A longing emptiness yawned deep inside Alex, and he felt a need to weep, a desire he had not experienced since he himself had been a young child.

Jess.

Chapter Eight

Carolyn was fixing the beaters into the hand mixer in preparation for whipping the potatoes, when the doorbell pealed through the house, announcing Alexander's arrival.

With a thunk, the beaters dropped from her suddenly nerveless fingers onto the countertop.

"It's Alex!" Jess cried jubilantly, tearing from the dining room, where she had been setting the table. "I'll get it."

Good thing, too, Carolyn thought wryly, picking up the beaters to try again to insert them into the mixer. To her consternation, her fingers were trembling so badly she had difficulty aligning the narrow beater flanges with the mixer's locking grooves.

What was wrong with her? Carolyn demanded of herself, glaring at her hands. Well, of course, she knew full well what was wrong with her: Alexander Forester was wrong with her, darn the chemistry of the ongoing attraction she experienced for him.

"Need some help?"

Carolyn started at the quiet sound of his voice, close, too close behind her; the beaters clattered onto the countertop once again.

"Don't ever creep up on me like that!" she exclaimed, spinning around to transfer her glare to him.

With her heightened tension, awareness of him was immediate and devastating. He looked good, dressed for his outing with Jess in tan brushed denims—which clung to his slim waist, narrow hips and long straight legs...a soft cotton-knit pullover shirt—which molded his flatly muscled chest and wide shoulders...and a nylon windbreaker—the sleeves of which he had loosely looped around his strong neck. And, as if the look of him wasn't bad enough, he smelled good, too. His scent combined an intoxicating mix of exotic pine and musky man.

Damn his attractive hide, he looked and smelled too good for her peace of mind, never mind her rioting senses.

"Feeling a mite jumpy, are you?" His voice held a self-satisfied–sounding purr.

"No, I'm not jumpy," Carolyn lied in a near snarl. "You simply startled me, that's all. I'm just not used to having a man in the house."

"Indeed?" The satisfied purr in his voice was even more pronounced.

She had blundered, and badly, Carolyn knew it. She didn't know quite how to go about getting around it. Fortunately, at that moment, Jess saved her the effort of formulating a suitable response.

"Hey, Mom," Jess called from the dining room. "I've finished setting the table. Are we going to eat soon? I wanna get going." She had already changed her clothes, out of her Sunday best and into jeans and a T-shirt emblazoned with the legend: Life's A Beach.

Carolyn sighed.

Alex chuckled.

She made a soft but rude sound.

He laughed out loud.

Suddenly furious, she spun around, grabbed the beaters and slammed them unerringly into the mixer slots.

"You may laugh, think it's all rather amusing," she muttered, setting aside the mixer, then reaching for the pot of potatoes on the stove. "But then, you're not in the position of raising a child on your own."

"That's right, I'm not," Alex said, reaching around her to brush her hand away from the pot handle. "I'll do that," he went on, picking up a hot-pad before grasping the handle. He drained the steaming water from the pot, then set it on another hot-pad on the counter next to the sink. "Anything else I can do for you?"

Go away.

Carolyn clamped her lips to keep the response from escaping her guard. "Ah . . . yes," she replied instead, turning her attention to the potatoes, to hide the betraying confusion in her eyes from the laser probe of his stare. "You can take the roast pan from the oven while I whip the potatoes."

She felt him, smelled him, unmoving beside her for a moment, a long tense moment, then gave a silent sigh of relief when he scooped up two more hot-pads and turned to the stove.

She might be a fool, Carolyn mused later as Jess and Alexander conducted an animated conversation across the dining-room table. But she was a competent fool.

The traditional Sunday midday meal was delicious. At any rate, Carolyn had to assume it was delicious, if the compliments she received from both her companions were anything to go by. She herself had eaten sparingly... and had tasted even less of the food she had prepared.

"Can we go now?" Jess asked eagerly, jumping up as she placed her napkin next to her plate.

"May we—" Carolyn had started to correct the girl, but that's as far as she got.

"Wait a minute, kid," Alex interrupted, frowning at Jess. "Don't you think we should show our appreciation for the wonderful meal your mother cooked, by offering to do the clearing-away?"

"Yeah, I guess so," Jess said, somehow managing to look contrite and disgruntled at the same time.

"No, really," Carolyn inserted, anxious to have him gone, if only to allow her to breathe normally again. "I'll let you skip kitchen duty today," she told Jess. "You run along. I don't mind."

"Thanks, Mom," Jess cried, grinning as she made a dash for the doorway into the hall. "C'mon, Alex, before she changes her mind," she called back in obvious teasing.

Alex didn't move for a moment, other than to arch one eyebrow at Carolyn. "You're sure?"

"Yes, of course." Carolyn searched until she found a smile of sorts to offer. "I have nothing better to do."

"You could join us in the shell hunt," he suggested.

"I'll pass, thank you." Carolyn had been reduced to grinding her teeth, wishing him out of the house, out of her sight, out of her system.

He heaved a sigh, but smiled. "Well, then, perhaps you'll join in when we get back."

"Get back?" She frowned. "Join in on what?"

Grinning in much the same way Jess had mere moments before, Alex pushed back his chair and stood. "Why, rinsing the shells, and then painting them," he drawled, still grinning as he sauntered from the room.

Carolyn stared at the empty doorway in mute horror. He was coming back to the house with Jess.

Oh, great.

Oh, wonderful.

Oh, hell.

She wasn't even aware of crunching the edge of the tablecloth with her fingers.

"It was nice of your mother to let you off the hook today," Alex observed, strolling along beside Jess as they crossed the highway and headed for the beach.

"Yeah." Jess nodded vigorously. "Mom's pretty cool."

And she makes me pretty hot, Alex reflected, too aware of the sudden discomfort he had suffered while standing behind her in the kitchen.

Carolyn, this new Carolyn, smelled altogether different than the woman he remembered, and the complete opposite of the women he had known in the years since then.

That younger Carolyn had worn a light, flowery scent, and the women since then had seemed to douse themselves with more expensive, supposedly more alluring perfumes.

But this new, more mature Carolyn exuded a devastating-to-the-male-senses scent, a combination of cooking aromas, feminine soap, shampoo and sheer, exciting woman.

It just wasn't fair to the average male.

The protesting thought brought a wry smile of self-knowledge to Alex's lips. The smile deepened as the breeze billowed Jess's unzipped jacket revealing the lettering on her T-shirt.

Life's a Beach.

And sometimes a real bitch, he concluded, his eyes clouding with tenderness as he gazed at the scampering girl.

Was Jess his?

Lord, Alex prayed so. Even with the bitter thought that Carolyn had deceived, and possibly betrayed, him, he badly wanted the girl to be his, of his flesh, of his blood, conceived in union with the woman he now readily admitted he had never stopped loving.

Oh, yeah, life could certainly be a bitch.

"Hey, Alex!" Jess called, ending his reverie. "Are you gonna help or are you just gonna watch?"

"I'm going to help," he assured her, following her example by dropping onto the sand to remove his running shoes. "Why should you have all the fun?"

Laughing together, they set their shoes to one side, then began to hunt shells in earnest. Jess produced an extra sand shovel for him; Alex offered to carry the large pail he had bought for her.

Throughout the warming afternoon, Alex was tempted to subtly question the girl, probe into the memories, not actually remembered, but very likely instilled into her consciousness by a loving mother.

But while the temptation was strong, the need great to garner more details of her parentage, Alex refrained, his conscience repulsed by the very idea of grilling, however gently, the girl's tender sensibilities.

Nevertheless, due to Jess's openness and obvious attachment to him, Alex did learn some, if less personal, interesting facts about her.

Jess innocently tossed them out to him as they dug up a sizable portion of the beach.

"I made the honor roll every report period so far this year," she said at one point, apropos of absolutely nothing said before.

"Congratulations," Alex said, feeling pride in her achievement swell inside him.

"Thanks, but I've got to admit that, though I study, it comes pretty easily." She tossed him a smile.

He tossed it back, thinking her intelligence must have been passed on genetically.

Content in each other's company, they dug in silence for a long spell. Again, Jess finally broke it, this time with a question.

"Did you ever go up to Ocean City when you were visiting here?"

"Sure," Alex replied, standing straight to stretch the kinks from bending out of his back. "We used to go up once a week for the concerts on the Music Pier."

"So do we!" she exclaimed. "Mom loves those concerts, especially when they're playing music from Broadway shows and the movies."

Alex smiled, recalling that Carolyn always had preferred show and movie tunes to the then-current rock and popular music, even though she liked that stuff, too.

"I liked those concerts the best, myself," he confided.

Silence again reigned between them—for all of thirty or forty seconds.

"I like the water slide."

Drawing a blank, Alex frowned. "What water slide?"

"The one on the boardwalk in Ocean City."

"Coulda fooled me," he confessed. "I didn't know there was a water slide on the boardwalk."

"You haven't been there for a while?"

Alex laughed. "I haven't been in Ocean City for a long while. Fourteen years, at least," he said, knowing it had been exactly that long ago.

"Well, you should see it. I mean, it's really big," Jess assured him.

"I'd like to see it," he said. "I've never been to a water slide, big or otherwise."

"You haven't?" Jess looked appalled, as if seriously shocked at his deprivation. "Geez, what have you been doing for fourteen years, living in a cave?"

"Close," Alex answered wryly, struck by the apt comparison of his office to a cave. "For most of that time, I've been working inside."

"You know what they say about all work and no play, don't you?" Jess asked, shaking her head in obvious despair of his single-minded diligence.

She looked and sounded so adult, Alex had to laugh. "You think I'm dull, huh?"

"No!" She set her hair flying with the fierce shake of her head. "I think you're pretty cool." She frowned, and went on, "But I think you oughta get out more often."

"Escape the daily grind?"

"Yeah," she said eagerly. "It's too bad it's not yet summer. I'd be out of school, and we could go up to the slide in Ocean City."

"Couldn't we go one afternoon after school?" he suggested, pleased at the way her pixie face lit up. But then the light went out of her, and her shoulders slumped. "What's wrong? Don't you want to go?"

"'Course I do," she was quick to assure him. "But it's been so cool lately that the slide won't be much fun."

"But I could still see the slide," he consoled her. "And we could stroll along the boardwalk a while, then have dinner somewhere before coming back."

"Yeah!" The light was back in her eyes, and his heart. "We could have dinner at the diner at the circle in Sommers Point. You ever been there?"

"Yes." He nodded, feeling as happy as she looked. "That diner is still there, then?"

Jess mirrored his nod. "And the food's good."

"It always was." He smiled in remembrance of the excellent meals he had wolfed down there as a youth and young man. "Is it a date?"

"I'll have to ask Mom." Her small face crinkled. "She's pretty strict about me being out on school nights. You know, after-school chores and homework and that stuff."

"Yeah, that stuff," he echoed, grinning at her. "That stuff is important, you know."

"Well . . . sure." Jess shrugged. "But, sometimes, there's stuff a lot more interesting."

"Hmm." Alex nodded. "I'll tell you what, kid. We'll pick a day, one on which you don't have as much schoolwork, and then we'll see if we can coax your mother out of your chores—just for that one day, you understand."

Jess lit up like a Christmas tree, and was nearly dancing in place with enthusiasm.

"Yeah, okay—" She paused, eyes going wide in sudden realization. "Hey, Alex, what about Friday? We never get homework on Fridays!"

Watching her, Alex felt his insides contract, then expand with sheer, unadulterated affection. Struck by an amazing urge to dance in place alongside her, but reminding himself that he was the adult here, he extended his hand instead.

"Hey, Jess, put it there, kid." When the girl eagerly, trustingly slid her palm onto his, Alex gave her hand a professional, businesslike shake.

"It's a deal."

"Awright!" Jess exclaimed, in turn slapping him a high five when he released her hand.

The sun was lowering when they abandoned their shell hunt, which had not been satisfyingly successful. The shells they had found were run-of-the-mill, not in the least spectacular, or even interesting.

"Don't look so disappointed," Alex commiserated with the discouraged girl. "There'll be other times."

Jess sighed. "Maybe we woulda had a better catch if we'd gone fishin' instead."

"Maybe," Alex agreed, deciding at that instant that he would do some fishing of a different kind later, after Jess was in bed.

Alex couldn't wait any longer. Speculation was eating him alive. He wanted answers, and he was determined on hearing those answers from Carolyn before the night was over.

Chapter Nine

Carolyn heard the shell hunters before she saw them. The sound of Alexander's laughter mingled with Jess's giggles wafted to her through the kitchen window she had opened when the afternoon sun warmed the day.

As it always did, the innocent trill of Jess's giggles brought a soft smile to her lips. But her smiling lips quivered because, as it always had, the deep masculine rumble of Alex's laughter sent a streak of awareness in a wild erotic dance down her spine.

It wasn't fair, she cried in silent despair. It simply wasn't fair that he should have this devastating effect on her senses after all these years.

Absently, Carolyn also registered the sound of running water, followed by their tramping footsteps up the stairs to the back porch. Alerted, she gathered together the fragments of her fraying composure, straightened her tingling spine, banished the tremor from her lips and met their entrance into the kitchen with a bright smile.

"How did it go?" she asked in a tone pitched to match her smile. "Find anything fabulous?"

"Naw," Jess muttered disgustedly, shaking her head. "Just the same old same old."

"Too bad." Carolyn braved a direct look at Alexander, and immediately knew she'd made a mistake.

He was standing behind Jess, and from over the girl's lowered head, his expression was open and unguarded, soft and compassionate.

"We did a fairly thorough job of digging up a good portion of the beach, though," he said in a bracing tone, while his eyes flashed a warning to Carolyn not to fuss over the girl. "Didn't we, kid?"

"We sure did!" Jess agreed, the disgust changing to renewed eagerness for the fruitless venture. "And now we're starving, aren't we, Alex?"

Alex laughed, and nodded in answer.

The erotic dance performance reprised along the length of Carolyn's spine.

Unfair? It was almost criminal.

"And a good thing, too," Carolyn said, somewhat surprised at the light note she managed to infuse into her voice. "You two weren't the only ones busily employed all afternoon. I made a pasta salad, a plate of finger sandwiches *and* whipped together a strawberry mousse for dessert. While I set it out, you two can wash up."

The sound of silence blessed the house.

Jess was asleep.

After the hilarity the girl and Alex had engaged in during supper and afterward, while they painted strange-looking animals and even stranger-looking faces on their cache of shells, Carolyn would have happily put her feet up and relaxed for a few hours before seeking her own bed, except for one distracting tension-causing fact.

Alexander remained firmly ensconced in her favorite chair, *his* feet resting on *her* footstool, perusing the pages of one of *her* magazines.

Other than tear the publication from his hands, and then toss him bodily from the house—a feat beyond her physical capabilities, anyway—or to be downright rude by flatly telling him to take himself off somewhere, Carolyn was at a loss as to how to get him out of the house.

Understandably, considering the circumstances, the silence quickly grew strained and overloud.

When he suddenly shut the magazine, the minimal sound of the pages slapping together had the effect on Carolyn of the maximum noise of a cannon shot.

She jerked erect in her chair.

He raised a quizzical eyebrow.

"I...er...you startled me," she explained in a breathless, nervous tone of voice.

A frown scored Alex's forehead as he got up and crossed to where she was sitting, uptight and rigid, on the edge of the velvet-covered love seat.

"Are you afraid of me, Carolyn?" he asked, his tone laced with impatience and a tinge of anger.

"Afraid? Of you?" Carolyn shook her head, and babbled on, "Why, no, of course not."

His raised his hand to her face, to brush his fingertips over her cheek. Carolyn flinched; his frown darkened, his eyes caught fire.

"I would never harm you." Though soft, his voice betrayed the emotions heating up inside him.

Carolyn lowered her head, shielding her eyes from his probing stare. "I know," she murmured. "I'm sorry, it's just that..." Her voice vanished, got lost in the sensations his stroking fingers sent skittering from her cheek to every pulse point in her body.

"Alexander." His name fell from her trembling lips on a breathless murmur.

"Caro." Her name whispered on his breath as he bent his head to replace his stroking fingers with his lips.

It was foolish, dangerous, impetuous, and Carolyn knew it, yet she could not keep herself from turning her head the fraction required to touch her lips to his.

She was disarmed on contact, and defeated the instant Alex took command of her mouth.

The flame of passion that had always flared between them blazed anew, even stronger, hotter than before. Carolyn's fear, trepidation, common sense went up in smoke.

The danger didn't matter. Nothing mattered. Nothing except this man, the one man who could make her feel alive, a woman, in every sense of the word.

Without a thought of protest, Carolyn allowed, no, *eagerly* sought his deepening kiss, the intimate caress of his hands, the evocative thrust of his tongue.

She was young again, eighteen, ripe and hungry for the possession of the man she loved.

The love seat was too small to accommodate his tall frame. Carolyn murmured a wordless acceptance when he caught her to him and slid onto the carpet.

The flame of passion leaped higher, flicking relentlessly against the aching inside her. Frantic to be with him, be one with him, she tore at his clothes, moaning encouragement as he tore at hers.

There were no words spoken, and no need for them; speech was superfluous. Actions said all that needed to be said: the stroke of his one hand up the inside of her thigh; the curling of his other hand around her breast; the silent message of his devouring mouth and tongue.

Alex came to her, into her body, in a desperate rush, breaking the barrier of a thirteen-year dormancy.

Carolyn gasped at the sensation, so similar in impact to her very first time with him.

Thrust to the hilt within her, Alex stilled, staring down at her with eyes clouded by confusion.

"Caro?" Even as he said her name, the confusion in his eyes changed to dawning comprehension and amazement. "I'm sorry," he said contritely. "It's obviously been some time since you've been with a man. I didn't mean to hurt you."

"It's all right. It didn't hurt," she was quick to assure him. "It . . . it feels wonderful."

"Does it?" Alex murmured, lowering his mouth to hers. "It feels wonderful to me, too," he whispered against her lips. "Like coming home."

"Yes. Oh, yes," she cried, arching her hips in a silent plea for more.

Alex was a strong man, but not strong enough to withstand her sensuous demand. Murmuring her name into her mouth, he began moving his body in an erotic dance of physical expression mere words could never convey.

The friction of their straining bodies sparked a tension inside Carolyn, coiling tighter and ever tighter until, certain she could no longer bear the pleasure, the tension coil snapped, releasing a flood of pulsating sensations so intense she cried his name aloud.

"Alexander!"

"Caro." His strangled cry of release vibrated simultaneously with hers.

Utterly spent, Carolyn gloried in the weight of Alexander's body, pressing her into the carpet. She reveled in the scratchy fibers abrading her back.

Alexander. Tears stung her eyes at the thought of his name. Yes, what he had said was true; being with him, joined with him in the most intimate of embraces, instilled a satisfying sense of homecoming.

Surrendering to him may have been wrong, probably was wrong for her, but she couldn't bring herself to care.

She loved him; she always had.

Alex lay on his back on the carpet, one arm flung over his eyes, his breathing harsh, his heart hammering, his body rejoicing in the beauty of the aftermath of lovemaking almost too perfect to be real.

But it had been real, more real than at any time since the last time with Caro.

Wrong, Alex's clearing mind avowed. This time with Caro had been even better than before.

And she had deceived or betrayed him.

Suddenly, the force of the realization struck a blow to the depths of his heart, mind and soul.

Alex wanted to crawl away from her, lick his wounds, grieve in silent anguish.

But Alex was strong, and strong men didn't crawl away, they stayed and fought for what was their own.

Lifting his arm, Alex turned his head to stare into the love-flushed and beautiful face of the only woman on God's earth that he had ever loved.

"You never married again?"

As quiet as it was, his voice startled Caro, and she met his stare with wide, wary eyes.

"N-no," she said, flicking her dry lips with the tip of her tongue. "How..." She swallowed, then tried again. "How did you know?"

"Simple." Alex gave her a tired smile. "Your name, Carolyn Forester, is on the magazine label."

"Yes, of course." She closed her eyes.

He opened them again in a hurry. "You know, in the heat of the moment, neither one of us gave a thought to protection. If you have conceived, will you tell me this time?"

"What?" Caro's eyes flew wider than before. "Alexander, what are you talking about?"

"Jess," he answered wearily, feeling more tired than ever before in his life. "She's mine, isn't she?"

"No!"

"Caro, don't lie to me now," he said in a voice ragged with emotion.

Either unmindful, or no longer aware of her nudity, she sat up, squared her shoulders, lifted her chin proudly and said with utter conviction, "I am not lying to you, Alexander. Jess is not your child."

He shut his eyes, shielding himself from the truth blazing from her eyes.

"I wish with all my heart that she were yours," she said.

Now it was Alex who opened his eyes in a hurry. Caro's impassioned whisper had the force of a shout. But what was the whispered shout saying—that she had neither betrayed nor deceived him?

Hurting inside, because he had so badly wanted Caro's child to be his child, and amazingly, because he already loved Jess as if she were his child, Alex heaved himself up and fixed her with a riveting stare.

"She's illegitimate?" His throat was so parched his voice cracked over the word.

"She is not!" Caro exclaimed, obviously incensed. "How dare you suggest such a thing?"

"I dare because I need to know!" Alex retorted in angry confusion.

"Why?" Caro demanded belligerently.

"Because I love her." There, it was said, out loud, and Alex didn't care that he had made himself vulnerable by his own admission.

"Do you?" Caro's voice and expression softened with tenderness. "Oh, Alexander."

"Who..." He hesitated, not wanting to hear, yet needing to know. "Who was her father?"

"A man I never met."

"Huh?" Alex blinked and shook his head as if to clear his thinking process. "You're not making sense."

Carolyn sighed. "I'm making perfect sense. You just don't know the particulars of Jess's story."

"All right." Still angry, and even more confused than before, Alex nevertheless maintained enough control to keep from shouting at her.

"So, enlighten me," he said with as much patience as he could muster.

Caro lowered her eyes, then jolted, as if amazed by the fact of her nakedness. "I have to dress," she said, moving to get up from the floor.

Alexander caught her by the wrist, keeping her in place. "I'm not leaving here until you tell me."

She went stiff, looked rebellious for an instant, then her shoulders slumped and she gave in.

"All right, but first I've got to dress...we've got to dress." Her eyes appealed to him for understanding. "What if Jess were to awaken and come downstairs? Would you want her to find us . . . like this?"

"No, you're right," he said, reluctantly releasing his hold. "Where can I . . . er, clean up?"

"The powder room in the hallway, beneath the stairs," she directed, scrambling up and collecting her clothes. "I . . . I'll be down in a few minutes." Clutching the garments in front of her, she took off at a run.

Alex performed his cleanup with the same swift efficiency he applied to every task. Unsurprisingly, he was finished long before Carolyn reappeared downstairs. In the interim, restless and impatient, he busied himself by making a pot of coffee, certain that he, if not both of them, would need it.

When it came down to the crunch, Alex knew full well that he didn't have a leg to stand on concerning the particulars of Jess's parentage. If he was not her father, and he honestly had no doubts about the veracity of Caro's claim, he was dead in the water—unless Caro chose to tell him the story.

Fortunately for his peace of mind, when she came to him in the kitchen, she apparently was prepared to confide in him. She gave not so much as a hint that her opening statement would rock him to his very foundation.

"Jess knows that I'm not her biological mother."

"What?" Alex was so shaken by her disclosure, he nearly scalded himself with the hot coffee he was pouring into a cup for himself.

The faint smile that fleetingly softened her lips told him she had expected his reaction.

"It's a long, sad story."

"Okay," he said, indicating the cup he had filled for her. "I've got nothing better to do. Sit down, relax, then tell me as much as you want me to know."

Carolyn hesitated, gazing at him in obvious trepidation, as if in actual fear of his response.

Further shaken by the fright clouding her spectacular green eyes, Alex deliberately put the distance of the table width between them.

"Please, Caro, sit down," he said in a tone as mild as he could manage. "I promise I'll be good."

His attempt at tension-relieving humor was admittedly lame, but it drew a weak smile from her.

"Okay." Seating herself across the table from him, Carolyn grasped the cup with both hands, drew a deep breath, then launched into an explanation.

"After our divorce, I decided to go back to school, get my college degree."

He frowned, uncertain about the possible connection between Jess's parentage and Caro's education.

She held up a hand. "Hear me out." At his slow nod of assent, she continued, "Since I was aiming for a degree in teaching at the primary level, I took a job at a day-care center for lower-income families." She paused to sip at the steaming coffee, then stared into middle distance, as if looking back over the years.

"Go on," Alex gently prompted.

"Not long after I started working at the center, I met a young woman, a widow with a two-month-old daughter."

"Jess?"

She nodded. "Jess." A tender smile curved her lips. "She was so beautiful, tiny and delicate, and such a sweet, pleasant baby." Tears filmed her eyes, but she pressed on, "Jess's mother, Judy, was a quiet, unassuming girl, alone and afraid. She and I became fast, and then firm friends. Scared, and needing someone to talk to, she confided in me."

"Jess was illegitimate?" Alex guessed, even though she had denied the charge earlier.

"Oh, no," Carolyn again denied. "Judy and Jess's father were married. They had eloped in open defiance of his parents' disapproval." Her lips curved downward. "You see, his parents thought Judy wasn't good enough for their son, since she was the product of rather unsavory parents."

She paused once again to take a swallow from her cup, this time to moisten her throat. Alex held his silence, allowing her all the time she desired.

"Judy insisted that they were happy, and making a go of their marriage, despite his family's objections. She told me they—Judy and her husband—were thrilled when Jess was born."

She paused once more, to heave a sigh that tore at Alex's heart, and warned him the worst was yet to come.

He was right. When Carolyn resumed speaking, her voice was strained with emotion.

"Wanting his child cared for by her mother instead of strangers, Judy's husband insisted she not return to her job. To make up the difference, he held down two jobs. He had no car, and to save money, he walked to and from both places of employment." Carolyn's narrative speeded up. "He was tired, and grew careless." She stared at Alex from tear-washed eyes. "He was struck down and killed while crossing a street. The authorities never found the hit-and-run driver."

"My God," Alex murmured. "And Judy, and Jess?"

"Alone," she said. "With no family, no friends to turn to. Judy went back to work, of course, and by necessity, had to leave Jess in the care of strangers." The look she sent Alex held an appeal for understanding. "I asked Judy to bring Jess and share the house you had so generously given me in the divorce settlement."

"I'm not surprised." Alex smiled. "You always did have a soft heart."

"Perhaps," Carolyn agreed, returning his smile.

"But you still haven't explained why Jess calls you mother," he said.

Carolyn's smile vanished. Pain flickered across her taut features. "Judy was not strong. Her health was unstable at best. Naturally, she was concerned about her daughter's future, should something happen to her. She asked me for permission to name me as guardian to Jess, in the event of her demise before Jess reached the legal age. I . . . agreed."

"And Judy died?"

"Yes." The word came on a sob that Alex felt to the depths of his being. "She . . . she . . . Alex, I think, believe, she didn't want to live without him! She was my friend, and I gave her my promise." Her breath was ragged and uneven as she skimmed a glance around the room. "I . . . I had always remembered this house, this city, as a place of happiness and hope." She swallowed. "So, when the Petersons decided to sell the house ten years ago, I—" she wet her lips, then rushed on— "I sold that beautiful house you gave me and bought this place, so I could earn a living at home." She was sobbing openly, tears pouring down her cheeks. "I've done the best I can."

In an instant, he was out of his chair, circling the table to drop onto his knees next to her, drawing her into the comforting protection of his embrace.

"Caro, my sweet darling," he murmured against her hair. "It's all right. You've done a wonderful job. Jess is a happy, beautiful child. And I'm so very proud of you."

"But you don't understand," she cried, pulling back, away from him. "Jess bears your name, too. I used your name, your position, unscrupulously, to adopt her. While I resented the dedication you gave to your work during our marriage, I didn't hesitate to use your name to get what I wanted."

"Good for you," Alex said, smiling at the shock of surprise in her eyes.

"You're not angry?" she asked, her voice catching with an endearing note of hope.

"No, I'm not angry. Far from it," he assured her. Raising his hands, he cupped her face. "Caro, oh, Caro, I've been such a fool. Such a stupid, selfish fool. All these years wasted while I chased my own ambition, thinking business success was the ultimate goal." His smile was bleak, self-derisive. "Now, when it's too late, I finally see that I had true success when I had your love."

"Who said it's too late?" she softly chided him.

Alex went still, while inside his chest, his heart went crazy with hope. "Caro, are you saying what I pray to God I think you're saying?"

"A little while ago, when you... ah... said it must have been a long time since I'd been with a man?"

Alex nodded, afraid to speak, afraid to breathe.

"It had been a very long time," she went on, her voice faint, whispery. "Alex, I love you. I've always loved you. I couldn't...couldn't ever give myself to another man.''

Alex closed his eyes, struck numb by a conflict of emotions. There was humility, strong and humbling. And there was exhilaration, wild and uplifting. He wanted to shout aloud his own avowals; he could manage only a dry croak.

''And I have never loved anyone but you. Caro, please, let me help you raise Jess,'' he pleaded. ''I love you. I love Jess. Let me be a part of both of you.'' He lowered his head, drew a breath, then put his future on the line. ''Caro, I'm asking you to marry me again.''

Carolyn smoothed her hand over his hair, drawing a shudder from him with her touch. ''Be certain this time, Alexander,'' she said, lifting his head to gaze into his emotion-darkened eyes. ''For, if we remarry, I won't let you off the hook again. I'll cling to you like a barnacle.''

''I hope so,'' he whispered, drawing her trembling form to his own trembling form. ''Because I'll be clinging just as strong to you.''

''What did I tell you, Dad, isn't it cool?''

Alex gazed into the raised, animated pixie face of his soon-to-be-legally-adopted daughter, and felt his heart contract with pure love.

''It certainly is,'' he agreed, laughing to conceal the thickness in his voice. He peered up at the multilayered water slide, and experienced a thrilling eagerness to run and play. ''Too bad the weather's cool, too.''

Three months had elapsed since the night Alex had banished his pride and laid bare his heart and soul to Carolyn. Three months filled with laughter and love. But, though it was only early September, the temperature had turned cool.

"Yeah." Jess heaved a disgusted sigh.

Carolyn, standing on the other side of Alex, anchored to him by his encircling arm, leaned forward to smile encouragement at her daughter.

"Next summer will come before you know it, honey," she assured the girl. "And we'll come back to Ocean City." She transferred her laughing gaze to her husband. "Won't we, darling?"

Alex shifted a sparkling look between the two most precious of females. "We will," he promised. "We'll do a lot of fun things together."

"Like fishing?" Jess asked eagerly.

"Like fishing," Alex echoed, joyously laughing inside at his own private joke.

*   *   *   *   *

Dear Reader,

Hello! Here I am again, back with my second Silhouette Summer Sizzlers story.

Summer. What does the word conjure up for you? Camping and hiking in the mountains? A visit to a national park? Or, perhaps, long afternoons beside the local pool?

All of the above sound like fun. But, for me, the mere thought of summer brings with it a longing for the seashore, with all its lures, real and imagined.

I close my eyes and I can feel it—a frisky breeze cooling the effects of a brassy summer sun. The beach, swept clean by the tide, dotted with spread blankets, sand chairs and brightly colored umbrellas.

And what else is on my imaginary beach? Our summertime hero, of course.

Picture him, tall and lithe, his supple skin bronzed by the sun, his hair ruffling in the breeze, his arresting eyes squinted against the glare.

Oh, be still my heart! I think I'm in love.

I hope you'll fall in love in this Summer Sizzler!

Stay well, and happy reading.

THE SHEIKH'S WOMAN

Barbara Faith

For dreamers and hopeless romantics.
May our tribe increase.

Chapter One

The plane circled, and below Catherine saw the watermelon-red buildings of the centuries-old city. Marrakesh, jewel of the Islamic world.

For years she had dreamed of it, had rolled the name around in her brain and on her tongue, Mar-ra-kesh, while in her mind's eye she conjured up a vision of palm trees swaying in the light of a desert moon, exotic smells and never-before-tasted fruit. And yes, though she would have been loath to admit it, a handsome, dark-eyed sheikh, an Omar Sharif type who would carry her off to his desert stronghold and make her his—at least for a weekend.

In her saner moments she had blamed her rambling thoughts on the freezing Chicago winter. Every morning that February, running from her one-bedroom condo to her car, she cursed the cold that seeped into her bones and the icy sleet that made driving so hazardous. No wonder she dreamed of Marrakesh.

Then last week, in the middle of Chicago's worst snowstorm in thirty years, Uncle Ross had called from New York to ask her to accompany him to Morocco.

"I'm going to a conference of American and Middle Eastern oilmen in Marrakesh," he said. "I'd planned to take my assistant, but at the last minute he canceled because his wife is having a baby. The conference is important, Catherine. I'll be representing the oil conglomerate and I'll need somebody to act as my hostess. Is there any way you can manage it?''

Marrakesh! She looked out at the snow and sleet and saw from her office window the people below, struggling to walk against the blast of wind. ''When would we leave?''

''Next week.''

''It's awfully short notice, Uncle Ross. I—''

''It's time you gave yourself a vacation,'' he said, cutting off her objections.

''Hmm.'' She smiled. ''How long would we be gone?''

''Two weeks. I really need you, Catherine.''

That did it. Uncle Ross, her father's brother, had taken her in when both her parents had been killed fifteen years ago. She had lived with him all through college, and though she'd been on her own for several years his home had always been her home. He managed the trust fund left to her by her father, and in every way that counted he had taken her father's place.

So it was decided. On Sunday she and her uncle would leave for Morocco.

Now here she was, and Marrakesh was everything she had dreamed it would be. The boulevards were wide and lined with stately palms. Mercedeses and an occasional Porsche raced past their long black limo, while robed camel drivers plodded along the side of the road.

The hotel where the conference was to be held, a beautiful, white-columned building set off the highway amid palm trees and flower gardens, was a fragrant oasis. Attendants in white robes and red fezzes took their luggage and escorted them to their rooms. As soon as she was in hers, Catherine went to stand on her balcony. Breathing in the clear desert air, relishing the sun on her face, she gazed at the distant Atlas Mountains. And smiled.

She slept well that night and awoke at dawn to a haunting cry. Quickly she gathered her robe from the foot of her bed, slipped into it and went barefoot to her balcony. Through the haze of morning light she could see the minarets and the mosques. She listened to the voice of the imam calling to the faithful, just as holy men before him had called this early morning prayer centuries before. And she shivered with pleasure because at last she was here, in this most mystical of cities.

Later that morning, when she met her uncle for breakfast, she saw that delegates from other countries had begun arriving and that the dining room was filled with men in both Western and Arabian attire. Over her coffee, Catherine stole glances at the robed men. None of them looked at all like Omar Sharif.

"Nothing for you to do today," Uncle Ross said as he signed the check for their breakfast. "Go sightseeing if you'd like to. Just be back for the reception tonight." He gave her an appraising look and with a slight smile said, "You know, my dear, these Arab men love tall blond women. I want you to look your best." He took a sheaf of bills out of his pocket. "If you didn't bring a gown that will knock out every Arab eye tonight, buy one that will. It won't hurt to have a beautiful woman like you by my side when I'm dealing with these Middle Eastern types.''

Catherine looked at him uncertainly, not quite sure how to answer. She didn't like the insinuation that he might have brought her along as window dressing.

She handed the bills back. "I'm sure the dress I have will be appropriate," she said.

"It's just that..." He hesitated. "I want you to enjoy yourself while you're here. I thought you might like a new gown."

"No," she said. "I have everything I need." Then, afraid that she sounded cool, she asked, "Are you sure there isn't anything I can help you with this morning?"

"Everything's under control," he assured her. "I'll meet you in the lobby at six-fifteen."

"Yes, all right." She hesitated, then bent to brush a kiss across his forehead.

In the lobby she paused to ask the concierge the way to the square. "I want to go to the Djemmaa..." She smiled and shook her head. "I'm sorry, I'm afraid I don't know how to say it."

"The Djemmaa El Fna. It is not too far, *mademoiselle*. If you will give me a few minutes I will arrange for someone to take you there."

"It's ten in the morning," Catherine said firmly. "And really, I prefer to go alone."

He frowned, started to say something, then with a shrug he walked with her to the door and said, "Once you reach the road you will turn to your right. In ten minutes you will reach the Djemmaa. But once again I suggest it would be—"

"Thank you," Catherine interrupted. And with a nod she stepped into the sunshine.

The lawns leading from the hotel to the road were manicured to perfection. The air smelled of gardenias. She hummed as she walked along, glad that she'd worn white sandals with her short white skirt and blue silk blouse.

Ten minutes later, just as the concierge had said, she arrived at the Djemmaa El Fna. She heard it before she saw it, the bustle and the noise of dozens of men, women and children, the bray of donkeys, the cacophony of music, of drums and pipes and organ-grinders. And the smells! Incense and myrrh, cinnamon and smoke, animal fur and camel dung.

It was like a circus, not the Ringling Brothers type, but a wild, noisy conglomeration of sights she had never seen before. Veiled women with hennaed hands jabbered to each other as they bargained for grilled chicken and mutton on sticks. Arab men in flowing robes shouted to make themselves heard over the voices of the buyers and sellers.

She watched acrobats dressed in bright pants and billowing shirts cartwheel by, and an organ-grinder with a trained monkey pushed his way through the crowd. There were stands that sold jeweled leather slippers with curled-up toes, gem-studded daggers, Berber blankets and intricately designed rugs. There were trick cyclists, jugglers and magicians, whirling dervishes and flame eaters.

She moved with the crowd, shrugging off a seller who pulled at her sleeve, clutching her purse closer to her body, too intrigued by everything to be afraid as she made her way past soothsayers and storytellers, men hawking leather wallets, belts and silver bracelets.

When she saw a small crowd gathered, she stopped to look, trying to peer around the man in front of her. With a laugh one of the men stepped aside. Another urged her forward and she saw a man sitting crosslegged on the ground. He was playing a flute. On the ground next to him was a basket. As Catherine watched, a cobra wafted up, flat-headed, thick bodied, swaying to the hypnotic rhythm of the flute.

She shrank back. The men around her didn't move. The cobra rose higher, three feet above the basket, flat head moving back and forth, back and forth until finally, to the high, thin wail of the flute, he slithered back into the basket. The snake charmer popped the lid on, then turned to another basket and opened it. Then he raised his eyes and saw Catherine. He smiled, and dipping into his basket he took out a long thin black snake and held it up to her.

"Pretty snake for pretty lady," he said. "You like? Take picture."

The man who had pushed her forward reached out for the black snake. Afraid, Catherine tried to move back. But robed men blocked her way.

"Only snake," one of them said, and the rest of them laughed.

"No! Please. Let me..." She turned and tried to push her way through the circle of men.

The man with the snake advanced. "Only fun," he said. "Not poison. Take nice picture. Snake won't bite pretty lady." And before Catherine could stop him he draped it over her neck.

For a moment she was too horrified to do anything. The snake moved, cold and dry against her skin. She cried out, "No! Take it away. Help!"

A man in a gray robe, his hair uncovered, his face angry, shouldered his way through the crowd. He grabbed the snake and flung it to the man on the ground, shouting, *"Baraka! Baraka!"* He put an arm around Catherine's shoulders and elbowed his way through the crowd again.

When they were away from the crowds, he turned her and, gripping her shoulders, asked, "Are you all right?"

"I . . . I think so." She tried to pull herself together, to quell the queasy feeling in her stomach. "Thank you for rescuing me. I—"

"What in the hell are you doing here alone? Where's your guide?"

"I don't have a guide."

"You came to the Djemmaa alone?"

Catherine nodded. "I thought it would be all right. And it was, until that . . . that man put the snake around my neck." She shivered and her face paled.

Her rescuer muttered under his breath. Taking her arm he said, "Come along, you need some coffee."

He was tall, well over six feet, broad-shouldered and impressive enough to have put the fear of God or Allah into the men who had surrounded her. The clean gray robe accentuated his black hair and dark skin.

His eyes, under heavy eyebrows, were brown touched with flecks of gold. His nose was straight, his mouth firm, unyielding. She guessed his age to be somewhere in the late thirties or early forties. He made Omar Sharif look like a sissy.

He led her to a restaurant, then up the stairs to an outside patio that looked on the scene below. Without asking he ordered coffee for both of them and a brandy for her. "Have you had breakfast?" he asked. "Do you want something to eat?"

"No, thank you."

The waiter came with his order. When she hesitated over the brandy the man who had rescued her said, "Drink!" and she drank.

Sounding angry, he said, "Who allowed you to come to the Djemmaa alone?"

Allowed? That made her bristle. "I wanted to see the Djemmaa and saw no reason I shouldn't."

"You are traveling alone?"

"No, I'm with my uncle. He's here for the conference of American and Middle Eastern oilmen."

"Ah." He looked at her and said, "I, too, am here for the conference. Please allow me to introduce myself. I am Tamar Fallah Haj."

"Catherine Courlaine," she said.

"Courlaine?" He frowned. "Your uncle is Ross Courlaine?"

"Yes. Do you know him?"

He looked at his coffee, added a teaspoon of sugar and took a sip. His hands were large, his fingers long and slender, the nails clipped and clean. "Only by reputation," he said.

"I see." She tried to think of something to say and, because she couldn't, asked, "Where are you from, Mr...."

"Fallah Haj," he said. "I come from El Agadir."

"I'm sorry, I'm afraid I don't know where that is."

"El Agadir is a small, oil-rich country that lies far north of the Atlas Mountains."

She remembered then that standing on her balcony she had gazed out at the mountains and wondered what lay beyond them.

He looked at her closely. She was fairly tall and more slender than he liked his women to be. Her skin was as smooth and pale as the petals of a camellia, her hair sun-streaked, her eyes a vivid blue. She was every man's dream of a beautiful, desirable woman, which made him wonder if that was the reason Ross Courlaine had brought her to Morocco.

She turned and looked at the scene below. "It's incredible, isn't it?" she said, almost to herself. "Is it always like this?"

"Yes, it is. Actually very little about the Djemmaa has changed in the past few hundred years." He hesitated, then because he wanted to see her reaction said, "Of course, slave girls are no longer auctioned here."

"Slave girls?" The delicate eyebrows raised. "You're kidding."

"Am I?" His lips twitched, but he didn't smile. "Years ago women were brought to Marrakesh from other parts of North Africa, Greece and Turkey as well as from Madagascar and the Seychelles." He gestured to the square below. "Imagine how it was," he said in a low voice. "Women dressed in diaphanous robes, being led one after another to a center platform. The men would gather around while the auctioneer took them onto the platform as the bidding began."

Horrified, Catherine could barely choke out, "That—that's barbaric!"

"Yes, I suppose it was." Tamar looked at her and suddenly it was as though he could see her in the square, her slim body revealed through a gossamer-thin robe, blond hair streaming down her back, blue eyes wide with fear. *I would have bid a million pieces of gold for you,* he thought. And felt his body tighten with an unaccustomed need. He wanted to take that pale hand in his, stroke her arm, touch her face. He wanted...

By Allah, what was the matter with him? With a muttered oath he looked at his watch and pushed his chair back. "I have a one-thirty appointment at the hotel. I will escort you there."

Not, "May I escort you?" Just, "I will." Once again Catherine felt herself bristle. On the other hand she didn't relish walking back by herself. She picked up her bag. With a lift of her chin and as much dignity as she could muster, she said, "Yes, you may escort me."

He looked at her, startled, then took her arm and led her downstairs. He shepherded her through the noisy square, and when he found a horse and carriage, helped her on.

Catherine was very much aware of him beside her. When the carriage made a sharp turn into the driveway of the hotel she was jostled against him, her shoulder brushed his, her bare leg slid along his thigh. She clutched the side of the carriage and wondered suddenly if Arabs wore trousers under their robes. And felt her cheeks flush at the thought.

He escorted her into the lobby. "Until tonight, Miss Courlaine," he said. He took her hand and brushed his lips across it.

And left her, a little breathless as she rubbed her fingers over the back of the hand he had kissed.

Chapter Two

White-robed waiters wove their way among the hundred or so assembled guests, bearing trays filled with fluted glasses of champagne for the Westerners, mineral water or juice for the Arabs.

The salon, lighted by crystal chandeliers, was as elegant as anything Catherine had seen in Paris or New York. The floors were carpeted in a deep royal blue. The walls were covered with gilded mirrors, magnificent hangings and gold-encrusted sconces. Tables inlaid with multicolor mosaics were laden with platters of delicacies—whole smoked Norwegian salmon, bowls of caviar, thinly sliced lamb, Russian eggs, delicate slices of sweet-and-sour duck, spiced and vinegar-flavored vegetables, along with an array of sweets to tempt the most avid dieter.

The Arab delegation predominated the gathering. They were unaccompanied by women. A few of the Westerners, oilmen from various parts of Europe as well as the United States, had brought their wives. But these women, perhaps intimidated by the robed men, stood together in small groups or clung to their husbands' arms and did not mingle. Catherine, near her uncle, was surrounded by a group of Arab men.

Tamar stood back from the crowd, watching her. The black silk gown she wore was a startling contrast to her blond beauty. In classically simple lines, un-adorned by jewelry, the dress was severe, stark. But when she turned to the man next to her he saw that the back was slashed almost to her waist. And at that tempting vee she had fastened a gardenia that was as smooth and pale as her skin.

As he had that morning, Tamar felt the sudden rise of heat flood his body. And a flash of anger that her uncle would allow her to expose herself that way.

A small crowd of men was gathered around Ross Courlaine, but even as they spoke to him or pretended interest in what he was saying, their gazes were drawn to Catherine. He sensed their desire, and he could almost hear their sighs. He wondered again if that was the reason her uncle had brought her.

"Is it Mr. Courlaine who holds your attention, my friend Tamar?" the man next to him asked. "Or is it the woman who draws your attention?"

"My attention is as yours, Hamid Nawab," Tamar answered, resenting the expression he saw in the other man's eyes. By Allah, if she was his she would not dress that way. No, if she was his he would veil her so that no other man could gaze upon her flawless face, and clothe her in robes to hide the perfection of her body.

If she was his.

Suddenly she raised her gaze and looked at him. Her eyes widened, and one slender hand lifted to her throat. It was as if she knew what he was thinking, as if, caught by an invisible bond, she could not look away. A shiver seemed to run through her. She mur-mured something to her uncle and, with a nod to the men who surrounded her, turned and moved toward the balcony.

Hamid spoke to him. "I wonder if Courlaine brought his beautiful niece to Morocco to distract us from the business at hand. Surely she is a woman to turn any man's head."

He puffed on his cigarette, his small eyes narrowing as he watched Courlaine. "Come," he said to Tamar, "I will introduce you."

Ross Courlaine, in his middle fifties, too thin of face to be called handsome, was nevertheless a man of distinguished looks. His gray hair was perfectly styled, his mustache neatly trimmed. His features were even, his skin smooth and pink.

"Ah, my good friend Nawab," he said when they approached. "It's good to see you again."

"And you," Nawab answered. "I would like to present Prince Tamar Fallah Haj."

"Of El Agadir," Courlaine said. "Yes, of course. I've been looking forward to meeting you, Prince Fallah Haj."

"I've wanted to meet you, too," Tamar replied. "But from what I have heard neither you nor your associates approve of the idea of forming a confederation with Arab interests."

Courlaine shook his head. "It's not that I disapprove," he said smoothly. "However, I believe that the balance of power should be held by the larger oil conglomerates."

"Like your own."

The other man smiled, but before he could answer, Hamid, his face contorted with anger, said, "You have come to Marrakesh to sabotage the meeting. You care nothing of our coming together in mutual understanding.''

''My dear Hamid—''

''No,'' Hamid said with a warning note in his voice. ''I will not allow you to ruin our efforts. You would join with certain countries and exclude others. I will block you, Courlaine. I will—''

''This is not the place for such a discussion,'' Tamar broke in. ''Tomorrow there will be time for your arguments.'' He took a glass of mineral water from a passing waiter and with a murmured, ''Excuse me,'' turned away.

Like Hamid, he suspected Ross Courlaine was up to no good. He would deal with him when he had to, but right now his mind was on something else. Or rather, someone else.

She stood by the railing, a slender woman sheathed in black. A woman from a different culture, one he could not allow himself to be interested in. Yet he was drawn to her, lured by the way the moonlight touched her hair and patterned the pale skin of her bare back. Her perfume wafted through the night air, and like a stallion picking up the scent of a mare his nostrils flared and his body heated with a terrible need. He must have gasped, for suddenly she turned.

''Oh,'' she said, startled. ''Mr. Fallah Haj. Good evening.''

''Good evening, Miss Courlaine. Weren't you enjoying the party?''

''Yes, but I...'' She looked away. ''I wanted some air.''

"Is this your first time in Marrakesh?"

"Yes." She gave a small smile. "It's a place I've always dreamed of seeing. When Uncle Ross invited me to come I couldn't resist."

"You've only been here for a day. It's too soon to ask if it comes up to your expectation, especially after your experience this morning.

"There is much to see." He moved to stand beside her. "The Koutoubia, the twelfth-century minaret that is as tall as the towers of Notre Dame, the Bahia Palace, the Saadian Tombs, many places."

"I want to see them all." She took a deep breath and he saw the rise of her breasts. "And the Sahara," she said. "I want to see the Sahara."

"It lies beyond the mountains."

"Where your home is."

He nodded. "El Agadir is built on a desert oasis. Though we have modern buildings and boulevards we are always conscious that the Sahara is at our doorstep. At night you can smell the desert, and you know there is much that remains timeless." And though he did not intend to, he said, "I would like to show you the desert."

"And I would like to see it." Caught up in the magic of the night she couldn't help feeling a strange attraction to this tall, dark man who was so foreign from anyone she had ever known. Attracted, but a little frightened by the smoldering intensity she saw in the gold-flecked eyes.

"Mr. Fallah Haj..."

"Tamar. My name is Tamar."

"I...we should go back to the reception."

"In a moment." And because he thought that if he did not touch her he would go mad, he brought his hands up and rested them on her bare shoulders. He felt her shiver and said, "Why are you trembling?"

"I . . . I'm not."

He smiled. This morning she had behaved like an independent American woman. Though the snake had frightened her she had quickly recovered, putting him in his place when he'd tried to order her about. Certainly this evening, dressed in sophisticated black, she had seemed a woman of the world. And yet when he touched her she trembled. That aroused him as nothing ever had.

He drew her closer and kissed her.

She stiffened and tried to push him away. He wouldn't let her go. Her lips compressed. He ran his tongue across them. She gasped and involuntarily her lips parted. He felt their softness, he tasted their sweetness. The hands that had come up to push against his chest relaxed against his robe.

He held her close in his embrace, encircling her waist to draw her nearer. He felt the bare skin of her back beneath his fingers, and his body caught fire. The kiss became heated, urgent.

"Stop!" she whispered against his lips. "Please."

His breath came hard and fast, but he let her go and in a voice that did not sound like his he said, "You should not dress so. You make a man crazy when you show yourself this way."

"It's a perfectly acceptable dress." She tried to sound defiant but her lips were trembling. "I . . . I have to go back to the party," she said.

"Catherine."

She hesitated.

"Your gardenia."

It had fallen from the vee in the back of her dress. Tamar picked it up. She held her hand out, but he shook his head and with a smile put it in the pocket of his robe.

"Tomorrow we will have lunch," he said. "I'm sorry if I have offended you, Catherine. It was not my intention. Please, let me make it up to you."

"You have meetings," she said.

"In the morning. In the afternoon I will escape and show you what I can of Marrakesh."

She wanted to see the city, and yes, it would be better, and certainly more entertaining, to see it with someone like Tamar Fallah Haj. But she had to be careful of him and of herself. His kiss had stirred something deep inside her. And that wouldn't do, it wouldn't do at all.

"One o'clock," he said, breaking in on her thoughts. "Yes?" And when she didn't answer, he said, "Yes!" and drawing her arm through his led her into the salon.

Ross Courlaine, deep in conversation with several Arab men, saw them enter. He raised his eyebrows, and a secret smile crossed his face. He nodded as though in satisfaction and resumed his conversation.

Catherine decided when she awoke the next morning that she would not go out with Tamar after all. He was not the kind of man she would ever be interested in. He was aggressive, forceful and macho, an Arab who very likely believed a woman's place was in the home behind high stone walls, veiled and robed and forever pregnant.

She scrunched down into her pillows. He was, of course, the most attractive man she'd ever met, and heaven help her, she had responded to his kiss like a high school girl. But she had enough sense to know he was a dangerous man to get involved with. She was only going to be in Morocco for two weeks. Just then the phone rang and when she answered it her uncle said, "Good morning, my dear, did I wake you?"

"No, I'm being a little lazy."

"You're entitled. It was a nice party last night, wasn't it."

"Mmm. Wonderful food."

"Everyone thought you looked lovely. I certainly did."

"Thank you."

"And I rather think Prince Fallah Haj did, too."

"Prince?" She sat up straighter in the bed.

"Didn't you know? He rarely uses his title, but yes, he has one."

Catherine heard the clink of a coffee cup against a saucer. "I saw you coming in from the balcony with him," Ross said. "I must say, dear, your cheeks were a bit flushed."

"They were not," she denied, and heard him laugh.

"Well?"

"Well what?"

"Do you like him?"

"I don't know him."

"Has he asked to see you again?"

"As a matter of fact he invited me to lunch today."

"You're going, aren't you?"

"I'm not sure."

"Of course you are. It wouldn't hurt my cause at this conference to have him in my corner. If he likes you…" Ross chuckled. "Well, you know. It wouldn't hurt to do a little public relations for your old uncle."

Catherine stared at the phone. Was this why Uncle Ross had brought her to the conference? So that she would be "nice" to whatever oilman he wanted on his side?

"Prince Tamar is a handsome man whose company you'd enjoy," Ross went on. "Go have lunch with him, and perhaps tonight the three of us will dine together."

"Well…"

"The meetings start in ten minutes, so I've got to run. Have a good day, Catherine. I'll meet you in the lobby tonight at seven. Wear something alluring."

And before she could answer he hung up.

For a moment Catherine didn't move. Surely she had jumped to a not very pleasant conclusion. But still… Even as she debated, uncertain whether or not she ought to meet Tamar for lunch, there was a knock. She threw on her robe and went to the door. "Yes? Who is it?"

"Flowers, *mademoiselle*," a young voice said. And when she opened the door he handed her a long white box.

Catherine thanked him, carried the box to the small table under the French doors and opened it. There were long-stemmed red roses, at least three dozen of them, fragrant and beautiful. And a handwritten card that read, "Though I am sorry if I offended you, I cannot be sorry for having kissed you. Until later. Tamar."

She fanned her lips with the card and smiled. Prince Tamar Fallah Haj might be dangerous, but there was no denying he was charming. She picked a rose out of the box and carried it with her into the bathroom, wondering as she did what she would wear to lunch today.

Chapter Three

She walked right past him. Only when he said, "Catherine," did she stop. Her eyes widened in surprise. Prince Tamar Fallah Haj in trousers, a white shirt open at the neck and a well-cut sport jacket was certainly something to look at.

"I'm sorry, I didn't recognize you without your robe." She grinned. "I mean in Western clothes."

He grinned back, and for the first time since she had decided to have lunch with him she relaxed.

"Is there somewhere special you'd like to go? A special kind of food you like, or will you leave it up to me?"

"It's your call," she said. "I don't know Marrakesh."

"Then I will show it to you."

The car that awaited them was long and sleek and black. Tamar helped her in then went around to his side. He was a good driver, for though they chatted while he drove, he kept his attention on the road.

His face in profile, especially when he frowned as he did when a Mercedes shot in front of him, showed a strength and forcefulness of character. His forehead was broad, his nose neither too large nor too small, his mouth... Catherine took a deep breath. His mouth was sensuously curved, his lips full. She remembered the feel of them against her own last night, felt a trickle of flame somewhere in her midsection and quickly looked away.

Maybe it was the climate, just being in this exotic country that excited her. Or maybe it was him. Whatever it was she had better watch her step.

The restaurant he took her to, La Maison Arabe, was tucked away in a garden. They were greeted by a robed man and led to a table under a flowering acacia tree.

"Here you may order either French cuisine or typical Moroccan dishes," Tamar told her.

"Moroccan," Catherine said. "Will you order for me?"

"Of course. Would you like an aperitif first?"

The champagne was served, and since this was a special occasion, he, too, accepted a glass. He touched it to hers and said, "To your stay in Marrakesh, *ma chère* Mademoiselle Courlaine."

She smiled, and he thought, *By Allah, there is something about her that stirs me as no other woman ever has. There is a delicacy about her, a shy sexuality that could drive a man mad. I find myself wanting to protect her, to please her in any number of small ways and take care of her. Yet at the same time I have this almost overwhelming urge to make love to her. What manner of woman is this? What is she doing to me?*

He ordered *bastilla,* pigeon pie filled with almonds, saffron and sugar nestled in layers of tissue-thin pastry, couscous, hot *nan* bread and roast lamb.

Whenever a new dish arrived he said, "You must taste this," and holding a fork to her mouth offered her small bites from his plate.

Catherine sampled everything. "Wonderful," she murmured each time she tasted a different dish. "Delicious." The tip of her tongue came out to dab at a piece of date at the corner of her mouth, and the breath caught in his throat.

He watched her eat, fascinated that one so slender could relish food quite so much. It pleased him, too, that she liked the Moroccan style of cooking.

"You've never been anywhere in this part of the world?" he asked when he had paid the check and they started to his car.

"No." She tucked the short flared skirt around her legs when she got in, and he caught a glimpse of smooth, white thigh. "But I've wanted to see it, especially Morocco."

He would like to show her everything, including Egypt. He would take her to the pyramids, sail down the Nile with her and watch the moon rise over the water from their stateroom. He would like... He tried to banish the thought. Catherine Courlaine was not a woman from his world, nor, he was sure, was she a woman who would agree to a two-week affair and when it was over be able to say goodbye with a smile. *Be careful,* he warned himself. *Be careful of this one.*

He drove along the boulevard to the ancient Ramparts, the Royal Enclosure and the Saadian Tombs, which sheltered the remains of the rulers of that dynasty. She asked dozens of questions, and her blue eyes were wide with curiosity.

Somewhere in their sight-seeing he gave her his hand to help her up a flight of stairs. When they reached the top he made no move to release her, nor did she try to pull away.

When he thought she might be tired, he stopped at a small café where they had strong Arabian coffee. "Thank you for taking me out today," Catherine said.

"It has been my pleasure."

"I'm afraid I've taken you away from your meetings."

"There was nothing of great importance this afternoon. Tomorrow, though, I will be in meetings all day." He hesitated. "I would like it very much if you would have dinner with me tonight, Catherine. There is a place above Marrakesh I think you'd like, with music, a show, dancing..." Dancing. It would be an excuse to hold her in his arms, to feel her body close to his.

"Good Lord!" She shook her head and with a rueful smile said, "I've been so excited by everything that I'd forgotten Uncle Ross wanted me to ask you to have dinner with us tonight."

"I wonder why he invited me."

Catherine looked a little startled. "I imagine it's because he wants to get to know you better. I mean because of the conference, because—"

"Of you?" His expression darkened. Had she agreed to come out with him today because her uncle had asked her to? Was that why she smiled at him and put her hand so trustingly in his?

Anger tightened Tamar's stomach. He tried not to show it. If this was her game then he would go along.

He would have dinner with her and her uncle tonight. He would watch and listen, but he would not be taken in by her beauty or her softness. He would play their game and would have no qualms about seducing her.

Catherine saw the change come over his face, but when he took her arm and said it was time to take her back she told herself she had imagined it. At the hotel he escorted her to the elevator and said, "Please tell your uncle I would like very much to have dinner with him tonight." He kissed her hand. And smiled. "And with you, of course, *ma chère* Catherine."

He was still smiling when the elevator doors closed. Then the smile faded and a look of cruelty crossed his face.

When he went into his room there was a message on his phone from Hamid Nawab. He asked for Nawab's room, and when the other man answered said, "This is Tamar."

"Where have you been? I have tried all day to reach you. Something has happened. A faction from Mali Bukhara is threatening the takeover of that new oil discovery off the coast of Tunisia. Courlaine is in on it. We've got to stop him."

"Are you sure?"

"Of course I'm sure!" There was panic in Nawab's voice. "My God, Tamar," he said, "do you know what this will do to the conference?"

Yes, he knew. The oil off the coast of Tunisia was reported to be one of the richest finds in recent years. Both Tunisia and Mali Bukhara had claimed the discovery as their own. The issue was one of the reasons for the conference. Most members of the delegation sided with Tunisia. But if the forces of Mali Bukhara were joined with the power Ross Courlaine wielded, there would be little the other delegations could do to stop them.

"I'm having dinner with Courlaine tonight," Tamar said.

"And you spent the day with his niece when you should have been here." There was the hint of suspicion in Nawab's voice. "That makes one wonder which side you are on, my friend Tamar."

"Do not wonder where my loyalties lie, Hamid Nawab. If Courlaine and his niece are conspiring with Mali Bukhara in this, I will expose them."

"When you do, and before they are turned over to the authorities, I would like a little while alone in the desert with Courlaine."

Tamar nodded, his face grim.

"And his niece," Nawab said.

Tamar clenched his hand so tightly around the phone his knuckles turned white. "I will take care of the niece," he said.

He put the phone down. If it was true that Catherine and her uncle were in this together he would let Hamid deal with the uncle. As for Catherine . . .

Tamar stood in the middle of the room, making himself take deep breaths, waiting until his rage was under control. Then he picked up the phone, asked for the florist shop and ordered a cluster of gardenias to be sent to Miss Catherine Courlaine.

Two could play this game, a game he planned to win.

*   *   *

Ross and Catherine were waiting for Tamar when he got off the elevator that night at eight. She looked very beautiful, he thought dispassionately. Her hair had been pulled off her face into a fashionable chignon. Her gown was red, which seemed fitting for a Jezebel, and she had pinned two of his gardenias on the slender strap of her right shoulder.

He wore a robe, a gray gabardine that looked as somber as he felt.

"Hello, there!" Courlaine hurried over to shake his hand. "I'm so glad you were able to join us for dinner. Catherine tells me the two of you had a fine afternoon together."

He looked at her then. She smiled. He looked away, afraid she would see all that was in his eyes.

"I thought we'd go to the Sahara Room," Courlaine went on. "If that's all right with you."

"That's fine." Tamar nodded. "A good choice."

"Well, then." Ross rubbed his hands together. "Shall we go?" He held the door open. Tamar took Catherine's arm.

Courlaine had rented a car with a chauffeur. The three sat in the back, Catherine in the middle. Ross chatted. When Catherine had an opportunity she touched the gardenias at her shoulder and said, "Thank you, Tamar. They're lovely."

"As you are, *ma chère*," he said smoothly, and saw Ross Courlaine's satisfied smile.

At the Sahara Room they were led into a brightly lit reception salon and toward an eight-foot-tall brass-studded door.

"Through here," the attendant said, and they passed into a huge tented room that seemed to Catherine straight out of the *Arabian Nights*.

A maître d' led them to a grouping of a sofa for two and a low chair. Ross motioned Catherine and Tamar to the sofa and said, "I'll take the chair."

A dim lantern swung above the table. There was the faint scent of incense, and of Catherine's gardenias. Ross ordered champagne. A band played. A French singer sang of love and romance. Ross said, "Why don't the two of you dance?"

"Of course." Tamar stood. "Catherine?" he said, and held his hand out to her.

On the dance floor she stepped into his arms. "Is anything wrong?" she asked.

"Of course not. Why do you ask?"

"I don't know. You seem . . . different."

"Do I?" He brought her closer. He felt the brush of her cheek against his, the slight crush of her breasts against his chest. For a moment heat flamed. He quelled it, forcing himself to think of her complicity in her uncle's plan, of using her femininity to distract him. Involuntarily his arms tightened, his muscles clenched.

She felt it and said, "Tamar? What is it?"

He forced a smile. "Holding you like this does strange things to me," he said. "With you a man could almost forget . . ." He lifted his powerful shoulders. "Many things," he said. "Many things."

The dance floor was dimly lit. He drew her to an even darker part of the floor and urged her closer. He brushed a kiss across her cheek, then kissed her mouth. She said, "Tamar?" and tried to step away, but he wouldn't let her go. Moving with the music, he put a hand against the small of her back and brought her against him. He kissed her again, a teasing kiss, nibbling at her bottom lip and the corners of her mouth. He kissed the tender skin behind her ear and ran his tongue around the curve of it.

He felt her heat and knew a moment of satisfaction. They moved slowly, slowly to the music.

She was unaware of the other couples, caught up in the feel of Tamar's hard, muscled body so close to hers.

"Catherine," he murmured against her lips, and she swayed toward him while the breath caught in her throat and a feeling unlike anything she had ever known set her afire.

The music stopped. He held her away. His eyes were dark with passion—and something else. Something she didn't understand.

"Come," he said, and led her to her uncle.

They had dinner and watched the show. A juggler was followed by a belly dancer, an attractive, overweight woman who rolled her stomach, writhed and undulated, slowly at first, then faster and still faster until her almost naked body was bathed in sweat.

Tamar caressed her bare shoulders and played with the tendrils of her hair at the back of her neck. She wanted to move away, could not move away.

The dance ended in a crescendo of drums, a shattering climax of sound. The dancer collapsed, face against her arms, hair spread out like a fan around her.

"My goodness." Ross smiled. "That was something, wasn't it?" He took a sip of his champagne. "What do you two have planned for tomorrow?"

"Unfortunately I have to attend the meetings tomorrow." Tamar toyed with his knife. "I understand the delegation from Mali Bukhara has plans that will upset the conference. If that's true I will join the others in trying to stop—" he paused "—whatever it is they're up to."

"Mali Bukhara is a rich and powerful country. It might be in one's best interests to do business with them."

"Oh? Do you think so?"

Ross leaned forward. "Yes, Prince Tamar, I do."

"Even though they're a warlike nation?"

Ross shrugged. "They have to protect themselves. Better to invade than be invaded."

The hand on the back of Catherine's neck tightened. Then abruptly Tamar let her go. "Five years ago they slaughtered half the population of Ridani."

"No, no," Ross said with a shake of his head. "They were only defending their frontier."

It took every bit of Tamar's control to say, "I suppose there are two sides to every story."

"Of course there are," Ross agreed. "It wouldn't hurt to listen to what the Mali Bukhara delegation has to say, would it?" He leaned forward, intent, holding Tamar with his gaze. "You wield a lot of power, Prince Tamar. Other men respect you, listen to you. I've heard you speak, I know you can sway others with your rhetoric."

So he had been right about the reason for the dinner tonight. Right about Catherine, too. She was the advance company, sent in to soften him up for her uncle, offered as a reward for his cooperation.

To confirm Tamar's suspicions, Ross glanced toward the dance floor and said, "Why don't you two have another dance?"

Catherine smiled at Tamar. Then her smile faded, for though his mouth curved there was something in his eyes that stopped her, a cruelty she had not seen before, an expression that chilled and frightened her. "I... I'm rather tired, Uncle Ross. Would you mind if we called it a night?"

"Not all all, my dear." He signaled for the check. When it came he paid it and the three of them left the tentlike restaurant. When they reached the hotel, Ross said, "Think I'll have a nightcap in the bar. You wouldn't mind showing Catherine to her room, would you, Tamar?"

"It would be my pleasure," Tamar said with a slight bow. "Thank you for the excellent dinner, Mr. Courlaine. I hope you will allow me to entertain you during your stay in Morocco." And though he smiled, Tamar's thoughts were grim. Entertain the man? Yes, it would be entertaining for one of them.

"Indeed." Ross clapped Tamar's shoulder. "We must talk again. I'm sure our interests are much the same." He kissed Catherine's forehead, said, "Rest well, my dear," and headed toward the bar.

Tamar took Catherine's arm. "Would you like anything before we go up?"

"No, thank you." She turned to him. "You don't have to take me up, I mean if you have something to do."

"The only thing I have to do is see you safely to your room." He steered her toward the elevators. When they got to her floor they went to her room and Tamar took her key. He opened the door and said, "I'd like to come in for a moment."

Catherine hesitated, then with a nod went into the room. She waited, facing him. He made no attempt to kiss her. "What is it?" she said. "Something has changed. You're different."

"Am I?"

"Tamar, what—"

He pulled her to him, not gently as he had when he'd kissed her before, but fiercely, with anger. His mouth covered hers and he held her there, demanding her surrender. Why did she struggle? Wasn't this what she and her uncle had planned?

He pulled her hard against him. She said no and pushed against his chest.

"This is what you want," he said against her lips.

"Not like this."

"What difference does it make how I make love to you as long as I do? How far did you plan to go with this, Catherine? Did you only mean to tease me along or would you actually have let me make love to you?"

She looked stunned, as though he had slapped her.

He glared at her, tired of games. "It won't work, you know. I'm not the easy mark you seem to think I am."

"What?"

"I know what you're up to. I know why you let me take you to lunch today. I know why you kissed me and why you acted as though you wanted me as much as I wanted you." He shook his head. "But as far as I'm concerned you and your uncle can both go to hell."

He turned and started toward the door. She went after him, grabbed his arm and turned him to face her. "What in the *hell* are you talking about?"

"I'm talking about how your uncle is trying to sabotage the conference. I'm talking about his thinking he could buy my cooperation with you." So angry he could barely get the words out, he managed to say, "It's why he brought you to Morocco, isn't it? He thought that if he needed something to swing the Arab delegation his way, a beautiful woman just might do it."

He tightened his hands on her arms. "And you went along with him. You seduced me with your softness, with your—"

She uttered a cry of outrage and drew her arm back. He grabbed it and thrust it behind her. "Don't try it," he said. Still holding her arm, he brought her closer. "Why?" he asked. "Why did you agree to help him?"

"I don't know what you're talking about." Her voice was low, shaking with emotion. Her face was ashen. "I came to Morocco because Uncle Ross said he needed me. He wouldn't... My God, Tamar, he wouldn't do what you're saying. How dare you suggest such a terrible thing?"

He almost believed her. Was she a dupe, being used without her knowledge? Or was this only a convincing performance?

He let her go and stepped away. "Tell him it won't work," he said. "Tell him I didn't fall for it. Or you." And wished to God he hadn't.

She stood there alone in the middle of the room after he left. He was wrong. Uncle Ross wouldn't use her that way. How could Tamar even think she would be part of such a thing? If what he said about her uncle was true . . .

Like a sleepwalker, Catherine sank down on the bed. Dear God, it couldn't be true.

"You know, my dear, these Arab men love tall blond women," he'd said. "Buy something that will knock out every Arab eye tonight," he'd said. "It won't hurt my case to have a beautiful woman like you by my side when I'm dealing with these Middle Eastern types."

Catherine covered her face with her hands. "No, oh, no." And she cried as though her heart was breaking. As indeed it was.

Chapter Four

Even before the sessions began that morning there were signs of trouble.

After an hour, the meeting was in an uproar. Some of the delegates threw up their hands and walked out. Hamid Nawab had to be forcefully removed from the meeting.

Ross Courlaine moved aside as the other men ushered Nawab from the room. For a moment the two men's eyes met. Nawab's were full of hate. Ross smiled.

But Tamar, who saw the interchange, did not smile. He knew Hamid Nawab, knew how dangerous the man could be. When Hamid had spoken of Ross Courlaine there had been venom in his words. If Courlaine knew what was good for him he'd watch his back.

When the head of the Mali Bukhara delegation got the floor and held it, Tamar left. It would be better to hold some private meetings later today, to gather his supporters around him, than to try to outshout his opponents now.

Hamid was waiting for Tamar. The man was livid, almost incapable of speech.

"Ross Courlaine!" he thundered. "That son of a camel, excrement of a hyena, spoor of a rat. The conference is in danger of dissolution, and it's his doing." Hamid's hands curled into fists, and he leaned across the table toward Tamar. "Courlaine has to be stopped, Tamar, for if he is not—" He paused. His face went still. "There he is, with that niece of his. I have a good mind to—"

Tamar put a cautioning hand on the other man's arm. "No," he said. "Now is not the time."

They were seated at a table on the other side of the room, Ross, smiling his bland smile, impeccable in a gray tailored suit, Catherine in a blue dress, blond hair soft about her shoulders. The muscles of Tamar's stomach tightened. It was all he could do not to rush to their table, to pull her away and demand she tell him the truth about her part in the scheme to destroy the conference.

"You are wrong, Tamar." Hamid's eyes narrowed as he watched Catherine and her uncle. "Now is the time." His words were almost a promise.

Catherine had seen Tamar as soon as she entered the dining room. He had looked her way, then quickly averted his eyes. This morning when she had awakened after an almost sleepless night she hadn't wanted to face either her uncle or Tamar. She had ordered breakfast in her room, but when it came she only drank the coffee and barely touched the fruit.

What Tamar had said last night about her uncle couldn't be true. The things Uncle Ross had said to her were merely a coincidence. Of course he wanted her to look nice. The men attending the conference were friends of his, it was only natural he'd want her to make a good impression. How dare Tamar accuse her of being party to some kind of a conspiracy, to suggest that her uncle would use her to further his own gains?

Perhaps she should tell her uncle what Tamar had said last night. Perhaps... But before she could speak, Ross broke in on her thoughts to ask if Tamar had taken her safely to her room. And when she said, "Yes, he did," her uncle smiled.

After lunch Catherine asked at the desk if they could arrange a guide to take her to the souks, then went up to her room to change. When she returned a robed and turbaned man approached her and said, "I am your guide, Mademoiselle Courlaine. My name is Cashan. I have a car outside."

"I didn't think it was far to the souks," Catherine said. "I thought we'd walk."

"It is much too hot a day, *mademoiselle*. Besides, there will be much walking once we reach the souks. It is better to save your energy for shopping, yes?"

"All right," Catherine said with a nod. He held the door open for her to leave and gestured to the waiting car. There was a driver behind the wheel, a man who didn't acknowledge her but looked straight ahead. Cashan opened the back door. For a moment Catherine hesitated. Then, telling herself she was being foolish, she took his proffered hand and stepped into the car.

They drove off and Cashan kept up a nonstop one-sided conversation. Once she said, "I didn't realize it was this far."

"Oh, yes," he said. "A little farther yet."

The car sped along the boulevard, then veered into a twisting labyrinth of streets. When she looked alarmed, Cashan said, "Short cut. Do not worry."

She felt a prickle of fear and tried to shake it off. The hotel had arranged for the guide. Surely he was all right. But still...

"Oh, dear." She tried to look exasperated. "I've forgotten something I should have told my uncle. Would you ask the driver to stop so I can make a phone call?"

"No place here to make phone call," Cashan said.

"Oh, but there must be. I insist—"

"No place," he said firmly.

Alarmed, she said, "Stop this car at once!"

He ignored her. "Faster!" he shouted at the driver. "We're almost there."

The car shot into an alley. When it slowed to avoid a cart loaded with pomegranates, Catherine grabbed the door handle. The door opened, but before she could jump Cashan pulled her back. While she struggled he took a scarf from the pocket of his robe and tied her hands.

"What are you doing?" she cried. "Stop the car! Let me go!"

"The next corner," he said to the driver, ignoring her.

The car was maneuvered into a wider alley. Ahead she saw a truck parked, the back doors open, a ramp ready. The taxi rode up the ramp and into the truck. She heard the truck doors slam, then they were rolling.

It was dark inside. Cashan said, "You see, Youssef, I told you it would be easy. Now help me with her."

The driver muttered an oath and got out of the car. When he leaned over her she kicked out at him. He grabbed her legs and held on when she fought. "She devil!" he growled. And to Cashan, "Quick, tie her ankles."

When it was done they threw her onto the floor of the car. The driver said, "How soon before we can get rid of her?"

"As soon as we reach the desert," the other man said.

She lay where they had thrown her, a shoulder and hip hurting from the fall. She was terrified, shaking with reaction. Dear God in heaven, what was going to happen to her? The desert? Were they going to abandon her? To let her die? But why? Why were they doing this?

Tamar, unable to sleep though it was long after midnight, lay stretched out naked on his bed. The afternoon's session had been no better than the morning's.

"*Zfft!*" Tamar snapped on the bedside lamp and reached for a cigarette before he remembered he'd quit smoking two weeks ago. Angry and upset, he decided to ring for room service and order coffee and a package of cigarettes. But as he reached for the phone it rang.

Without preamble Ross Courlaine said, "Is Catherine with you?"

"What? What are you talking about?"

"Is she there?"

"No, damn it. What—"

"She isn't in her room. I've been trying to call her, she doesn't answer, and a few minutes ago..." Ross stopped to take a breath. "A few minutes ago I received a phone call from a man. He said...he said they had Catherine."

"Look, Courlaine, if it's another ploy of yours to use Catherine to get to me—"

"You don't understand!" Ross cried. "She's missing. She—"

"Forget it, Courlaine. It isn't going to work." Tamar slammed the phone down. Too angry to sleep, he got out of bed and began to pace. He didn't know what kind of game Ross Courlaine was playing, but saying that Catherine was missing was a low thing to do, even for him.

The phone rang again. Tamar snatched it up. "Listen, Courlaine," he shouted. "If you—"

"It's Hamid. You talked to Courlaine?"

"I just hung up on him. Why?"

Hamid chuckled. "So, the fox is worried, is he? Good."

Tamar stiffened. "He told me that Catherine was missing."

"And so she is."

The breath caught in Tamar's throat. "Hamid..." He tried to keep his voice neutral. "What have you done?"

"I thought the lady might like a little vacation in the desert," Hamid said. "I will let her uncle stew awhile.

Tomorrow he will receive a phone call telling him what he is to do if he ever wants to see her again."

Tamar clenched the phone and tried to speak calmly. "Well, well, my friend. You surprise me."

"I told you I didn't intend to stand by and let that son of a camel ruin the conference."

"What will happen to the woman?"

"She will be held until I have what I want."

"And if you don't get what you want? If Courlaine refuses to be intimidated?"

"Then it will no longer be of concern to me."

Jaw clenched, bile rising in his throat, Tamar managed to say, "Where are you now?"

"In my room. It has been an exhausting day." Hamid yawned. "Tomorrow will be interesting, my dear Prince Tamar. I want to be rested enough to enjoy it."

Tamar forced a laugh, but it cost him. "Sleep well." He put the phone down and stood for a few moments, taking deep breaths, trying to think rationally. But by Allah, this wasn't the time to be rational. Catherine had been kidnapped. He had to act.

He dressed quickly, a shirt, trousers, dark robe. Money, a lot of it, credit cards. He slipped a small revolver into the pocket of his robe, a slim silver dagger into one boot.

He left his room and headed for the stairs. When he reached Hamid's floor he went into the hallway. There was no one around. He found Hamid's room, took out a credit card, inserted it into the door, heard a click when the lock gave and stealthily, quietly moved inside.

He waited until his eyes adjusted to the light, then slowly went toward the bed. He leaned over it, made out the figure lying there and with a cry loud enough to raise the dead, grabbed Hamid by his throat and shook him.

The other man reared up out of the bed, or tried to. Tamar, one hand still grasping Hamid's throat, reached for the bedside light and snapped it on.

"You son of a bitch!" he roared, hitting Hamid. "Where is she? What have you done to her?"

Hamid Nawab's eyes were wide with fright, and he was wheezing. "My God," he said. "Why are you acting this way? You hate Courlaine as much as I do."

"But I don't take my hate out on women." Tamar hauled Hamid out of bed. The man was naked except for a pair of shorts. Tamar grabbed the robe that had been carelessly thrown over a chair. "Get dressed," he ordered.

"Why? Where . . . where are we going?"

"To find Catherine." He yanked Hamid closer. "And when we find her, pray that she has not been harmed. Because if she has I will kill you, Hamid Nawab. By Allah, I will kill you."

Catherine lost track of time. At some point she'd been taken out of the car, which had driven off. Now she was alone in the back of the moving truck.

Time passed. The road was bumpy. She tried to force herself to be calm. Why had she been kidnapped? What were they going to do to her?

Suddenly she remembered that first morning when she had gone to the Djemmaa el Fna, sitting in the restaurant overlooking the huge square. Tamar had told her of the women who, centuries before, had been sold as slaves to the highest bidder. Was that what was happening to her now?

She told herself she was being ridiculous. This was the twentieth century. Things like that didn't happen today. Did they? Maybe Tamar had only told her that to frighten her.

Tamar. She said his name aloud, finding comfort in the sound of it. Would he care that she was missing, or would he think it was another of her uncle's tricks? She remembered the scorn in his eyes, that last disdainful kiss. And thought, *No, he won't care. He won't care at all.*

And because she believed it she curled up on the floor of the truck and wept.

Chapter Five

Hamid mumbled directions to a section of shabby back streets far away from the luxury hotels and the palatial homes of the well-to-do. It was a dangerous area, home to cutthroats and thieves. And the men who kidnapped Catherine.

They entered a dark alley. When Hamid whispered, "There, that is it," Tamar stopped the car. He got out, went around to the other door and grabbed Hamid, whose hands he had bound, and pushed him. "Call out," he whispered.

"Cashan!" Hamid said in a croaking voice. "Cashan!"

A hand pushed aside a corner of the curtain that served as a door. "Who is it?" A whisper. "What do you want?"

Tamar shoved Hamid so hard that he collided with the other man, knocking him back. Before the man behind the curtain could right himself, Tamar grabbed him.

"What have you done with the woman?" he growled in a voice that threatened violence.

Cashan shot a look at Hamid. But Hamid, terrified, huddled on the dirt floor in a corner of the shack without speaking.

"Where is she?" Tamar roared. "Where is the American woman? Where have you taken her?"

With an oath Cashan pulled a dagger from the pocket of his dirty robe and struck out at Tamar. Tamar dodged, grasped the man's arm and twisted hard. Cashan grunted in pain. Tamar shot two fast jabs into his midsection. Cashan doubled over.

"Now!" Tamar shook the other man. "Tell me what you've done with her!"

Hands over his stomach, Cashan managed to say, "I . . . I only did what Hamid Nawab told me to do. I delivered her to the men he hired."

"Where is she now?"

"I don't know. They were going to take her to a . . . a nomad camp."

"What will they do to her?"

"Their orders were to hold her until they hear from me. In five days they may do whatever they want with her. Sell her, keep her." He lifted skinny shoulders. "They are a nomadic tribe. Once they move on no one will ever find the woman."

It was all Tamar could do not to go for the man's throat. "Do you know where the tribe is now?"

"I know where they were two weeks ago."

"Take me there!"

"No," Cashan squealed. "They are dangerous people. They might kill me."

"I will kill you if you don't." Tamar hit him and felt no pity when the man crumpled to the ground. He dragged him toward the curtained door where he yanked off a piece of dirty cloth. He tied Cashan's hands behind his back. Then he shoved Cashan toward his car.

"Don't leave me here," Nawab cried out. "Untie me. Let me go."

"I'll let you go straight to hell!" Tamar said between clenched teeth, and turning his back on the man who had once been his friend he pushed Cashan into the car.

Before he left the city he stopped long enough to make a phone call. "It's Tamar," he said when the phone was picked up. "I am on my way to El-Gandouz. Meet me there with ten men, camels, supplies and weapons. We are going into the desert."

To Catherine. He got into the car and prayed to his god and to hers that he would find her. And that he wouldn't be too late.

The truck stopped. Catherine waited, scarcely daring to breathe. The doors opened and she was momentarily blinded by the daylight. A man jumped into the truck. He pulled her to her feet, dragged her to the opening and handed her to another man. When he pulled a knife out of his robe, she uttered a cry and he laughed. "Don't worry," he said. "I'm not going to slit your throat. At least not yet." Stooping, he cut the rope that bound her ankles.

"The animals are here, Ahmed," another man said, and when Catherine turned she saw that they were at the edge of the desert where robed men, five or six of them, waited next to some camels.

The man who had hauled her from the truck gave her a push. She would have fallen had not another man grabbed her.

"We must give her food and water," he said.

He helped her to the shade of a date palm. She sank down, shaking with reaction and fear. Where were they taking her? What were they going to do to her?

"My uncle..." Her throat was so dry she could barely speak. "My uncle is a rich man," she managed to say. "He'll pay you whatever you ask. More than you're being paid by whoever—"

"Shut up!" Ahmed, hands on his hips, face threatening, glared at her. "Another word from you and I will shove a gag in your mouth. From now on you will speak when you're spoken to. You will do what I say and if you know what is good for you, you will do it quickly."

She took the canteen the man gave her and drank her fill. He left, to return in a few moments with an orange and a piece of flat bread.

"You must eat because you will need your strength in the days ahead," he said.

"Where are you taking me?"

"Into the desert." He looked over his shoulder. "When we receive word from the person who arranged this we will release you."

From the person who arranged this. But who? Who would do such a thing? And why?

Sick with fear, she ate the orange and the bread. The food gave her strength enough to believe that she wasn't helpless.

"Get up!" Ahmed yanked her to her feet and shoved her toward the camels. He grabbed Catherine's arm and thrust her into the saddle of a kneeling camel.

A man said, "Aren't you going to tie her hands?"

Ahmed laughed. "Why? I doubt even hanging on with two hands she'll be able to stay in the saddle."

She was able to, but just barely, especially when the lead camel driver shouted at the animals, *"Yala! Yala!"* and they broke into a trot.

She clung to the reins and hung on. When at last the animals slowed she saw that they were surrounded by rolling dunes and endless stretches of sand. She had wanted to see the desert, but dear Lord, not this way.

I'll get through this, she told herself again and again that hot and endless day. *I will survive.*

His men were waiting for him when he reached El-Gandouz.

"It is as you ordered, Prince Tamar," the head man, whose name was Bouchaib, told him. "The supplies and the arms are packed and ready. We can leave any time."

Tamar greeted the others, all good men who had been with him for a long time. Some, like Bouchaib, had served his father before him. He grasped Cashan's shoulder and propelled him forward. "This camel's vomit will be our guide," he said. "Watch him, Bouchaib. Do not let him escape."

Bouchaib took a step forward. "He will be carrion bait if he tries."

Cashan tried to shrink back. Tamar didn't blame him. Bouchaib was big, almost seven feet tall, with shoulders as broad as a camel's behind. His face, weathered by the sun and scarred from the battles he had been in, had been known to put the fear of Allah into braver men than Cashan.

Tamar shook his head. "He must be kept alive to guide us."

"Where do we go?"

"To a nomad camp." Tamar looked out at the desert and tried to quell the fear that came with the thought of Catherine somewhere out there, taken by Allah only knew what kind of men. "Men have kidnapped a foreign woman," he said. "An American. We must find her."

"Where is the camp?" Bouchaib loomed over Cashan, his scarred face threatening.

"Near...near the oasis of Ben Sabah," Cashan said. "Almost a two day ride from here."

"If you are wrong," Tamar said to Cashan. "If you lie about the location of the nomad camp, or if through stupidity you cannot find it, I will kill you. Do you understand? I will kill you."

The other man cowered. "I...I..." He tried to speak. But Tamar had already turned toward the camels.

We're coming, Catherine, he thought. *And we will, with the help of Allah, find you.*

That night when they stopped Catherine slid forward over the camel's neck. A man pulled her off and half dragged her to the small cluster of palms where they would rest for the night.

"Drink," he said, and held a canteen to her lips.

Barely conscious, she managed to drink a few drops. Her lips were cracked, her skin sunburned. She was dizzy, sickened by the unaccustomed motion of the animal and by the long day in the heat. She lay under the palms and closed her eyes, unmindful of the murmuring voices of the men around her.

Uncle Ross would have called the police. They would be searching for her.

She had a sudden vision of dozens of police cars racing across the desert, lights whirling, sirens blasting. But cars couldn't travel in the desert, could they? Did the police in Morocco have camels? Did they come riding out onto the sand like a squadron of Lawrence of Arabias? Or once you were taken into the vastness of the desert did they know it was hopeless and simply write you off as missing and presumed lost?

As she was lost.

Too tired to cry, she turned on her side and lay motionless, despairing.

Tamar knew he pushed his men hard, driving them on when they should have stopped, needed to stop, but he had to do it. They camped for only three hours in the dead of night. In the first light of dawn they were off again, whipping their camels forward with cries of, *"Yala! Yala!"*

They ate without dismounting, drank pint after pint of water. And kept going.

"We are almost there," Cashan said again and again the next afternoon.

"You said that an hour ago." Tamar pulled his camel close to the other man's. "Are you playing games with me or are you lost? I will—"

"My lord Tamar." Bouchaib held up his hand in a signal to stop. "There are camel droppings, and ahead I see scrub plants. Perhaps we draw near the oasis."

Tamar started to spur his animal, but Bouchaib said, "No, wait. It would be best to attack at nightfall. In darkness we will take them by surprise."

Tamar hesitated. As much as he wanted to go charging into the nomad camp he knew that Bouchaib was right. The night would be in their favor.

"Hang on, Catherine," he whispered. "Be brave. I'm coming."

She was taken to a black tent that smelled of grease and camel dung. A robed woman with a tattooed face and henna on her hands brought her a bowl of what looked like stew. Catherine asked, "May I have a fork?" The women turned away and sat at the tent opening with her back to Catherine.

Catherine looked at the food. It wasn't an appetizing sight, but she was hungry, starving. It tasted like last week's dog food, but she ate it.

When she finished she said, "I'd like some water, please."

The woman turned and looked at her. "Water," Catherine said again, and realizing the woman didn't understand cupped her hand and pretended to drink.

"L'ma," the woman said. She called out, *"L'ma! L'ma!"* In a few minutes another woman brought a gourd. The water was cool, and Catherine drank her fill. When she finished she poured what was left into her hands and tried to rinse her sunburned face. Her blue dress was soiled and torn and she needed a bath. She motioned to the woman that she wanted water to bathe in, but this time the woman turned her back and stared at the camp.

The day faded into darkness. From outside the tent she could hear the movement of the camp, voices raised in talk, children calling out to one another, the occasional barking of dogs.

The panic she had known when she'd first been kidnapped had become a sickening knot of fear. She thought about her uncle and knew how frantic he must be. And of Tamar, Tamar who had nothing but contempt for her. But as angry as he had been, Tamar wasn't a man who would hire others to do his dirty work.

But if not Tamar, then who was behind this? Was it someone who hated her uncle enough to use her to get at him? The thought chilled her. So did the uneasy feeling that perhaps Tamar had been right, perhaps Uncle Ross had been trying to disrupt the conference.

At last, exhausted by the two-day journey into the desert, Catherine rested. The noise of the camp had diminished, and except for the occasional yap of a dog, everything was quiet.

The woman who guarded her sat like a stone at the tent opening. Perhaps tomorrow she'd be able to overpower the woman. Tomorrow... And with that thought her eyes drifted closed and she slept.

She was awakened by bloodcurdling cries that brought her upright. Shots were fired, men shouted. She rushed to the tent opening. Her guard was gone. Catherine stared in horror at the scene before her.

In the light of smoldering camp fires she saw men on camels racing into the camp, rifles raised, firing as they came, screaming a terrifying war cry. Other men, sabers drawn, slashed at the nomads, who tried to defend themselves. One of thé men who had captured her took aim at one of the riders. Before he could fire a saber slashed and he went down. Then suddenly, above the bedlam and the din of gunfire, she heard her name. "Catherine! Catherine!"

She turned, shocked, sure she had only imagined it, and heard the cry again. Without conscious thought, she raised an arm and cried out, "Here! Here!"

One of the robed men wheeled his camel and started toward her. At that moment she saw Ahmed. He lifted his gun, but before he could fire she screamed, "No!"

The man racing toward her turned, fired, and Ahmed fell almost at her feet. Before she could retreat the rider swung an arm down and pulled her up in front of him on his saddle.

"Balak!" he shouted to the other riders. "Move out! Ride!" And gripping Catherine's waist, thighs pressed tightly to hers, he raced out of the camp.

There was no time to think, nothing to do but hang on. Had she gone from the frying pan into the fire? Was this a rescue, or was her rescuer yet another desert bandit? Behind her she heard the gunfire and the pounding of camel hooves as the other men caught up.

"Keep riding!" the man who held her urged. "Don't stop!"

Tamar! She turned so she could see his face. His head and forehead were covered. He looked as wild and fierce as a desert pirate come to rape and to ravage. Or to rescue?

In the darkness of that wild night his eyes met hers. For a breathless moment they looked at each other, then he said, "Hang on," and whipped his camel on, forward into that dark desert night.

Chapter Six

Pounding hooves coming closer. Rifle fire. Bullets pitting the sand, whistling over their heads. Screaming war cries. Behind her Catherine felt Tamar swing around and heard the burst of his gun. One of the men riding with them cried out and slumped forward in his saddle. Another rider slowed to support him, grabbed the injured man's reins and urged the camel on.

Catherine gripped the saddle. Aware of Tamar shielding her with his body, she tensed with fear for herself and for him. She didn't know how long they rode before the firing stopped. When it did she leaned back against Tamar, shaking with reaction from the pursuit, the horror of the battle scene in the nomad camp and her sudden rescue. If indeed it was a rescue.

They rode into the silence of the desert night until at last Tamar raised an arm and called out, *"Baraka! We have gone far enough. They are no longer in pursuit."*

He signaled his camel to kneel, then dismounted and helped Catherine off. She staggered, a little disoriented by what had happened. He steadied her. "Are you all right?" he asked. "Did they hurt you?"

"No. I . . . I'm all right. How did you find me?"

"Later. I must see to my men." He turned and called out, "Who was hurt? Is it bad?"

"Mohammed took a bullet in his shoulder," someone answered.

"It is not bad," the wounded man said. "I can continue."

"Are you sure? Let me see." He looked to make sure they were no longer being pursued, then hurried to the side of the wounded man.

Bouchaib knelt next to Mohammed. He took his *ghutra,* his head wear, off, tore a strip of cloth from it and quickly bound the man's arm. "It will hold," he said.

"Can you ride, Mohammed?" Tamar asked.

"Of course, my lord. This is only a scratch."

Tamar and Bouchaib exchanged a look. "He will do," Bouchaib said. "What about the woman? Is she all right?"

"Yes. What happened to Cashan?"

"I knocked him out of his saddle as soon as we rode into camp. The nomads will know he led us to them and finish him off. They're a bad lot, Tamar. I would feel better if we went on."

Tamar turned to Catherine who stood nearby, anxiously looking at the wounded man. "They will send others to search for us," he told her. "We have to go on. You'll ride with me."

She nodded. She still wasn't sure why he'd come after her. Had her uncle sent him? Was Uncle Ross waiting for them? She had so many questions, but before she could ask any of them Tamar helped her onto the camel. He mounted behind her, and holding her around the waist as he had before, called out, "Up!" With a jarring lurch, a moan and a wheeze, the camel rose.

They rode for what seemed like hours. Her eyes drifted closed and several times she came awake with a start, aware of the movement of the camel. And of Tamar's arms around her, his muscled thighs pressed tightly against hers.

"Rest against me," he said close to her ear. "I will not let you fall."

And though she told herself she wouldn't sleep, her eyes shut. In that nether land between sleep and waking she remembered her fantasy about Marrakesh and what it would be like to be carried off into the desert by an Omar Sharif kind of man. That her fantasy had become a reality frightened even as it thrilled her. Where was Tamar taking her? What did he plan to do with her?

They rode until daybreak. When they saw an oasis, Tamar called out, "We will stop here and rest."

When his camel knelt he lifted Catherine down, took a water bag from his saddle, handed it to her and said, "Drink."

She drank and after she handed the water bag back to him said, "How did you find me?"

"The man who kidnapped you led us to the camp."

"But why was I kidnapped? Was it for ransom? What—"

Tamar held up his hand, stopping her. "Later we will talk." He opened a saddlebag, took a blanket out and handed it to her. "Rest now, Catherine. You're safe."

"But I—"

"Later," he said firmly. Then he called, "Bouchaib!" and when the tall man with the dangerous smile came, Tamar said, "This is Bouchaib. Go with him. He will take care of you."

The tall man took her arm and led her to a cluster of date palm trees at the side of a small pool of water. He took the blanket from her, spread it under a tree and said, "Now you will rest."

"I'm hungry."

He reached in his pocket, took out a handfull of dates and handed them to her. "This will have to do for now," he said. Before she could say anything else he strode away.

With a sigh Catherine sank down and turned to look at the men who had ridden with Tamar. One of them had built a fire, two others led the camels to the pool to drink. The wounded man lay under another cluster of trees. Beyond the oasis was the endless stretch of desert sand.

This was all so strange. She had been picked up from the world she knew and transplanted to a place that was completely foreign to her, kidnapped, then rescued and carried away by a man she scarcely knew, a man who considered her uncle his enemy.

Why had he come to her rescue? And now that he had, what was he going to do with her?

She yawned, too tired to think or to question, curled up on the blanket and went to sleep.

* * *

After tending the wounded man, Tamar looked to
where Catherine rested. Excitement flared. She was
here in his desert land. Where he was in control.

Last night he had been wild with fear that he
wouldn't be in time to save her. For as long as he lived
he wouldn't forget the moment he caught sight of her
standing at the entrance of the tent, firelight on her
face, fear in her eyes.

Nor would he forget the feel of her against him as
they rode out of the nomad camp. Even then, in the
danger of that mad escape, with the nomads breathing down their backs, he had thrilled to her body so
close to his. Her hair had blown from her face, and he
buried his face in the fullness of it.

He went to where she slept under the palms. Her
face was dirty, her hair tousled. The blue dress she
wore was stained and torn. One hand was curled by
her chin. She looked very young and helpless, and
again came the feeling of masculine power. And yes,
excitement because she was here in the desert with
him, and because he knew that before this was over he
would possess her.

He posted a man on guard duty, told another to replace him in two hours, and found a place under the
palms near Catherine, close enough so that if he
reached out his hand he could touch her. And when at
last his eyes closed he slept with the vision of her behind his lids.

When he awoke a little before noon he saw that she
was sitting up. Not moving from where he lay, he said,

"Good morning," then, *"Sabbah al khair,* Catherine."

"Good..." She hesitated. "I don't know what you said."

"Sabbah al khair," he repeated. "It's a greeting, it means morning of gladness." And knew that it was indeed a morning of gladness because she was safe and here with him. "The response," he went on, "is *Sabbah annour."*

"Oh," she said.

"You must learn Arabic." He didn't smile. "It will help you while you're here."

"But we'll go right back to Marrakesh, won't we?"

Instead of answering, he said, "Perhaps you would like to bathe."

"Yes, but—"

"I will have one of my men drape some blankets in front of a section of the pool." And when she looked doubtful, he said, "You have nothing to fear from my men."

And from you? she wanted to ask. But did not.

He went to his men who were up and moving about the camp. In a little while a shelter had been erected for her. When Tamar returned with a robe he said, "Your dress is torn. You can put this on when you have bathed."

He started to turn away but before he could she said, "Tamar, wait. I have so many questions. Did my uncle tell you I was missing? How did you—"

"He called me the night you were taken. I didn't believe him at first because I thought it was another of his schemes, that between you, you had planned it."

"My own kidnapping?"

Her blue eyes flashed, but before she could go on, Tamar said, "Right after your uncle's call a man by the name of Hamid Nawab phoned. I knew by what he said that it wasn't a hoax, you really had been kidnapped. I went to his room and..." He hesitated, and a look of such coldness came into his eyes that without realizing she had, Catherine stepped back a pace. "And I convinced Nawab to take me to the man who had kidnapped you." His brows came together in a frown. "How did it happen, Catherine? Were you on the street alone? Did he force you to go with him?"

"No," she said, and explained what had happened. Then she continued, "I haven't thanked you for coming after me. So much happened so fast, the noise, the gunfire... I heard you call out and then I saw you and I..." She shook her head. "I couldn't believe it was you, Tamar. I don't know why you came after me, but thank God you did. I'm so grateful."

He took a step closer. "It isn't your gratitude I want," he said in a low voice. Her eyes widened with shock, but before she could respond, he handed her the robe, along with a bar of soap and a towel. "The robe is the smallest I could find," he said. "It will be better than your dress."

She looked at the robe, then at him, a little uncertainly. With a murmured, "Thank you," she retreated behind the cover of the blankets where she stripped to her undergarments. The water was cool and when she was sure no one could see her she took off the panties and bra, washed them and hung them on the low branches of a sedge plant to dry. Then she lay back in the water.

It isn't your gratitude I want. His words circled round and round in her head, frightening her but at the same time ... She shivered and splashed water on her heated face.

She wasn't going to think about it or worry about it now. She was safe and at the moment that was all that mattered.

Today they'd start the return journey, and while she wanted civilization the thought of the trek across the desert was not a pleasant one. She had gotten used to the rolling gait of the camel, but the heat! My God, how could anybody stand the heat?

It would be better with Tamar, she thought. He would let her rest when she was tired, give her water when she needed it.

She bathed, then washed her hair. Still reluctant to leave, she lingered until she caught the smell of food frying over the camp fire. Her underwear was almost dry. She put it on, then her sandals and the white robe. It felt strange but not uncomfortable. It was far cooler than her dress.

The men were gathered around a fire when she came from behind the cover of the blankets. They had been talking, but they stopped when they saw her. And stared.

So did Tamar. He had envisioned her in colorful silken robes, not this plain homespun cotton. But seeing her in the plain cotton robe, with her face scrubbed and her damp hair curling around her face, he felt the breath catch in his throat. Were it not for her fair coloring she might have been an Arab woman. But an Arab woman would have been shy among men who were not of her own family. If she had been Arabian her face would have been covered so these other men might not see her beauty. If she had been his woman...

The thought disturbed him, and in a voice made harsh by his conflicting emotions, he said, "Come and eat."

"How long will it take us to get back to Marrakesh?" Catherine asked over her second cup of coffee.

"From here? I'm not sure. Perhaps three days."

"That long?" Catherine sighed.

"But we're not going to Marrakesh."

She stopped, the cup halfway to her lips. "What did you say?"

"We're not going to Marrakesh." He met her startled gaze and turned away to pour more coffee. "The men who kidnapped you might be following us. If they are, it would mean another battle." He sipped his coffee, taking time to convince himself as well as Catherine that what he planned was for her protection. "So I have decided to take you to my home," he said.

She stared at him. "But you can't do that. I want to go to Marrakesh. Uncle Ross will be worried. I can't go to...?"

"El Agadir," Tamar said. "My home."

His home. At the edge of the desert, he had said.

"I want to go to Marrakesh," she said firmly. "Immediately."

"You will be safer in El Agadir." He stood, ignoring her protest. "It is a three-day ride. We leave in thirty minutes."

She stood. Almost toe to toe with him, her blue eyes flashing fire, she said, "I insist that we return at once to Marrakesh."

"You insist?" He gave an ungentlemanly snort. "From now until this is over you will do what I say. I have rescued you, therefore you are my responsibility."

"I don't want to be your responsibility!"

"Nevertheless you are. Now come. I have no more time for talk."

He took a roll of cloth from one of the saddlebags. "Wrap this around your head," he said. "Try to cover as much of your face as you can."

Catherine snatched the cloth from him, turned her back and wrapped it turban fashion around her head. But when it came to draping it over her face, the material kept slipping.

"Let me do it." Tamar turned her toward him. He brought the white material down so it partially covered her forehead, and when that was done tilted her face up and loosened the cloth on each side so it almost covered her cheeks.

"Don't be angry," he murmured. "I only want to protect you."

She stood very still and told herself that the brush of his fingers on her face didn't faze her. But when he tugged the swatch of cloth down and touched her ears, a small chill shivered through her. His eyes met hers and flared with sudden heat. She stepped back. "I don't want to go with you," she whispered.

"No," he said, "but you will."

One of his men killed the camp fire, another packed the food and a third took down the blankets that had sheltered her bath. To Bouchaib, Tamar said, "Saddle one of the pack animals for Miss Courlaine."

"Yes, *sidi.*" Bouchaib raised one scarred eyebrow. "She has spirit, she will not be an easy one to protect."

"Nevertheless, she will obey my orders."

"Of course. And you are taking her to El Agadir rather than to Marrakesh only for her own protection."

"What other reason would I have?"

"What indeed?" With a sly smile Bouchaib turned away and went to his camel.

Tamar glared after Bouchaib. Damn the man! Of course he was taking Catherine to El Agadir to protect her. And yes, because with Catherine as his... No, he didn't want to use the word *prisoner*. With Catherine as his *guest* he could bring Courlaine to his knees. He could save the conference and the future of both Eastern and Western oil interests.

Two noble reasons, he told himself as he turned to his camel. *And what of the other reason, Tamar? Why do you hide the real reason, even from yourself? Why do you not admit you want her in your home, in the land that you rule?*

He watched her with narrowed eyes while a fire kindled within him and his body hardened with need at the thought of how it would be. He would dress her in gossamer silks and teach her the ways of a proper Arab woman. And yes, by Allah, before this was over he would make her his. For whatever time they had together, Catherine would be his.

He stared over the rolling dunes and thought what it would be like with her, of early mornings and endless nights of making love to her, with her. Catherine.

When he looked back he saw that Bouchaib had saddled and brought one of the pack animals to its knees. In careful English he heard Bouchaib say, "This is a mild-mannered beast, Miss Courlaine. He rarely spits, and if you keep your legs well back he will not take a bite out of you."

Catherine took a step back. She gave Bouchaib a baleful look and glared at the camel. Then with a muttered curse she climbed into the saddle.

And Tamar, with a smile of satisfaction, mounted his own animal.

The next few days were the most challenging of Catherine's life. Determined not to let Tamar see how uncomfortable she was, she refused to complain. But the endless hours exhausted her. Her bottom hurt, her hands were sore from gripping the reins, and the camel's lurching gait made her queasy.

Each night when they stopped it was all she could do to swing her leg over the saddle and walk to the nearest palm.

The trip became a test she was determined to face no matter what it cost her. She would not let Tamar see her weaken. Whenever he asked, "Are you tired? Would you like to rest?" she would shake her head and avert her eyes.

She didn't believe she would be in danger if she went to Marrakesh. Tamar was taking her to El Agadir for reasons of his own. Perhaps by making her his prisoner he could force her uncle to do something.

Tamar rode at the head of his men. In a black robe, with his head covered, he was straight out of the *Arabian Nights*.

She had to get away from him and to the safety of Marrakesh. She didn't know how, she only knew she had to escape. For if she stayed with Tamar she would be lost. There would come a time when he looked at her with his dark desert eyes and she would be unable to resist.

As if reading her thoughts, he swung his mount around and rode to her. "You're tired," he said. And indicating a few scrub plants and a cluster of palms, he called to his men, "We will stop for a while."

He rode beside her until they reached the palm trees. He brought his camel to its knees and reached to help her. And said, "Come. You must rest."

His hands encircled her waist, and when he lowered her to the sand her body brushed against his. Heat flared in his eyes. And though she whispered, "Let me go," he tightened his hands on her waist and held her there.

"Please." She gripped his wrists to push him away. His skin was hot. A shock of awareness surged through her veins. She swayed toward him.

He said, "Catherine."

With a gasp she pushed him away. And knew she had to escape.

Chapter Seven

"Tomorrow we will cross the mountains," Tamar told Catherine when they stopped beside an oasis for the night. They were alone; his men had camped over a rise of dune. "From there it will be only a short trek. By night we will be home."

His home, not hers. She turned away to look into the flames, not wanting to meet his gaze, to have him know how desperate she was, how determined to escape.

She knew almost nothing about El Agadir, but it was his country. He would be in control there. If he decided to keep her, there would be little she or anyone else could do about it. If she was going to escape, it had to be tonight.

She looked up, pinpointing the North Star, and found herself wondering if the sky had ever been quite so beautiful before, the moon so bright. She hated the desert during the day, but there was a softness about it at night when the light of day slowly faded and the air cooled. The rise and fall of the dunes became a moonscape of light and shadow, the air as pure as God or Allah had intended it to be.

"You're very quiet," Tamar said, breaking into her reverie. "What are you thinking?"

"How beautiful the desert is at night."

He leaned back on his elbows. For a little while he didn't speak, then he said, "For me there is no place like it in the world. Though I often travel to Europe and to your country, I find that after a while I long to be here. The desert is in my blood, as much a part of me as life itself." He put a few more branches on the fire. "Perhaps it is because my mother was Bedouin. I was raised in El Agadir, but I went to school in Casablanca and later to your Princeton University. But all through my growing up, there would be a time each year when my mother and I would go into the desert to live with her people. I came to love the desert, to feel a part of it."

He looked at Catherine over the flames. "No matter where I go I will always return. This is where I will raise my children."

For you are a desert man, she thought. *This is where you belong.* She did not. The desert was foreign to her. She wanted to be in civilization, to see bright lights, have ice in her tea, hot showers, cool wine and a two-inch-thick steak.

"We're very different," she said, and looked across the flames at him. He had taken off the *ghutra* before he bathed in the small pool beneath the palm trees. His hair was still damp and in the light of the fire it glistened.

He was a handsome man. He had wonderful eyes, eyes that could look into the very soul of a woman. His mouth, the curve of his lips that could be both sensual and cruel, held the promise of pleasure. A pleasure that in spite of herself she hungered for, yet would never give in to.

"I know how hard the desert has been for you," Tamar said. "It will be better once we are in El Agadir."

He waited, and when she did not speak, he went on. "You're angry with me because I'm taking you to my home. I understand that, Catherine, but no harm will come to you there. You are my guest—"

"I'm your prisoner," she broke in. "You're forcing me to go with you against my will just as that man did in Marrakesh. You're no different than he was."

"No different? He kidnapped you!"

"And what do you think you're doing?"

"Keeping you safe." *Keeping you for myself.* "Protecting you." *From any other man but me.* "Shielding you . . ." He stopped. Damn! He couldn't think rationally when he was with her. He *did* want to protect her. *And what else, Tamar?* he asked himself. *Do you doubt that once she's in your home you will make her yours? Do you really believe she will come willingly to your bed?*

He had never taken a woman by force; he never would. But he wanted this woman more than he had wanted any other.

With a curse he reached to draw Catherine beside him. "Don't compare me to that animal. I want to protect you, to keep you . . ." Keep her until his body was sated. A week? A month? Would a month of loving Catherine get her out of his system?

The thought of how it would be when they lay and loved together on his bed made him tighten his hands on her shoulders. She stiffened and said, "Let me go!"

He stared into eyes that had gone smoke-gray in the reflection of the firelight and with a groan pulled her closer and covered her mouth with his.

She tried to turn away, but when she did he clasped the back of her head and held her there, held her while he took her mouth and kissed her. Though she pushed hard against his chest he wouldn't let her go. He kissed her again and again, hot, moist kisses, his mouth hungry, demanding a response she refused to give.

She fought him, but slowly, slowly, heat snaked down through her belly. She told herself she wouldn't give in to him or to the feeling that turned her knees to jelly and weakened her resolve. Though she whispered, "No, let me go," the hands that came up to push him away clutched his shoulders to hold him closer.

"I won't do this," she whispered. "I don't want—"

"I know. I know." He kissed her again, more gently this time, and with his hand on the small of her back brought her so close she felt his muscled thighs.

She uttered a small sound of protest. Or was it of need? And fought against that need even as a heat unlike anything she had ever known threatened to consume her.

Suddenly from the direction of where the camels were tethered came the laughter of the men on the other side of the dune. Sounds of reality that brought her to her senses. *Oh, God,* she thought. *What am I doing?*

She wrenched away. "No," she whispered. "No."

He reached for her and she backed away. "I don't want this," she said in an unsteady voice. And with more resolve, "I don't want you."

His face went still. Without a word he turned and went toward the dune. Without looking back he climbed it and disappeared over the other side.

Catherine stood where she was, so filled with mixed emotions she couldn't think. But, oh, she could feel. Her body trembled with reaction and a desire unlike anything she had ever experienced. She had wanted Tamar. She buried her face in her hands. And knew she had to escape.

Tamar lay a short distance from the other men, gazing into the camp fire. What was it about Catherine that turned him from a sane and rational man into a man so primitive he had almost taken her there on the sand?

She was beautiful. So beautiful. With blond hair streaming down her back and her eyes gone smoky with desire, she stirred him to a rise of passion that had been almost impossible to quell. It had taken every bit of his willpower to turn and walk away.

He told himself he felt like this because he had been without a woman for a while. And knew that he lied. He didn't want any other woman, he only wanted Catherine.

An hour passed, two, and at last he stood and walked to the top of the dune to look at the place where she slept. The fire smoldered; the moon came from behind the clouds. He narrowed his eyes, trying to see. Catherine wasn't by the camp fire. Perhaps she had gotten up to stroll around the camp. Perhaps...

He heard a sound. A murmured, "Up, damn it!" What the hell? Then he saw her astride one of the camels.

He called out, "Catherine!" But she wheeled the animal and headed into the night.

Behind him he heard Bouchaib call out, "What is it? Are we attacked?"

"The woman," Tamar called over his shoulder. "She's escaping."

He ran, slipping and sliding down the dune, raced to where the camels were tethered and grabbed an animal's reins. He brought it down and, without taking the time for a saddle, mounted and cried, "Up!"

The animal lurched. Tamar turned in the direction Catherine had gone. He had to find her before she disappeared into the dark vastness of the desert. For she would surely die. El Agadir was in the opposite direction. There was nothing in the direction she had taken, not a village, not an oasis, nothing but desert for a hundred miles.

He raced on, frantic, searching. At the top of a dune he paused long enough to look around. He saw a movement ahead of him. Catherine! Yes!

He caught up to her and pulled her from the camel, evading her blows. They rolled in the sand, and he captured her beneath his hard length. Fearfully she stared into his angry face, and with a groan he kissed her.

He exulted in the knowledge of his strength, his power to bend her to his will. And knew he could conquer her. He kissed her again and again, kissed her until the smoldering fire in his body burst into a flame that screamed for release.

Catherine shook her head, and her breath came in painful gasps. But still, knowing this was a battle she couldn't win, she fought him.

My God, he suddenly thought. *How valiant she is, how brave. How defiant in the face of my strength.*

"Oh, don't," she whispered.

He hesitated, poised above her. Moonlight touched her face. Her eyes were bright with tears. A terrible shudder ran though him; he knew he couldn't do this to her. Not to Catherine.

He let her go. She didn't move, she only lay there beneath him. Waiting. He saw the rise and fall of her breasts. Time stood still. He brushed her hair back, he rested the palm of his hand against the side of her face.

She said, "Tamar." And again, "Tamar." A sigh quivered through her. She reached to lay a trembling hand against his chest.

"Catherine," he said. "I—"

A cry split the night air. "Tamar! Prince Tamar!"

For a moment he didn't move, then with a strangled sound he pushed himself away from her and stood. "Here," he called out.

She lay where she was, shaking with reaction before she slowly got onto her hands and knees, then stood and saw the man on the camel racing toward them.

"You found her," Bouchaib called out. "Thanks be to Allah."

Tamar took her hand and felt her tremble at his touch. He led Catherine to his camel and brought the beast down. "You will ride with me," he said. And to Bouchaib, "Bring her camel."

A sudden weakness came over her. She swayed and would have fallen had not Tamar supported her with an arm around her waist. She was suddenly exhausted, filled with so many conflicting emotions, unable to think. Her attempt to escape had failed, but what was far worse, her body had betrayed her. In another moment she would have given in to the man who was her captor. Did he know? Had he felt her weakness? Her readiness to yield? If it happened again would she be able to resist him?

Tamar helped her onto the camel, and for a moment, their eyes met. He said, "Catherine?" Then, because Bouchaib was watching, he turned and mounted behind her.

But, oh, she was aware of his body against hers, of the jolt that brought them closer when the camel lurched to its feet. Aware of the rolling gait of the beast, of the shifting desert sands and desert smells. And of Tamar, holding her. She felt his breath on the side of her throat, his hand on her waist, the brush of his arm against her breasts.

When they reached the camp he helped her dismount and without speaking led her to the fire. To Bouchaib, he said, "We leave at dawn. Tell the other men."

"You will tie her?" Bouchaib asked, looking at Catherine.

"I couldn't do that."

"What if she tries—"

"She won't." He wanted to gather her in his arms, to hold her gently and calm her fears. But he said nothing; he did nothing.

"Let me go, Tamar," she pleaded.

Slowly he shook his head. "I cannot," he said.

They crossed the mountains the following morning and when they had descended once again to the desert, Bouchaib, who had been assigned to guard Catherine, said to her, "In three hours or less we will reach El Agadir. You will be comfortable there."

But still a captive.

What would happen when they reached his home? Would she be strong enough to withstand him? To fight her conflicting emotions?

By late afternoon she was too tired to speculate on her fate. Her back ached, her bottom hurt. She wanted a bath and fresh clothes, something decent to eat and a soft bed to sleep in. She would worry about what was going to happen to her after a good night's sleep.

Occupied with her thoughts, she was caught unawares when the column halted.

"There," Tamar said. "Below and to your right, there is El Agadir."

The last bright rays of the setting sun blinded her, but as the sun sank lower behind the dunes she saw it, like a shining jewel in the midst of the desert. Towers and turrets, mosques and minarets, rainbow colors of mosaic turned golden in the fading light of day.

"Look upon my home, Catherine," Tamar said in what was almost a whisper. "For that is where you belong."

She turned to look at him, but before she could speak he turned his mount and rode to his men.

And in the last rays of the sun they descended to the kingdom of El Agadir.

Chapter Eight

The city was surrounded by a walled parapet, the gate guarded by soldiers in bright red uniforms with smartly tailored jackets festooned with gold braid and buttons.

"Baraka!" one of them said when they saw the robed men approaching. "Stop, please. May I ask—" He saw Tamar then, stepped back a pace and saluted. "Prince Tamar! You have returned, thanks be to Allah."

"Shukran." Tamar smiled. "May I pass?"

The guard smiled in return. "Indeed, yes, my prince. This is your land, and your subjects await."

"This is the capital of El Agadir," Bouchaib told her when they passed through the gate. "Beyond and to the east are other cities and seashore resorts. The land that encompasses the oil wells lies to the south. The country itself compares in size to your state of Massachusetts."

They proceeded parallel to a wide, palm-tree-lined boulevard. Expensive foreign cars and limousines sped past small camel caravans like their own, as well as donkey carts and pack mules. As they neared what appeared to be the business section of the city, robed men and women crowded the sidewalks. Many of the women were veiled and had their hair covered. They were swathed from head to foot, all but their eyes hidden from view.

But there were other women who weren't veiled, women in Western clothes. A few of the younger ones wore blue jeans.

"I thought all of the women here were veiled," Catherine said in surprise.

Bouchaib grunted. "Prince Tamar made many changes when he took over at his father's death. Though the more traditional families prefer their women to be robed and veiled, it is no longer a law. Now a woman can go to study such subjects as engineering and medicine." He shook his head. "Changes. It makes one wonder what the world is coming to. I fear it will lead to the downfall of our society."

Or the salvation, Catherine wanted to say. But didn't. She had pigeonholed Tamar as an Arab chauvinist who believed women should be robed and veiled, barefoot and pregnant. Finding out that wasn't quite the truth unsettled her.

The city wasn't anything like she had expected, either. The marble and glass office buildings and the government buildings Bouchaib pointed out were modern. There were the usual mosques and minarets, a hospital, schools and a library.

When at last they left the boulevard the caravan started up a steep hill, rounding curve after curve of paved highway until at last they stopped at a lookout point. When they did Tamar rode up beside Catherine.

"There is my home," he said, pointing upward.

Catherine blinked. His home? It was a palace straight out of a fairy-tale dream. Turrets pointed toward the sky, and the sun glinted off towers and Moorish arches covered with gold mosaic. The thought struck her then that Tamar really was a prince, a desert sheikh who ruled with absolute power over this, his land.

He said, "Come, Catherine," and she followed in a daze, up and up until finally they approached an arched entranceway.

Armed men waited to block their way. One of them, a handsome dark man with a wide mustache that curled up at each end, saluted and said, "We did not expect you to arrive by camel, Prince Tamar." He looked curiously at Catherine. "You came through the desert from Marrakesh? Over the mountains?"

"Yes, Amin. It has been a long journey and the men are tired."

"I thank Allah for your safe return. I will phone the palace that you are coming."

"Tell them I bring a guest and to prepare for her."

"Yes, my lord Tamar."

Catherine, too spellbound to say anything, simply followed where Tamar led. And where he led was beautiful indeed.

Stately royal palms and terraced gardens filled with colorful splashes of red hibiscus and sunflowers, yellow chrysanthemums, dahlias and a rainbow of roses. The air was scented with frangipani blossoms, with blossoming orange and apricot trees. Rolling green lawns gave way to lily ponds and small stone bridges over bubbling streams. Scented water sprayed from a mosaic fountain and trickled through rock gardens.

Mesmerized by it all, Catherine barely heard Bouchaib say, "The men and I will leave you now, Prince Tamar."

Tamar reined in his camel. "Thank you, my friend. It has been a long journey. I know you are glad to be home."

"As we all are," Bouchaib answered with a nod toward Catherine.

"Thank you, Bouchaib." Tamar reached out to shake his hand, then saluted the other men and said, "Be sure that a doctor attends to Mohammed's arm."

"I will see to it at once." With a nod to Catherine, Bouchaib and his men rode off. Tamar brought his camel down, dismounted, then brought Catherine's camel to its knees. Taking her hand, he helped her off.

"We will walk from here," he said. And when still Catherine stood looking about her, he murmured, "This is your home while you are here, Catherine. If there is something you need, anything you desire, you have only to ask."

"Tamar..." But before she could say more, servants appeared in the arched entryway of the palace. They bowed, all the while glancing curiously at Catherine.

Tamar took her hand and led her forward. "This is Miss Courlaine from the United States," he said. "She will be our guest for a little while." He nodded toward an older robed woman. "You will see to her needs, Fatmah. Please send someone to the bazaar to buy a few robes, also rolls of cloth. Arrange for a seamstress to be here in the morning."

"I will attend to it, Prince Tamar."

"I'm sorry there was no way to prepare for your comfort before, Catherine. But unfortunately the oasis wasn't equipped with either a telephone or a fax machine. In a day or two I'm sure we'll be able to make you comfortable."

"I don't plan to stay longer than a day or two," she said with some asperity.

"Longer than that, I think." His smile didn't reach his eyes. Catherine was here now, and she would stay until he decided to let her go. Until his body was sated with all of her pleasures, his nostrils filled with her scents. Until he had made love to her a thousand and one times.

Filled with emotion, barely controlling his voice, he said, "Go along with Fatmah. Dinner is at seven. She will come for you then. I'm sure by then she will find something suitable for you to wear."

Catherine wanted to say she'd sooner eat grass than have dinner with him. She would have, too, but the idea of real food was too much to resist.

"Very well," she said in a properly cool voice, and followed the woman Fatmah through a labyrinth of corridors. Each one was more beautiful than the one before, with walls that were covered in intricately designed mosaic work, gold-filigreed arches that led into patios scented with lemon-tree blossoms and fountains that sprayed pastel-colored water.

At last they entered a flower-filled courtyard. Fatmah stopped in front of a tall, carved door and in careful English said, "Your quarters are through here, *madame.*"

Cool marble floors and tall marble columns greeted Catherine in the foyer. When Fatmah said, "This way," Catherine followed up a few steps into one of the most beautiful rooms she had ever seen. The colors, pale yellow and beige, gold and burnt orange, were soft, yet vibrant. There were two sofas, low and plush, made for Cleopatralike reclining, hassocks, tasseled floor pillows, beautifully carved tables and low-hanging lamps that cast a golden glow over the room.

"The bedroom is here." Fatmah opened a door, and Catherine entered a room of such delicate beauty it took her breath. The large round bed on a raised dais in the center of the room was covered with ivory-pink silk. The white carpet was cloud soft and deep, the chaise in front of the floor-to-ceiling glass doors a deeper shade of pink than the bedspread.

There were reclining chairs, low padded benches and a dressing table. One wall was lined with a glassed-in closet, another wall was mirrored. There were white roses on the dresser, and pink camellias floated in a crystal bowl on the nightstand.

"The garden is through here." Fatmah opened the glass doors. "It is private, the swimming pool is yours alone. You need have no fear of prying eyes." She turned to offer Catherine a smile, and with a gesture said, "The bath is this way."

Catherine took a deep breath and followed. But at the door of the bathroom she stopped. For the past three days all she had thought about was having a tub bath. But this wasn't a tub, it was a Roman bath surrounded by a greenhouse! Leafy-green ferns, gardenias and wild orchids bordered one side, and a small waterfall bubbled from the back.

"I will run your bath, *madame?*"

Catherine stared. She tried to swallow her astonishment and failed. "Yes, yes, please."

She went into the bedroom and sank down on the chaise. This was all too much, a technicolor dream from which she would awaken any minute. She'd known people with money. Uncle Ross had money. But never, ever had she seen anything to match the splendor of the palace. It was mind-boggling, intoxicating. If a person wasn't careful a person might be carried away by such luxury. A woman might...

No, she told herself, rising from the chaise. Not this woman! Not for all the Roman baths in Arabia.

But ten minutes later, submerged in scented water with the strains of a Mozart concerto filling the room, Catherine looked at the mirrored ceiling and with a grin murmured, "This isn't half bad, Miss Catherine."

It would take some getting used to, but of course she didn't plan on staying long enough to get used to it. A few days, perhaps a week. Then she would insist that Tamar let her go. How frantic Uncle Ross must be. She would phone him the minute she got out of the tub. But meanwhile...

She lay in the warm water and closed her eyes. How easy it would be to be seduced by these surroundings. She thought of Chicago in the winter, of snow and slush, of the wind blowing off Lake Michigan, of cold hands and freezing toes. And sank lower into the warm water.

In a little while she shampooed her hair with the fragrance of jasmine and rinsed it under the waterfall. She had just finished when Fatmah knocked and called, "May I come in?" And when Catherine, holding a towel around her, said she could, Fatmah approached with a silk wraparound.

"I have put several robes in the closet, *madame*. Also there are slippers and a few other things. It is a poor selection, but perhaps something will do for this evening. Tomorrow the dressmaker will come and finer robes will be made. There is makeup on the dressing table and scents you can choose from. I will return at seven to escort you to dinner. Is there any other way I can be of service?"

"Yes," Catherine said with a nod. "I would like to make a telephone call."

Fatmah lowered her eyes. "I'm afraid that is not possible, *madame*. There is no phone in your room."

"Then please take me to where there is a phone."

"I cannot, *madame*."

"But why? I have to..." But Fatmah had already turned and left the room.

With an oath, Catherine towel-dried her hair. It was six. In another hour she would see Tamar. He'd let her make a phone call or there would be hell to pay.

Tamar waited in a small salon for Catherine to arrive. That she was here in his home filled him with excitement, as well as a certain trepidation. He had never before brought a woman to the palace. Whatever relationships he'd had were conducted somewhere else. The Italian actress had a villa in Capri. For the year their affair lasted they met either there or at the apartment he kept in Florence.

He had entertained Monique, the lovely French model he'd been involved with before the Italian actress, at his home in Cannes. Gweneth had an estate in the Cotswolds, Pilar a home on the Costa del Sol.

Never before had he been inclined to bring a woman to El Agadir. But, strangely, this was where he wanted Catherine. He wasn't sure why, he only knew it was important to him that she be with him in his home.

The room he was in now was one of his favorites. It was where he felt the most comfortable. As a boy he had often dined here alone with his mother, as tonight he would dine with Catherine.

Here were paintings his mother had loved, a brilliantly colored Matisse, a Monet, and Delacroix's beautiful *Women of Algiers*. One of the women in the painting, with sad dark eyes and a softly mysterious expression, had always reminded him of his mother. Though draped in silks and satins, with rings on her fingers and pearls adorning her throat, Delacroix's woman looked as unhappy as at times his mother had been. For though she loved his father she had never really belonged in the palace. The desert was where she wanted to be, and it was there she died.

Occasionally he dined here alone, but until tonight he had never shared this room with anyone except his mother.

Fatmah opened the door. "My lord," she said, and with a bow motioned for Catherine to enter.

She stood in a pool of light from the shaded lantern above her head, dressed in a deep, rich blue robe almost the color of eyes made mysterious by a touch of kohl.

He said, "Please, come in." And when she moved toward him he caught the scent of jasmine.

"This is a beautiful room," she said, looking around.

"Yes." Did his voice catch? Did she sense what pleasure it gave him to look at her? "We'll eat in a little while," he said. "I thought you might like an aperitif first. What will you have?"

"A glass of wine, please."

"Certainly." He went to a carved cabinet and when he had poured her wine said, "Blue suits you, Catherine. As does the style of the robe. You look very beautiful."

She acknowledged the compliment with a nod, took a sip of the wine and said, "There isn't a phone in my room. I'd like to make a call."

"Oh? And who do you want to call?"

"Uncle Ross. I've been gone for five days, he must be frantic."

Tamar hesitated. "If you will agree to tell him you're my guest and that you will let him know when you decide to return, I will allow the call."

Allow? Tight-lipped with anger, Catherine said, "All right. If that's the only way I can talk to him."

He rang for a phone. When it was brought to him he dialed the hotel and asked for Ross Courlaine. When Courlaine came on the line, Tamar said, "This is Tamar Fallah Haj. I'm calling from El Agadir. Your niece is with me." Then, "Of course. Here she is."

"Hello," Catherine said. "Yes, I'm all right, Uncle Ross. But the trip in the desert was difficult. I'm tired and I thought I... I'd rest here in El Agadir for a while. I'll let you know when I can... when I'm going to leave."

They talked for a few more minutes before she handed the phone to Tamar. "He wants to talk to you," she said.

Tamar took the phone. "Yes," he said with an ironic smile, "I agree it would be best for Catherine to stay with me until she has rested."

He handed the phone to Catherine. When she said good-night and returned the phone he said, "Your uncle seemed pleased that you were here."

"He was relieved that I was safe."

"Of course."

Her brows drew together in a frown before she turned away, angry again because he seemed to be implying something and because she wasn't quite sure what it was. Uncle Ross was relieved that she was safe. He understood how exhausted she must be from her ordeal. Of course he'd want her to rest.

Still angry, she turned to look around the room. When she saw the paintings she went to look more closely at them. The Delacroix drew her. For a few moments she didn't speak, but at last, her voice hushed, she said, "This is truly wonderful."

"Yes, it is. It reminds me of my mother."

Curious, feeling her anger fade, Catherine asked, "What was she like?"

"Sad, I think."

"Like the woman in the painting."

He hesitated, taken by surprise. "Yes," he said. "Like the woman in the painting."

"Yet she has everything, the woman in the painting, I mean. Beautiful clothes, jewels, rich surroundings." Her head cocked to one side, Catherine studied the painting. "But she isn't really *there*, is she? Her thoughts are somewhere else. That's what makes her so unhappy."

"Perhaps as my mother did, she, too, longs to return to the desert."

Catherine looked at him, a little surprised by the sadness in his voice. She moved to the adjacent wall covered with intricately designed mosaic patterns. She touched the patterns with her fingertips, following the design as she moved along.

Behind her, Tamar said, "It tells a story."

"Oh?"

"A few years ago I was here alone and I began to study it. You have to look very closely to see what it is."

There was something strange in his voice. Catherine looked at him, one eyebrow raised in question, before she turned back to the wall.

At first she saw only the beauty of the brightly colored mosaic and the way the colors and the figures flowed like a score of music where one note follows another.

Then Catherine recognized a man and a woman standing a little apart from one another. In the next design the man held his hand out, and when the woman took it he led her into a garden of twisted golden trees and ruby-tipped plants. Here his hand rested on her shoulder, then it covered her breast.

Catherine took a sip of wine. Aware of Tamar behind her, she hesitated. Should she continue to study the mosaic or turn away? But she was intrigued, strangely spellbound.

The trees and the flowers of the garden thickened, almost hiding the couple. Catherine had to look closer, studying the elaborate design until she could find them amid the gold and the green, the bronze and the blue. She drew her breath, for now she saw clearly, now she understood the eroticism of the scenes, the woman entwined in the man's arms, then retreating, then beckoning him forward. The woman astride him while his hands touched her breasts. The woman prone, golden arms outstretched, golden thighs welcoming him.

Hot color rushed to Catherine's cheeks. She stared at the designs, unable for a moment to look away, fascinated, aroused. Embarrassed because she knew Tamar was watching her.

"Lovers," Tamar murmured. And she felt the heat of his breath against her skin.

She held the cool glass of wine to her fevered cheek and in a voice gone husky managed to say, "Interesting."

"Yes, it is." His hands were warm through the fabric of her robe.

She didn't move, she scarcely breathed.

He turned her toward him, his eyes searching hers. "Catherine," he whispered. "Catherine?" Just then there was a discreet knock on the door.

A quiver of breath ran through him. Still holding her, he said, "That will be our dinner."

When he let her go she stepped back a pace. He said, "Come." The door was opened and two servants bearing trays entered.

Tamar took her hand and led her to one of the low sofas in front of an equally low table. "Tomorrow we will dine on the food of my country," he said. "But tonight I thought you might like something you are more accustomed to. I ordered steak. Medium rare. Yes?"

Catherine caught a whiff of it and smiled for the first time that evening.

"A Caesar salad, baked potato with sour cream." Tamar returned her smile. "I hope you will enjoy it."

She did. Somewhere beyond the room came the softly melodic music of a zither. Except for murmurs of appreciation, there was little conversation until they had finished and the dishes were cleared. For dessert there were fresh strawberries served with brown sugar and thick cream. And baklava.

"I don't think I can eat another bite," Catherine said when she finished the strawberries.

Tamar picked up a piece of the sweet. "But you must sample the baklava, yes?" He held it up to her.

"I don't think so. I—"

"Just a small taste," he coaxed. And rubbed the honeyed sweetness of it across her lips.

His face was close to hers, his eyes on her eyes. She took a bite. It was very sweet. She licked her lips and he said, "Another."

Her heart skipped a beat. She couldn't look away. Nor could she refuse when he held another morsel to her mouth. She bit into it and felt a few small crumbs on her bottom lip. Before she could lick them away she felt the brush of Tamar's thumb on her lip.

"Lick," he said. And she did.

He fed her another small piece and again she felt the brush of his thumb. This time without his asking she licked the sweetness from it. And heard the hiss of his breath, saw his eyes darken and smolder. A rush of feeling as sweet as the candy warmed her, and not even knowing that she did she leaned toward him.

He sampled the baklava from her lips. He said, "Catherine," and his arms came around to crush her against him, holding her there while he drank his fill of her mouth.

When he eased her onto the sofa she murmured a protest. But he kissed her again, a deep and searching kiss that took her breath and weakened her resolve. As though from a distance she heard the slow, sweet music of the zither.

When at last he let her go she opened her eyes and found herself looking beyond him to the mosaic wall. The figures seemed more clearly defined, more real now as their bodies entwined in the act of love. The golden figure of the man touched the golden breasts of the woman. She opened her golden thighs...

Tamar's hand on *her* breast, heat between *her* thighs...

She closed her eyes to block out the figures, fought for sanity and for the strength to push him away.

"I can't do this," she whispered.

"You can," he said.

He took her mouth again. His hand was gentle upon her breast, caressing, coaxing a response she was too weak to deny.

"No," she said again. "Please, Tamar," she begged. "Please let me go."

He looked at her, his eyes hooded with desire, the breath coming fast in his throat. A shudder ran through him. He let her go.

She sat up, pushed herself away from the sofa. For a moment he did nothing. Then with a sigh he went to her. Resting his hands on her shoulders he said, "You want to make love with me, Catherine. You know that sooner or later you will surrender to me."

"No," she whispered. "No, I don't. I won't."

She looked at the golden figures on the wall again. And knew she lied. Knew that, like them, sooner or later she and Tamar would lie together.

Her throat so dry she could barely speak, she said, "I want to go now."

"Of course." He called for a servant, and when the man came he said, "Tell Fatmah to come at once."

"Yes, *sidi*."

They didn't speak while they waited. When Fatmah came he said, "Miss Courlaine is tired. You will take her to her rooms and see to her needs."

Fatmah touched her fingers to her forehead, and with a nod to Catherine, said, "Please, *madame*."

Catherine started toward the door, but halfway there she stopped and looked at Tamar.

He crossed to her and took her hand. She felt the brush of his lips on her skin, the heat of his breath. When she withdrew her hand she was shaking.

"Good night," she managed to whisper. And quickly followed Fatmah out of the room.

Chapter Nine

Though Catherine's bedroom was cool she was too warm to sleep well.

She dreamed in strange fantasy patterns, scenes that followed one into the other like the unfolding of a fan, peopled with shadowed images moving against a background of burnished gold.

In her dream she called out to her lover. He came closer and she felt the touch of his hand on hers, the brush of his lips against her palm. He kissed her quivering lips and caressed her golden breasts.

When at last she awoke and found that her dream lover had vanished, she wanted to weep.

Far too troubled to go back to sleep, Catherine pushed the tousled hair from her face and went to stand in the open doorway that led to the garden. In this hour before dawn everything was still. Not a leaf moved, not a bird sang. Morning dew lingered on the roses near the door, mist rose from the pool.

She slid the door open and stepped into the garden. The grass was damp beneath her feet. The pool looked cool, inviting, and she wished she had on a bathing suit instead of the short white cotton nightgown. She sat on the edge of the pool and dangled her bare feet in the water. Finally, unable to resist, she lowered herself into the pool and began to swim in long, lazy strokes.

The cool water was like satin against her skin. She took a deep breath and let herself sink below the surface, down into the deep silence, and stayed, suspended, until she knew she had to breathe again.

When she broke through to the surface some of the tensions of the night were gone. She swam again then hoisted herself up and out.

Light was breaking in the east. The air was fresh, a little cool. She wished she had thought to bring a towel. All she could do was push her wet hair from her face. The white cotton gown clung to her body, and she hurried to her bedroom, anxious to get into a hot shower.

From somewhere above her head a bird sang. She looked up, and when she saw it bobbing on a palm frond she paused to listen. With a smile she turned to enter her bedroom. And saw Tamar standing in the open doorway.

He wore a dark robe. His hair was damp. He needed a shave.

She stopped, frozen, hand to her throat, barely aware of the birdsong, the scent of roses or the grass still damp under her feet.

"I had to see you," he said.

She hugged her arms as though to shield herself.

He took a step toward her, murmuring, "You're cold. Let me warm you." And before she could move away he drew her into the bedroom and into his arms.

"No." Catherine struggled against him. "Let me go, Tamar. You have no right—"

She tried to pull away but he tightened his arms around her. "I dreamed about you," he murmured against her cheek. "About us. Every time I closed my eyes I saw you etched into the mosaic, beckoning to me, welcoming me with golden breasts and golden thighs."

The breath caught in her throat and she began to tremble so violently she might have fallen had he not been holding her.

"We made love in my dreams," he said. "You were like quicksilver in my arms, you set me on fire with your passion."

"It was only a dream," she whispered. This couldn't be happening. Two people could not share a dream. Could they?

"When I touch you I grow weak. When I'm away from you the sound of your voice sings in my head and your scent lingers in my nostrils. You're not like anyone I've ever known. I tell myself you're too independent, yet I find myself admiring the way you sometimes speak back to me, the way you lift your chin when you're angry and want to put me in my place." He drew her closer. "I know we're different, Catherine, I know this is impossible, and yet... and yet..." He covered her mouth with his, and in his kiss there was all of his longing and the passion of his dreams. And hers.

When she responded, when her lips parted and her body softened and swayed against his, he picked her up and carried her to the bed.

"No," she whispered. "No, I..."

"You're cold." He raised her arms and pulled the white gown over her head. She stiffened and tried to cover herself but he wouldn't let her go. Instead he eased her down on the bed and pulled the sheet up to cover them both, "Let me warm you."

She shivered with cold and with fear but still he held her, whispering words she didn't understand, his voice low, compelling, soothing. He held her gently and rubbed her back with slow, even strokes.

In a little while, lulled by his voice and the warmth of his hand against her back, she felt herself begin to relax. She closed her eyes, drifting on the edge of a dream. And in that dream she became not Catherine but the woman patterned in mosaic, a golden woman who waited to welcome her lover's embrace.

The hands that should have pushed him away lingered on his shoulders. He kissed her and her lips parted under his, for this was the dream they had shared, a dream more real than life.

He cupped her breast. He said, "So cool. So soft."

He took her mouth and kissed her long and deep before he began to trail a line of kisses across her cheeks. He nibbled her earlobe, and when she shivered he licked the curve of her ear, and his tongue was hot and moist. He kissed her shoulders, the hollow of her throat, and lifting her so that her breasts were closer he held her there for a moment, his eyes worshipful. Then his tongue darted out to touch a hardened peak.

It was as though she had been touched by a hot wire. She cried out, tightening her hands on his shoulders, and made as though to escape from the tortured pleasure she knew was to come.

He began to feather small, hot kisses against her skin, coming closer and ever closer to that small peak awaiting his touch. At last he took it between his teeth and flicked his tongue against it. He teased, he suckled, and with his tongue he circled and stroked. He felt the heat of her skin and her growing excitement. And rejoiced when her arms came up to encircle his neck and hold him there.

He was on fire, trying to hold back because he wanted to please and ready her. He claimed her mouth again, wild with passion, licking her lips with his hot tongue, biting a little, healing with his kiss.

He cupped her breast and she writhed against him, exciting him beyond thought, beyond reason. Engorged, swollen with desire, he ran his hand down over her belly and her hips. He said, "Open your thighs for me." Beautiful thighs. Golden thighs. And when she did he cupped her there, stroked and caressed her there, moaning at the sheer pleasure of such intimacy. He came up over her. Raising his robe, he grasped her hips and with a cry thrust himself against her. Into her.

His golden woman.

He buried himself in her warmth, holding her close as he rose over her, powerful and strong. She clung to him, moving as he moved, rolling her head back and forth against the pillow, gasping with pleasure. The sound of it, those small sounds that told him she loved what he was doing to her, pushed him to the brink. He tried to hold on. He said, "Catherine, Catherine," and moved against her, deeper, deeper. Sweet torture. What sweet torture.

Suddenly her body began to tremble. She cried his name, and the sound of it shattered the silence of the morning and cast him over the edge of reality.

He took her mouth. He tasted her cry. And as violent as the blast of a hurricane wind it came, explosive, hard, taking his breath, his strength and all that he was.

He slumped over her, lost in her, glorying in her. Her hand came up to stroke his hair. He captured it and kissed the tips of her fingers. "Are you all right?" he whispered. "Did I hurt you?"

"No. Oh, no."

"I should have taken more time. The next time..." He closed his eyes. The next time and the next unfolded before him. Early mornings like this morning. Love-filled nights, holding Catherine, making love with Catherine. For as long as she was here she would be his. When the day came that he knew he must release her, he would. But until then...

He raised himself so that he could look at her. "I will bathe you."

She shook her head, embarrassed.

"You were cold when you came out of the pool, you need a hot bath." Before she could answer he got up and went into the bathroom.

Leaving her alone with so many mixed emotions. Why had she let this happen? Could she have prevented it? Could she, when she saw him standing there in the doorway, have simply ordered him out? Should she have succumbed so quickly? Shouldn't she have put up a fight? Defended her honor?

He came out of the bathroom, a big black towel wrapped around his waist and started toward her. "What?" she asked, when with a laugh he scooped her up in his arms and carried her into the bathroom.

Steam rose from the bubbling, scented water as he eased her into the pool. Gypsy music played somewhere in the background. He turned away to take the towel off and Catherine drew her breath in. His shoulders were broad, the planes of his back long and smooth, his buns firm and round. Squeezable. Kissable. He turned and she sank into the water up to her chin and closed her eyes.

You're losing it, she thought. *The desert sun has done you in, addled your brain, shaken up your libido. You're not like this, remember? You're a cool and collected twenty-nine-year-old professional woman. Yeah, twenty-nine going on sixteen, suddenly aware you've got hormones.*

He stepped into the water and settled himself in front of her. She opened her eyes. *Okay,* she admitted, *this is probably the best-looking man I've ever seen, with a Greek physique and great buns, but this is pure insanity. You're his prisoner, remember? He brought you here against your will.*

But he didn't make love to you against your will, a voice inside her head whispered. *Or did you only pretend all those sighs and murmurs? Was the dream you dreamed real or imagined?*

The warm, scented water swirled gently around them. He moved closer and cradling her in his arms said, "I know you have been angry with me because I brought you here, but I couldn't let you go, not until I knew what it was like to hold you like this, to make love with you as we did a moment ago."

Catherine took one of his hands between hers. Not looking at him she said, in a voice so low he could barely hear, "And will you let me go now?"

The arms that held her stiffened. She heard the catch of his breath. "Now?" he said. "Oh, no. Not yet. Not yet. While you're here with me you are not my prisoner, you are my beloved and all that I have is yours."

For as long as this lasts, she thought, but did not say.

He chose a bar of soap from the selection at the side of the pool, lathered his hands and began to soap her breasts.

"Tamar..." She clasped his wrists.

"No, I want to do this. You must not stop me. You must only enjoy."

His hands were gentle on her skin, massaging with the soap, stopping to linger on her nipples, drawing soap bubbles out, then flicking them away with the tips of his fingers.

She closed her eyes and gave herself up to his hands, hands so smooth upon her skin. He rubbed her shoulders, her throat.

She said, "Tamar?" and he heard the tremble in her voice.

"Yes, *laeela?*" He reached to touch between her legs. "What is it?"

"I don't know what you do to me." Her eyes drifted closed. "When you touch me, when you kiss me—"

He covered her mouth with his. "Like this?" he asked against her lips. All the while stroking, stroking.

"Oh, please." She pushed against his hand. "Oh, please."

"Please what, Catherine?" He eased his tongue into her mouth. She moaned and her tongue touched his. And she was lost, lost in the warm, swirling water and the splash of the waterfall. Lost in the mouth that claimed hers, the hand that so gently caressed. In the feel of his body close to hers, the strength of his arousal.

With a cry he lifted her out of the pool onto the thick white carpet. "You have bewitched me," he whispered when he knelt beside her.

She raised her arms to him, and when he lay close she enfolded him. And cupping his face between her hands, she said, "I want this, too. I want you, Tamar."

He looked at her, the golden flecks in his dark eyes brighter than she had ever seen them. He kissed her. He said, "Catherine, Catherine," against her lips. And with a cry of need he joined his body to hers.

It was too fast. Heaven and hell. A passion so wild it took her breath. He drank from her lips. His mouth hot, feverish, he kissed her breasts, sucking hard, taking the small peaks between his teeth to lap and to tease.

He drove deep, his breath ragged, his face tortured. He rained kisses over her face, her throat, her breasts. He cupped his hands beneath her to bring her closer.

"Tamar, Tamar..." Sensation after sensation rocked her. She clung to him and turned her face into his shoulder to smother her cries. He plunged, he withdrew to plunge again as wave after wave of pleasure shattered and broke her. And when with a hoarse cry his body convulsed over hers she held him, sharing this moment, this incredible moment with him.

For a long time they lay without speaking, breath mingled with breath until at last he said, "I have never felt what I feel with you." He raised himself on his elbows and looked at her. "I do not think I can let you go, my Catherine."

"But you will." She touched the side of his face. "Some day you will."

Chapter Ten

The days passed in bedazzled pleasure. Catherine had never known such happiness, had never shared this kind of intimacy with anyone before. She went to sleep each night in Tamar's arms and woke to his touch each morning.

He was a caring lover, at times tender beyond words, at other times so fierce and strong he took her breath. There were nights when they hardly slept, nights when he couldn't stop loving her. Each time he touched her she turned to him with a cry of gladness, wanting this loving as much as he did.

Bolts of the most beautiful cloth Catherine had ever seen were delivered to the palace. A seamstress arrived to make kaftans and robes. Matching slippers were purchased, along with impossibly delicate undergarments and nightgowns.

"And jewels," Tamar said. "You must have jewels."

A ruby ring and a matching pendant that hung from a silver chain between her breasts. Diamond earrings. A gold necklace and a jade ankle bracelet.

"A slave bracelet," Tamar said with a smile when he fastened it around her ankle. "As long as you wear it you will belong to me."

Her delight in these things was as hard to resist as was Tamar. At night he would select one of the nightgowns for her to wear to bed, a long white ruffled concoction of silk and lace, a pale green floating chiffon, a scandalously short ruffled black satin. When she had put the gown on he'd smile and say, "Yes, that is nice. You look quite beautiful in it. Now come here and let me take if off."

Once Tamar took Catherine to the highest room in the palace. He opened the French doors and, holding her hand, took her out onto the balcony. "There is my desert," he said with a gesture. "The place I love the most in the world."

It was so beautiful it took her breath, and for a moment she couldn't speak. It stretched as far as she could see, mile after mile of rolling dunes, shades of mauve and pink and gold in the last rays of the setting sun.

"I've never seen such colors," she said. "It's beautiful."

She stayed out on the balcony for a little while, watching the shadows of evening fade to darkness. It seemed very strange to her that she was here on the edge of the desert, so far from her own home and from everything she had known. From the apartment in Chicago, from her office overlooking Michigan Boulevard. She had called the office from the palace to say that she wasn't sure when she would return. Her two partners had been curious about what had occurred. But all she could say was, "I'll let you know."

How could she tell them when she didn't know herself? It was as though she had been given a hand of cards to play; she would play them until there were no more cards left. And then? Then she would go home, to the life she knew, to her life before Tamar.

The thought of leaving him made her tighten her hands on the balcony railing. These last few days had been the closest to heaven she ever hoped to get, an idyll of a romance both she and Tamar knew could not endure.

He had brought her to El Agadir against her will and made her his prisoner. She knew that now he would release her if she asked him to, but she would not ask, not yet. For the moment she was a prisoner of her own desire, unable to resist, unable to turn and walk away from him. She would eventually, she told herself as she gazed out at the desert night. In another week, or the week after that. But not yet. No, not yet.

That night when they were in her room she selected a gown of ivory satin that clung like a well-fitting glove to the curves of her body when she put it on.

He gripped her shoulders and in a voice that shook with all he was feeling, said, "What is happening to us, Catherine? What magic do you weave around me? What spell have you cast?" He held her, his eyes searching hers. "You're all I think about," he murmured. "We make love, my body is sated, yet in a little while I want you again. It isn't only that, the wonderful way we make love, it's everything about you. I love the way you smile, the sound of your laughter, the way you walk. When I'm not with you I long for the sound of your voice. I look around a room when you're not there and I am appalled at how empty it seems."

He tightened his hands on her shoulders, his face intense, almost angry. "My life is well-ordered, my future planned. But now, for now..." With a low groan of need he pulled her into his arms. He held her as though he would never let her go, he kissed her as though drawing breath from her breath.

He showered her face with kisses as he carried her to their bed. He turned her onto her side, and resting his head on her arm he kissed her breasts through the fine satin, kissed until she thought she would go mad. But when she protested he whispered, "A little more. Only a little more."

She curled her fingers in his hair, her body on fire, writhing with need. At last he took the gown off and when he did he began to suckle, to tease and caress. Until Catherine, almost incoherent with need, begged, "No more. Oh, please. No more."

He stroked her to calmness and began to feather kisses over her belly, her hips and her legs. He made little love bites inside her thighs, then licked to soothe the skin there as he moved closer to the apex of her legs. When she put her hands on his shoulders to push him away he gripped and held them to her sides. And kissed her in that most intimate of places. Kissed her until she thought she would go mad, kissed her while she pleaded for him to stop. Then not to stop.

He reached to stroke her breasts, to gently pinch her nipples. And all the while his mouth, his hungry mouth, caressed her.

It came like a crash of thunder, like lightning zinging through her, like the shattering of glass. Her body lifted and surged. She cried his name and when she did he came up over her, and while still on that thin edge of ecstasy he took her, hard and fast, took her while she sobbed his name and their breaths mingled as one when they kissed.

"Oh, love," he said over and over again. "Oh, love."

Later, in the quiet of the night while still he slept, Catherine crept out of bed and went to stand on the balcony. A quarter moon had risen over the desert and she thought as she stood there that she had never seen a night as beautiful as this night. And wept because this was not, nor could it ever be, her home. And because someday soon she would leave Tamar.

Once Catherine tried to explain her past. "Uncle Ross took me in," she said. "He gave me everything. He's been like a father to me, Tamar." And finally, because it had to be said, "I know you don't like him, but—"

"It isn't a matter of liking or not liking." Tamar cut her off. "Your uncle sabotaged the conference. The conference would have eased the tensions that have been with us for years and brought about more understanding between nations. But because your uncle conspired with the oilmen from Mali Bukhara our hopes for peace and understanding were shattered. But what is worse," he went on, "what I can never forgive, is that he tried to use you."

"I don't believe that," Catherine said. "I'll never believe it."

"Doesn't it seem strange to you that once he knew we had met he invited me to have dinner with the two of you? Or that when he knew you were here in El Agadir he told you to stay as long as you wanted to?"

"No! And it wouldn't seem strange to you, either, if you knew what a kind and decent man he is."

By dinnertime that evening they had made up. But neither of them mentioned Ross Courlaine.

Five members of the delegation that had been in Marrakesh arrived the following day. Only one of them, Sheikh Rahma Al-Shaibi, had brought his wife, a slender woman near Catherine's age. At least that's what Catherine thought, because Zenobia Al-Shaibi was veiled. Her hair was hidden by a brown scarf, and a heavy brown robe covered her from her neck to her toes.

"You and the wife of Sheikh Al-Shaibi will join the men for dinner tonight," Tamar told Catherine when they were alone. "She will, of course, be veiled."

Catherine raised an eyebrow.

"And so must you be."

"You mean that I have to wear a veil? But I'm ... I'm an American."

"You certainly are." He smiled, then the smile faded. "Nevertheless, you are my guest. The men will suspect that you are my woman. Therefore it is only proper that when they are present you be veiled."

You are my woman. The rest of the words faded. She heard only those four words. *You are my woman.*

Am I? she wanted to ask. *Am I, Tamar? Is that who I am? Is that who you want me to be?*

But she said nothing.

That night while she was dressing Fatmah brought her a selection of veils. One was the same shade of blue as the robe she had chosen to wear. She held it up to her face, just below her eyes. It seemed very strange to her, not unattractive, just strange.

When she was alone she made up her eyes, outlining them with kohl, using more mascara than she usually did. And finally she covered her face with the veil.

Fatmah knocked and called out, "It is time, *madame*." And Catherine, after a last look in the mirror, followed the woman out of the room.

Tamar, the men and Zenobia Al-Shaibi were in the formal dining room. At the doorway she hesitated, but when Tamar said, "Good evening, Catherine," she murmured a greeting.

He watched her come toward him, robed and veiled in a blue that matched her eyes, her hair free about her shoulders. The effect was stunning. He heard the man beside him catch his breath, heard another man whisper, "Praise Allah. I have never seen a woman as lovely as she."

She drew closer. *She is lovely,* Tamar thought. *So lovely she takes my breath.* Her eyes, outlined with kohl, were filled with mystery and womanly allure. He felt himself go weak with need and wondered how he could last through the evening without touching her, what excuse he could give for escaping with her.

Dinner was announced. He sat at the head of the table, she was at his right. She had picked up enough Arabic since she had come to Morocco to catch some of the conversation, though the men ignored her as well as Zenobia.

Finally the man seated across from her said, "This has been a fine dinner, Prince Tamar. Now I think it is time to discuss the reason we are here. I'm sure the ladies will excuse us."

Zenobia Al-Shaibi stood like an obedient rabbit. Catherine took her time. She nodded to each of the men and to Tamar said, in what she hoped was a deceptively sweet voice, "May I be excused, my prince?" She knew he would understand her anger and outrage.

He rose and bowed. "Until later," he said with a grave look.

Catherine nodded as she started across the room. Just as she opened the door she heard a man say, "Now, gentleman, what are we going to do about Courlaine?"

With her hand still on the brass knob, she hesitated. Then she went out and closed the door, but not all the way. She stood there a moment, heart beating hard. Zenobia Al-Shaibi had disappeared down the corridor. Neither Fatmah nor the other servants were anywhere to be seen. The corridor wasn't well lit. She stepped into the shadows close to the door and strained to hear.

"There is talk of reconvening the conference," someone said.

"But it will do no good if that bastard Courlaine attends."

"Or the men from Mali Bukhara he plots with."

"We can make sure Courlaine does not attend."

"You speak of murder?" a shocked voice asked.

"No." Coolly spoken. "Execution."

"Killing isn't the answer," Tamar said.

"It is the answer and the solution," another man declared. "With Courlaine out of the way there is a good possibility Mali Bukhara will back off."

"We have no choice." A different voice. "We have to get rid of him."

"I know a man..." The man speaking lowered his voice. "A paid assassin..."

Catherine crept closer, straining to hear, but now all of the voices were lowered to conspiratorial whispers.

Carefully she closed the door and stood with her back against it. Uncle Ross! My God! They were going to kill Uncle Ross. She had to stop them, had to warn her uncle. But the use of a phone had been forbidden to her unless Tamar was present, as he had been when she spoke to Uncle Ross and when she called her office. Somehow, some way, she had to convince Fatmah to let her use a phone.

She ran down the corridors to her quarters. Once there she rang for Fatmah. But her pleas were unsuccessful.

Catherine paced back and forth. The room seemed too small. She went out into the garden, trying to think of a way to warn her uncle so he would leave Marrakesh. But how? Dear Lord, how?

Should she appeal to Tamar? Tell him she had overheard the plan to kill her uncle? He cared about her, surely he wouldn't hurt the man who for years had been her surrogate father. But could she take that chance? If she appealed to him and he refused she would have lost whatever opportunity she had of warning her uncle.

There had to be another way. There was an airport in El Agadir. If she could get away from the palace, get to the airport... But she had no passport, no papers.

The hour grew late; she knew that soon Tamar would come. And that he would want to make love.

She undressed quickly and got into bed, but it was after two before she heard her door open.

He said, "Catherine?" and when she didn't answer he came to stand by her bed.

She heard him sigh, then he gently touched her cheek and whispered, "Sleep well, my *laeela*. Sleep well, my darling."

Then his steps moved away from the bed and she heard the quiet closing of the door.

Only then did she begin to cry, for what had been and what could never be.

Chapter Eleven

Catherine had breakfast alone in her room the following morning. While she was eating a message came from Tamar saying that he had arranged for a car to take her and Mrs. Al-Shaibi on a tour of the city that morning at ten.

"I missed you last night," he wrote. "But we will make up for the missing tonight. Yes?"

She touched the note to her lips. Never in her life had she been as torn as she was now. She loved her uncle and felt a fierce loyalty to him. And yes, God help her, she was in love with Tamar. Now she had to choose between them. But was there a choice? If Uncle Ross was in danger she couldn't stand by and do nothing. If it meant turning her back on Tamar, having him believe she was betraying him, then so be it.

There had to be a way to reach Marrakesh. She couldn't let Uncle Ross be murdered.

A few minutes before ten Catherine left her room. She wore a robe, but she neither covered her hair nor wore a veil, unlike Mrs. Al-Shaibi, who was waiting for her at the palace entrance.

Catherine followed her into the back seat. They made only surface conversation. Zenobia talked about the weather. She said the city was interesting, but she was shocked to see that some of the women wore dresses instead of robes, shocked again when Catherine told her women attended the university.

"That would never happen in Bela Hamaan," she said.

At noon the driver stopped at a restaurant. "Prince Tamar has suggested you have lunch here," he said.

Zenobia looked surprised. "Can we enter unescorted?"

"Yes, *madame,*" the driver answered. "It is done frequently in El Agadir."

Zenobia looked uncertainly at Catherine. "My husband won't like it," she said.

"Does he need to know?"

The woman's dark eyes widened. Then, surprisingly, she laughed and said, "Perhaps not. Besides, he is too preoccupied with other matters for me to disturb him with something so trivial."

There were other women in the restaurant, some with men, some unaccompanied. One or two of them were veiled, the others weren't.

Zenobia shyly unveiled then began chatting with Catherine.

"I will see my parents when I go to Marrakesh tomorrow." Zenobia took a piece of flat bread. "I haven't seen them in over a year. They are vacationing there and my husband has given me permission to join them. He is sending me in his private plane."

Catherine stared at her. "You're . . . you're going to Marrakesh?"

Zenobia nodded.

"Will you take me? May I go with you?"

"Take you? I don't understand."

"I have to get to Marrakesh."

"Then of course you will come with me, if Prince Tamar agrees."

"But he..." Catherine hesitated a moment, then making a decision said, "He won't say it's all right, Zenobia. You see, Prince Tamar brought me to El Agadir against my will. Things are different now, but no, it wouldn't be all right with him to let me go to Marrakesh." She leaned closer, her eyes intent on the other woman's. "There is a reason I must go," she went on. "My uncle is there. He's in danger. I have to get to him. I—"

"Prince Tamar made you his prisoner?" Zenobia asked in a whisper.

"Yes."

"That is a very bad thing." Zenobia looked at her hands. "Any time you are made to do something against your will it is a very bad thing." She raised her eyes and looked at Catherine. "I would help you if I could, *madame,* but I don't see how I can, not if Prince Tamar refuses to release you." Looking thoughtful, she took a bite of her shish kebab. "If you were able to leave the castle without being seen..." She shook her head. "But even if you could, someone would surely see you getting on the plane. With your coloring and your blond hair everyone knows who you are."

"But if I covered my hair—"

"And wore a veil." Zenobia's eyes widened with excitement, and she clapped her hands. "You could take the place of one of my servants."

They stared at each other. "Two servants are to accompany me," Zenobia went on, leaning closer as though afraid someone might hear. "One is close to your height. If you were well covered and kept your eyes lowered..."

Catherine's heart skipped a beat. "It might work. But when your husband finds out he'll be angry. I don't want to get you in trouble."

"It is trouble I can handle." There was a tone of unexpected toughness in Zenobia's voice. "I have been married for almost ten years. In that time I have learned a few things. I will deal with my husband later, after he finds out what we have done. It is you I'm worried about. If Prince Tamar disapproves of your going to Marrakesh, will it not harm your relationship?"

Harm it? Catherine thought. Yes, beyond repair. Tamar would think she had betrayed him. Nevertheless, she couldn't stand by and do nothing to save her uncle. "I have no choice," she said. "I have to get to Marrakesh. But what of your maid when your husband discovers what we've done?" Catherine asked. "Won't it be dangerous for her?"

Zenobia thought for a moment. "I will call my brother today and ask him to send a plane. If I can arrange it, my maid Zohra will fly out a few hours after we do. Thus she will be in Marrakesh when my husband returns." She touched Catherine's hand. "Do not worry, it will be all right."

She tried not to think how angry Tamar would be when he discovered her gone. How hurt.

And so it was that she decided to make one last effort to ask him to let her go.

It was late when Tamar came to Catherine's room that night. She had dressed for bed and was resting on the chaise in front of the open doors that led out to the garden. A dim light glowed from a bedside lamp.

"Catherine?" He hurried to her and when she made room for him on the chaise he sat beside her and gathered her into his arms. "I've missed you," he said.

"And I've missed you." She buried her face in his shoulder, smelling the crisp freshness of his robe and the good, clean man scent of him.

"I had hoped we could meet at dinner but it wasn't possible."

"Business to discuss?" she asked.

He looked uncomfortable.

"Your guests are the same men who attended the conference in Marrakesh, aren't they?"

"Yes." Then changing the subject, Tamar asked, "How was your day with Mrs. Al-Shaibi?"

"Very nice. I like her." Catherine played with the tassel on one of the cushions. "She's going to Marrakesh tomorrow."

"Oh? I didn't know that."

"Her family's there. She's going for a visit." She looked at Tamar. "I'd like to go with her."

"To Marrakesh? No! I mean, not yet. Perhaps in a few weeks we can both go."

And because she knew it would do no good to argue, Catherine let the subject drop. She *would* go to Marrakesh, with or without his approval. But when she did it would be over between them, for by her leaving she would be betraying everything they'd had together.

When she sighed and lay back on the chaise, Tamar asked, "What is it, Catherine? Are you so unhappy here with me?"

Catherine took his hand. "No, Tamar. The days I've spent here with you have been some of the happiest of my life. I'll never forget..." She shook her head, unable to go on.

"*Laeela?* What is it? What is making you unhappy?"

"Nothing. I'm being silly. I missed you last night and this morning."

"Then we have much to make up for." When he kissed her, Catherine put her arms around him, her face against his. *I love you,* she wanted to say. *I think I've loved you from the first time we kissed. Even when I tried to run away from you, when we were in the desert, I knew I loved you. Even as I leave you I know that I love you.*

And because these were words she could not say she tried to tell him with the lips that returned his kiss and with the warming of her body against his. When he eased down the straps of her gown and began to caress her breasts she leaned to fill his hands, murmuring, "Oh, yes. That's so good. Like that, yes. Take off your robe, Tamar. Let me touch you."

The corners of his mouth quirked. "I should warn you, *madame,* I have nothing underneath."

"Mercy!" With a smile she drew her gown over her head and said, "Neither do I."

When he pulled his robe off she lay with her hand flat against his chest. His skin was warm to her touch. She curled her fingers into his chest hair, and easing him back against the chaise leaned to kiss him.

The kiss warmed, deepened. They lay side by side, holding each other close. She was filled with tenderness for him, touching his face, sweeping small kisses across his throat and his shoulders. And Tamar, as though sensing there was a difference in their love-making tonight, did not try to hurry her.

He breathed his pleasure into her mouth. *"Laeela,"* he whispered against her lips. "My dearest love."

And so they lay, quietly pleasing each other, until when he knew he could no longer stand her gentle stroking he made as though to rise over her.

"No," she said. "Let me."

She came up over him, and as she eased herself down onto him she remembered the woman etched into the mosaic. *I am like her,* she thought. *I'm taking my lover as she took hers.*

Now, as the golden man did, he reaches to touch my breasts. His fingers are warm against my flesh. He strokes gently as he nears my nipples. Oh, how sweetly he touches them. How his touch excites me!

She gripped his shoulders and surged against him. She heard the rasp of his breath, felt the tension of his body, the muscles straining to hold back. She leaned back, her hair swaying against his thighs with the rhythm of her movements.

"Catherine..." Gasping for breath. "By Allah, Catherine, what are you doing to me?"

"Loving you," she whispered. "Loving you."

He closed his eyes, and a look of tortured pleasure tightened his face. He surged upward against her, seeking her breasts again, rolling his head from side to side as though he could not bear the pleasure she gave him.

He cried out in words she didn't understand, words of passion, words of love. Driven beyond reason, she whispered, "I love you! I love you!" And with one final surge they climbed the precipice and tumbled to the other side of passion.

They lay in each other's arms, gasping for breath, waiting for their heated bodies to cool. He kissed her and smoothed the tumbled hair from her face. He said, "My dearest *laeela,* my dearest love."

"Hold me. Oh, please hold me."

He tightened his arms around her. "Always, my Catherine." He stroked her, and again and again he told her how dear she was to him and what being with her like this meant to him.

"I pray to Allah that when I am ninety we will still be like this, my Catherine. Holding each other, loving each other as we have tonight."

She turned her face into his shoulder and bit her lip with the effort not to cry. How could she leave him? How could she not?

She clung to him, and again, sensing her sadness, he said, "What is it, Catherine? Why makes you unhappy."

"I'm not unhappy." She sat up and, forcing a smile, said, "How about a swim?"

"Yes, that's a good idea. Come."

And together, hand in hand, they went into the garden to the pool. The night was clear, the sky filled with millions of stars that seemed close enough to touch.

He put his arms around her and when they kissed they sank together beneath the surface of the pool, naked body pressed close to naked body. And when at last they rose, Tamar said, "I never knew that anything could be as it is between us, Catherine. I know we are different, that we come from different backgrounds and live different lives. But I think we must always be together. I want you to be my—"

She put her fingers against his lips, stopping him. And though her heart was breaking, she said, "It's too soon, Tamar. Let's wait." She kissed him. "Let's wait just a little while."

"A little while," he said. "But the next time I speak so you must let me finish."

The next time. "Yes," she said. "The next time I will."

When they left the pool they went to her bed. They made love again, and finally, holding her close, Tamar slept. But Catherine did not. She lay with her head on his shoulder and thought of what tomorrow would bring.

At nine the following morning when Fatmah entered with Catherine's breakfast, Catherine said, "I'm not feeling well. I'm going to spend the day in bed and I don't want to be disturbed."

"I will tell Prince Tamar. He will send for a doctor."

"No! It...it's really nothing. A female disturbance. I'll be better tomorrow."

"If you are certain, *madame*."

"I am." Then hesitating, Catherine said, "But thank you, Fatmah. Thank you for everything."

The woman looked at her uncertainly. Then with a nod she left the room.

Catherine ate quickly. There was nothing to pack, nothing she could take with her. She left the jewels he had given her in the jewel box. The only thing she kept was the jade ankle bracelet.

A slave bracelet, he had called it. *As long as you wear it you will belong to me.*

At ten-thirty there was a knock at her door, and when she opened it a woman entered. "Quickly, *madame*," she whispered. "My mistress is to leave in a few minutes." She pulled the dark robe over her head, removed her head wear and heavy veil and handed the things to Catherine. "Come," she said, "I will help you."

There was no time to think. Catherine put the woman's robe on. The woman slipped into one of Catherine's robes and covered her hair with an extra scarf before she helped Catherine cover her hair.

"Now the veil, *madame*." She handed the thick dark cloth to Catherine, and when she had fastened it in place she took a pair of small shaded glasses from the pocket of the robe Catherine wore.

"I sometimes wear these," she said. "They are only shaded, not dark, but they will help disguise your eyes."

"Thank you." Catherine put the glasses on. "You're very kind. I don't know how I can thank you..."

"Zohra," the servant said. "My name is Zohra. But now we must hurry. I will guide you to the servants' entrance. There Seferina will be waiting."

Catherine looked once more around these rooms that for a short time had been her home. What would he think when he discovered her gone? How would he react? Would he think she had been taken against her will as she had in Marrakesh? It was bad enough, leaving him this way, but to have him think she was in danger... No, she couldn't do that.

"Wait," she told the woman. She ran into the bedroom, took up the notepad by the bed and quickly wrote, "Forgive me." Just that, for there was no more to say. She signed a C and left the note by the side of the bed they had shared only a few hours before.

The two women slipped into the corridor. Zohra motioned for Catherine to follow. Neither woman spoke. Catherine had not been this way before. Here the corridors were darker, twisting and turning this way and that until they reached an open door.

A woman stepped out of the shadows as they approached. She and Zohra spoke a few words before Zohra bowed to Catherine and slipped into the shadows.

"*Taali!*" Seferina said. "Come!"

They stepped into the sunlight, and ahead of her Catherine saw a long black limousine. Zenobia Al-Shaibi was already inside. Her husband waited beside the car.

"Hurry," he called out. "My wife is anxious to leave."

Catherine's mouth went dry. If he recognized her... What if he spoke to her?

"Be quiet," Seferina whispered. "Do not speak."

"Zohra," he called out. "Are you sure you've packed all of my wife's things?"

"I attended to the packing," Seferina said quickly. "I assure you, *sidi*, everything is in order."

"Then get going. I have to get inside to a meeting." To his wife he said, "Call me tonight. Seven sharp."

Keeping her head down, her face averted, Catherine followed Seferina into the limo. Sheikh Al-Shaibi nodded, the limo drove away, and Zenobia said, "We will be all right now."

"I can never thank you for what you're doing," Catherine said.

Zenobia laughed. "But this is a little adventure, yes?"

It took twenty minutes to get to the airport. They drove right up to the waiting plane. Zenobia whispered, "Do not speak, Catherine. When we get out take my arm as though you are helping me."

They got out of the car.

"Assist *madame* to board," Seferina told Catherine. "I will see to the baggage."

They went up the steps into the plane, which was furnished like a well-appointed living room. Seferina came aboard. The plane began to move. "Soon we will be airborne and all will be well," Zenobia said.

Catherine nodded, too filled with conflicting emotions to answer.

The plane raced down the runway, motors roaring. Then it lifted into the air, up, up.

Catherine looked out the window. Below she could see the palace. The sun was shining, and as the plane dipped to circle she was momentarily blinded by the brightness of the gold mosaic gleaming on the Moorish towers. She saw the terraced lawns, her private garden and the pool where she and Tamar had swum naked last night.

Now it was tears that blinded her. She whispered his name, and because she could not help herself put her face in her hands and wept.

Chapter Twelve

It was late that afternoon before Tamar could break away. He knocked on Catherine's door, and when she didn't answer he looked in and called out, "Catherine? May I enter?"

Still she didn't answer. Perhaps she was in the garden, perhaps in the pool. That brought a smile, for if she was he would join her.

But she wasn't in the garden or the pool. His brow wrinkled in a worried frown. Fatmah had said Catherine hadn't been feeling well. Had something happened? Had she been taken to a doctor? He ran into the bedroom, he saw the note on the nightstand next to the bed and snatched it up.

"Forgive me," he read. He stared at the words, unable to grasp their meaning.

Catherine had left him.

Last night they had made love. No, it had been more than that. Last night they had loved each other. He closed his eyes and saw her as she had been, over him, her head thrown back, blond hair streaming down her back. So gloriously beautiful. Loving him.

"She has left me." He said the words aloud, as though by hearing them spoken he might better believe. But why? And how? The only way out of El Agadir except by camel caravan would be to fly. But she had no money, no passport. The only way would have been by private plane, the way Al-Shaibi's wife... He sucked his breath in. Yes, that had to be it. She had gone to Marrakesh with Zenobia Al-Shaibi.

And why? Because of her uncle. Because somehow she had overheard the plot to kill Ross Courlaine.

She'd had to choose between him and her uncle, and she had chosen her uncle. God, that hurt!

It hurt that she believed he would be party to murder.

He hadn't agreed with the men who plotted to kill Ross Courlaine. He had pleaded for Courlaine's life, not out of compassion for the man, but because he was Catherine's uncle.

"We can arrange to have him deported," he'd argued again this morning. "We will stop him by official means rather than murder."

"Execution," Rahma Al-Shaibi said, "not murder."

"Besides," Omar Ben Ismail from Al Hamaam said, "it has been arranged."

"Stop it!" Tamar insisted.

"I will try."

But what if Omar Ben Ismail had failed to reach the assassin in time? By now Catherine would be in Marrakesh. If she was with her uncle... If the assassin tried to kill him... Tamar ran to his office. He phoned Courlaine's hotel in Marrakesh. In Courlaine's room there was no answer. He called the airport. "Have a plane ready to leave in thirty minutes," he said. Bouchaib was next. "We're going to Marrakesh," he told Bouchaib. "We leave at once."

In his own rooms he quickly changed. He took what papers he needed for diplomatic immunity and slid a gun into the waistband of his trousers.

And prayed he wouldn't be too late.

Zenobia kissed her cheek when they arrived at the hotel and said, "May Allah protect you, Catherine."

"There's no way I can ever thank you for helping me."

"No thanks are needed. I hope one day we will meet again." Zenobia smiled a tentative smile. "Perhaps in El Agadir."

"That was only a dream." Catherine took Zenobia's hand. "Goodbye, my friend."

She removed the veil and hurried into the hotel. She asked one of the men at the reception desk if he knew where her uncle had gone. When he said he didn't, she asked for a room.

"I have no money," she explained. "No identification."

"No money? But my dear..." He looked at her, and his eyes went wide with shock. "My word! You're Miss Courlaine! I didn't recognize you. You were kidnapped more than a month ago! Are you all right?"

"Yes, thank you."

"Praise Allah that you are safe. Where have you been? Your uncle will be overjoyed. Oh, dear, I see you have no luggage. I believe your uncle is taking care of your things, but if you need anything, clothes, toiletries, anything at all, simply charge them to his account."

Catherine thanked him, then followed a bellman to a room on the same floor as her uncle's. When he left she washed her hands and splashed cold water on her face. When she had changed she tried to phone her uncle's room again. Finally, three hours after she had arrived, her uncle answered.

"It's Catherine," she said immediately. "I'm here at the hotel. I have to see you."

"Of course, my dear. I wasn't expecting you. How are—"

"I'll be there in a minute," she said. "Don't let anyone else in."

"But what—?"

But Catherine had already put the phone down. She ran into the hall and to her uncle's room.

He opened the door. "Catherine!" He kissed her cheek. "How good to see you. When did you arrive? Is Prince Tamar with you?"

"No." She closed the door behind her. "You're in danger. You've got to call the police."

"What are you talking about?"

"There's a plot to have you killed. I heard..." She stopped to catch her breath. "Men came to El Agadir to see Tamar," she said. "I heard them talking. Someone has been hired to kill you."

"To kill me?" His face blanched. "Why...why would anyone...? Are you sure?"

"Yes, I'm sure. It has something to do with the conference, with your association with Mali Bukhara."

An expression of alarm crossed Ross's face. He began to pace. "The deal is almost done," he said.

"Another day or two at the most, and we'll wrap it up."

"But Mali Bukhara is a warlike country, Uncle Ross. Why would you become involved with them?" Catherine looked at him. "Surely you can't be associating yourself with men like that."

"You don't understand, Catherine. There's money to be made in dealing with an oil-rich country like Mali Bukhara, more money than either you or I have ever dreamed of."

"But you have money, Uncle Ross. You don't need—"

"Yes, I do." He faced her, his expression tense, his body taut as a coiled spring. "Things have been going badly for me the last couple of years. I haven't wanted to tell you, but I made some bad investments. I played the stock market, recklessly, I realize now. When I lost I tried to recoup, so I took a chance and gambled— rather heavily I'm afraid—that next time I'd win. I didn't. I had to...to borrow money from the conglomerate."

Sweat beaded his upper lip. "Perhaps *borrow* isn't the right word, but I...I meant to pay it back. You can see I was in a bind, that I had no choice. I had to deal with Mali Bukhara."

"But there was my trust fund," Catherine said. "If you'd told me you were in trouble I would have given you the money."

"There isn't any money."

She looked at him, unbelieving. "What...what do you mean?"

"It's all gone. I'm sorry, my dear, but you have to understand how desperate I was. I didn't want you to know. I thought I could pay it back. I promise you I will. I'll come out of the deal with Mali Bukhara with close to ten million dollars. I'll pay back every cent of what I've...I've borrowed from the conglomerate and from you."

Not borrowed, she thought. *Stolen. What you have stolen from the people you represent and from me.* She sank into a chair. This was her father's brother. The man she had trusted above all others. And now, because she had to know, she asked, "Why did you want me to come to Marrakesh? Was it to help you or to..." It was hard, so hard to get the words out. "Or did you think you could use me to help sway someone like Tamar into siding with you?"

"It wasn't that way at all, Catherine. Not really."

"Not really?" She felt suddenly very tired, bereft. But she had come to try to save his life. That had not changed.

She forced herself to stand and face him. "You have to leave," she said. "Your life is in danger."

"They wouldn't dare make an attempt on my life."

"You can't wait around to see if they mean it. You have to get out of the country. Today."

"No!" Ross faced her. "I can't! In another day, two at the most, I'll be a rich man. I won't leave. Perhaps you misunderstood. Perhaps—"

Someone knocked and said, "Room service."

Ross started toward the door.

"No!" Catherine cried. "Don't open it."

"It's all right. I sent down for a sandwich just before you came."

"Uncle Ross, wait!" Catherine shook her head. "Don't open the door."

He hesitated, then quickly crossed to the desk and took a small revolver from the drawer. "I've changed my mind," he called out. "I don't want anything."

"But everything is prepared, sir."

"No, I—"

A shot rang out. The door crashed in. Two men sprinted into the room. Catherine screamed.

As though in slow motion she saw Hamid Nawab and a man behind him. Hamid Nawab looked at her just as the other man fired.

Ross took a step forward. He looked puzzled, unbelieving. His assailant fired again. Catherine saw a splash of blood on her uncle's chest. The splash became a circle. He tried to grab the arm of a chair. She ran toward him. He fell before she could reach him. She saw the gun raised again.

"No!" Hamid Nawab cried. "Not the woman!"

"But she's seen us!"

She looked into the black barrel of the weapon and knew she was going to die. In that instant, that small fraction of an instant, she thought of Tamar. Did she whisper his name? Did she say, "Darling. Oh, darling, I'm sorry, sorry for what we could not have, what we will never have..."

She watched the finger tighten on the trigger and closed her eyes. *Let it be quick,* she thought. *Let it be merciful.*

The blast seemed to shake the room. But she felt nothing. She opened her eyes. The man with the gun stared at her, then as she watched he slumped to the floor and fell facedown.

"Catherine!" Tamar rushed into the room, a gun in his hand, Bouchaib beside him. Her knees buckled. Tamar grabbed her before she fell. "Are you all right?" he cried. "Did they hurt you?"

"How did you..." A wave of dizziness weakened her. "Uncle Ross! They shot Uncle Ross. Is he..."

"He is dead, *madame,*" Bouchaib said, his fingers on her uncle's pulse. With a shake of his head he got to his feet and looked at Hamid Nawab. "What do you want me to do with him?" he asked Tamar.

"Keep him here. Call the police."

"I didn't want him to shoot her," Hamid wailed. "I told him not to, I told him..."

Bouchaib shoved Hamid into a chair.

"Wait here until the police come," Tamar told Bouchaib. He picked Catherine up in his arms. "Do you have a room?" he asked.

"Down the hall," she said weakly. "The key is in my pocket."

He took it out. "Tell the police they'll find me there," Tamar said to Bouchaib as he stepped around Ross's body and shouldered his way out the door.

By now people had gathered in the hall. The manager pushed his way through. Tamar stopped long enough to say, "The police have been called. Miss Courlaine's uncle has been shot. She's in shock. I'm taking her to her room."

He hurried down the hall. Once inside he laid her on one of the twin beds and asked, "Did they hurt you?"

She shook her head, unable to speak, trembling with reaction. She saw again the terrible look of surprise on her uncle's face. The moment when she knew she, too, would die.

She looked at Tamar. And now, beyond the grief and the shock of her uncle's death, came the realization that Tamar and the men who had come to El Agadir were responsible for the killing.

He saw her expression change. He reached for her hand. She pulled away from him.

"You did it," she whispered. "You and those other men. You murdered him."

"No!" he said vehemently. "I didn't. Whatever I felt about your uncle, I wouldn't have hurt you that way."

"I don't believe you. You did it." She buried her face in her hands, sickened by all that had happened.

For a moment or two Tamar didn't speak. But at last he said, "I didn't plan your uncle's death, Catherine. But if you don't believe me there's nothing more to say, is there?"

She didn't answer. She couldn't look at him.

He went to the window. With his back to her, he asked, "How did you come to Marrakesh? Was it with Mrs. Al-Shaibi?"

"Yes."

"Would you like me to call her?"

"No. I don't want to see anyone."

"The police will be here in a few minutes to question you. I'll stay until they arrive."

For a little while he had honestly believed something could come of his and Catherine's relationship. Though they were different in many ways, he'd dared to dream they could make a life together. But because of Ross Courlaine's death there was no hope of that now.

When the police came Catherine would implicate him in the murder of her uncle, and though he could prove neither he nor the other men had any part in it, it would be an embarrassment. And certainly an irreparable break between them.

The police came in, a captain, a slim man in his late forties, and two of his men. The captain took a small black notebook out of his pocket and began to question Catherine.

"Can you tell us what happened in your uncle's room?" he asked.

"It was all so...so sudden." She got up from the bed and sat in a chair facing him.

"You had been away from Morocco?"

"Yes, I'd been visiting Prince Tamar in El Agadir."

"Ah. And you arrived today?"

"Yes."

"It seems strange that your arrival coincided with the murder of Mr. Courlaine."

Her expression didn't change, but Tamar saw her hesitate. *Now,* he thought. *She will tell him what she thinks is the truth and I will be implicated.*

"Not all that strange," she said, looking at her hands. "Sheik Al-Shaibi and his wife were also guests of Prince Tamar's. When Mrs. Al-Shaibi told me yesterday that she was going to come to Marrakesh to visit her parents I decided to come with her.''

"Did you recognize either of the men who broke into your uncle's room?''

"Yes, I recognized Mr. Nawab. I met him a month ago during the conference my uncle attended here in Marrakesh.''

"And the other man?''

"I never saw him before.''

"He was the one who fired the shot that killed your uncle?''

"Yes. And he...he was going to shoot me. I...I saw his finger start to...to squeeze the trigger.'' Her teeth were chattering, and she was shaking. "That...that's when Prince Tamar broke into the room.''

The captain snapped his notebook shut. "You've had a bad experience," he said kindly. "We can continue tomorrow. How long do you plan to stay in Morocco?''

"I'd like to...to leave as soon as I could.'' She had her arms around her waist, holding herself, trying to control the terrible shaking.

"There will be more questions. You'll have to make a statement. Mr. Nawab will be brought to trial.''

"But that may not be for months,'' Catherine protested. "I have a job, I...I have to return to my own country.''

"I will see what I can do.'' He turned to Tamar. "The man you killed was a hired assassin, Prince Tamar. I'd like to ask you exactly what happened, what you saw when you went into the room.''

"Of course," Tamar said. "If you'll just give me a moment alone with Miss Courlaine."

"I will wait in the hall."

When they were alone, Tamar said, "You didn't tell him about what you overheard, about your suspicion that I was a party to your uncle's murder. If you believe it—"

"I believe it." She looked at him. "He said the man was a paid assassin. I heard..." She was shaking so badly she couldn't go on.

"Then why didn't you tell him, Catherine?"

"Because of what we had," she said in a low voice. "Of what I thought we had."

"That hasn't changed."

"Hasn't it?" She met his eyes for a moment, then looked away. "I...I'm tired, Tamar. If I don't rest I'm going to be ill."

He didn't want to leave, not like this. "We need to talk. I have to tell you—"

"There's nothing to say. Please..." Her voice broke. "Please, just... just go."

He was desperate to hold her, to beg her to believe that he had no part in the murder of her uncle. But he had no choice, not when she looked at him the way she did, her face set, her eyes so cold.

He had his hand on the doorknob. Trying one more time to reach her, he said, "Catherine?"

She didn't answer.

He had no choice. He left the room.

Catherine drifted in and out of an almost sleep, afraid to close her eyes, again and again seeing her uncle murdered before her eyes. And jumped when, at a little after nine that night, someone knocked on her door.

"Who...who is it?"

"It is I, Zenobia. May I come in?"

She had thought she didn't want to see anyone, but suddenly she was glad Zenobia had come. She needed a woman to talk to, a woman who would understand the grief of death.

"My dear." Zenobia put her arms around Catherine. "What a terrible experience for you. My husband told me what happened. I'm so sorry." Taking Catherine's arm, she led her to bed. "Sleep now," she said. "I will stay."

Catherine's eyes filled with tears. "You...you don't have to."

"I want to. I insist." She pulled the sheet over Catherine. "Sleep, Catherine. I will be here."

At last exhaustion had its way, and Catherine slept.

It was while they were having breakfast in her room the next morning that Zenobia said, "My husband told me of the plot to assassinate your uncle."

Catherine stopped, coffee cup halfway to her mouth. "You know then."

"It was very wrong of them, Catherine. Thanks be to Allah and, yes, to Prince Tamar that they did not go through with their plan."

"But they did! My uncle is dead, murdered."

"But not by the delegates, Catherine. It was what they wanted, and surely it was wrong. Prince Tamar fought them from the beginning, and finally they agreed that it would be best to have the Moroccan government deport Mr. Courlaine and to protest to your government against the men he represented.''

"But I thought Tamar... He wasn't responsible for my uncle's death?''

"No, Catherine. I swear on the heads of my children that I have spoken the truth.''

She stared at Zenobia. Her heart thudded against her ribs. She jumped up. "I have to see him, tell him I was wrong. I have to...''

She was halfway to the door when Zenobia stopped her and with a laugh said, "It really would not be proper to leave wearing only a nightgown. I suggest you call him first.'' She handed the phone to Catherine.

Catherine took a steadying breath and said, "Prince Tamar Fallah Haj's room, please.''

"Prince Fallah Haj has checked out, *madame.*''

"He... he checked out?''

"Yes, *madame.* Early this morning.''

"I see. Thank you.'' She put the phone down. "He's gone,'' she told Zenobia. "He isn't here.''

"What will you do now, Catherine?''

Catherine shook her head. "I don't know,'' she said. "I don't know.''

Chapter Thirteen

Affairs of state kept Tamar busy, at least for the first few days after his return from Marrakesh. Though he exhausted himself with long hours in his office, at night he couldn't sleep. Often he would get out of bed in the middle of the night and go to the rooms Catherine had occupied.

Her scent lingered there, on the clothes she had left behind, on the pillow where her head had rested. He would move slowly about the rooms, breathing in the image of her.

Once he lay on the chaise, and in his mind's eye he saw her as she had been on their last night together. He remembered how the moonlight touched her face as she rose above him. He could almost see her eyes soften with desire and hear the whisper of her voice saying, "I love you. I love you."

Each night he asked that his dinner be served in the small dining room where he and Catherine had eaten that first night. Again and again while he only picked at his food his gaze went to the mosaic wall that had so fascinated Catherine. Taking his coffee he would stand in front of it, studying the figures outlined there, following scene after erotic scene of their lovemaking. Until at last, fevered with the memory of what had been, he would turn away.

Never before had he felt this pain of loneliness. Never before had he longed for the sight, the presence of that one person who could assuage his loneliness.

His need for Catherine went far beyond his physical need of her. He missed the essence of her, the sound of her voice, her smile, her endearing femininity, her humor. She was everything he wanted in a woman. And he had lost her. The thought racked his soul.

There were times when he thought of going to Marrakesh after her, of taking her by force the way he had done when he'd rescued her the first time. Of throwing her on a camel and heading into the desert where he would make her love him again.

But even as the thought came, Tamar discarded it. Catherine was the woman of his heart. Never again would he force her to do anything against her will.

And finally he could no longer bear the memory of her here in the palace. Perhaps in the silence of the desert, he would be able to forget her.

Catherine arranged for her uncle's body to be flown to Chicago for burial. She would return later to try to settle his financial affairs, as well as her own, but for now, she couldn't leave Marrakesh.

She made a formal statement to the police and signed what seemed like endless forms. Almost ten days passed before she was free to leave. When the decision was made she called Zenobia and said, "Everything is done here. I'm going home."

"Have you heard from Prince Tamar?"

"No."

"You have not tried to reach him?"

"No, I haven't."

So much soul-searching, so many times she had been tempted to tell him she had been wrong in thinking he had been a part of her uncle's death. But she was afraid if she heard his voice she would be lost. For though she loved Tamar, she knew there was little chance they could ever make a life together. They were such different people, from such different cultures. She had accused him of her uncle's murder, and she wasn't sure he could ever forgive her for that.

But there were times when the thought of him, and of how it had been, was like a physical ache. She awoke in the night calling his name. And wept because they weren't together.

She slept little the night before she was scheduled to return to Chicago, and awoke a little after five to the voice of the imam calling the faithful to morning prayer.

Pulling on a robe, she went onto the balcony, and as she had that first morning in Marrakesh, gazed out over the minarets and the mosques of the city.

She had wondered that other morning as she looked out toward the mountains what lay beyond. Now she knew, for she had been there. She had seen the endless miles of dunes turned golden in the setting sun. She had found her desert prince.

And dreamed a dream of what might have been.

She had a life in Chicago, friends, work that challenged her. How could she turn her back on who she was to become someone else?

The plaintive cry drifted over the city. She pulled the robe closer.

At night when he slept beside the camp fire he remembered another night, another camp fire. He remembered her defiance, her bravery, the feel of her body against his when he kissed her. And later, when she had tried to escape and he had caught her and pulled her from her camel. She'd fought him, there on the sand, and suddenly he had wanted her as he had never before wanted a woman.

Catherine! his heart cried. *Catherine, I need you.*

In the early evening of his fourth day at the oasis, at the time when the blue faded and the sky caught fire in a brilliance of flamingo red and the sand became golden in the last rays of daylight, Tamar looked out upon the desert and saw two riders coming toward him.

Bouchaib, he thought. *He has come to make sure I'm all right.* But who was the other rider? One of the men from his desert home?

They drew closer, but not close enough that he could distinguish their faces. They stopped. One of the riders lifted his arm in a salute, then turned and started back the way he had come. The other rider came toward him.

Hands on his hips, Tamar watched the rider approach. But the last rays of the setting sun were in his eyes, and he was momentarily blinded. He shaded his eyes with his hand, and as he watched he saw the rider reach up and pull the head covering off.

"Catherine!" The cry tore from Tamar's throat. He ran toward her. She whipped the camel into a trot, bouncing up and down in an effort to stay on.

He reached her. She pulled on the reins and when the animal stopped she began to slide out of the saddle. Tamar reached up and caught her in his arms.

"You're here," he cried. "Praise Allah, you're here."

She tried to speak, but he stopped her words, kissing her again and again. And held her as though he would never let her go.

That night when the moon was full and fat and yellow they lay together under the shelter of the palms.

"I love you," Tamar said. "I'll never let you leave me again."

"I'll never want to." Catherine raised herself up on one elbow. Stroking his hair from his forehead, she said, "We're very different, you know."

Tamar smiled. "Yes, we are. You are a woman, I am a man, and I thank Allah for the difference."

It was Catherine's turn to smile. "You know what I mean."

He curled a tendril of her hair around his finger. "Yes, I know. But if we love each other..."

"We love," she said.

He kissed her, and when he let her go, he said, "We will marry as soon as we return to El Agadir. That is where we will live, but we will travel, too. When you are lonesome for your own country, when you have a taste for your famous cheeseburgers and French fries, we will go back for a visit. But wherever we go, my Catherine, we will be together.''

''Will I have to wear a robe and a veil?''

''Only sometimes.'' He kissed her gently, slowly. Against her lips he murmured, ''Only because it will excite me to take them off.''

She lay naked in his arms. ''My love,'' he whispered. ''My *laeela*.''

He kissed her golden breasts, he caressed her golden thighs.

And it seemed to Catherine when he joined his body to hers that, carried on the desert breeze, she could hear the sighs and whispers of all the lovers who had gone before.

* * * * *

Dear Reader,

The Moroccan city of Marrakesh has always intrigued me. From the first time I saw it on a map I conjured up visions of dark-eyed men in flowing white robes, of intrigue and mystery and warm desert nights.

When at last I visited Marrakesh I knew my daydreams had become reality. It was everything I had hoped it would be, exotic beyond my imagination, filled with foreign sights and smells, with soothsayers, belly dancers, snake charmers, whirling dervishes and, yes, with handsome dark-eyed men.

Because it was the perfect setting for a love story, it's where I begin *The Sheikh's Woman*. There, in that most fantastic of cities, my heroine, Catherine, meets her desert man, Prince Tamar Fallah Haj. When Catherine is kidnapped Tamar goes after her. He rescues her, but instead of taking her back to Marrakesh, he makes her his captive and takes her across the high Atlas Mountains to his desert home.

There in his Moorish palace, amid luxury unlike anything she has ever known, Catherine becomes a prisoner of love. Though she tries to fight her growing attraction to this desert prince, she can't deny the desire that flames between them.

The Sheikh's Woman was an exciting story to write; I hope you'll find it exciting to read. Happy desert dreams!

Barbara Faith

MILLION DOLLAR SWEEPSTAKES

Available in July from

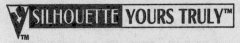
THE CASE OF THE LADY IN APARTMENT 308
by Lass Small

Ed Hollingsworth's observations about the lady in apartment 308: great figure, nice smile when she does smile, strange friends, kooky habits. His first thought had been *eviction* but now Ed's hoping to take his investigation directly behind sexy Marcia Phillips's closed door....

WHEN MAC MET HAILEY
by Celeste Hamilton

Hailey on Mac: He's cute, a great kisser...but a single dad! I've already been down that road before.... *Mac on Hailey:* My friends think I should date someone nice, maybe find a mom for my young daughter. The one hot number I keep coming back to is Hailey's....

Love—when you least expect it!

YT796

**Coming this August
from Silhouette Romance**

Expanding upon our popular Fabulous Fathers series, these
irresistable heros are going even farther beyond daddy duty...
for the love of children and unforgettable heroines!

UNDERCOVER DADDY
by
Lindsay Longford
(SR#1168, August)

Detective Walker Ford had always loved Kate McDaniels, but
she'd married his best friend. Now she was widowed with an
infant son—and they desperately needed his help. Walker had
sworn to protect the baby with his life—but who would protect his
heart from the boy's beautiful mother?

Don't miss this Super Fabulous Father—only in

Silhouette ROMANCE™

You're About to Become a

Privileged Woman

Reap the rewards of fabulous free gifts and benefits with proofs-of-purchase from Silhouette and Harlequin books

Pages & Privileges™

It's our way of thanking you for buying our books at your favorite retail stores.

PROOF OF PURCHASE

SPT-PP159

Offer expires October 31, 1996

Harlequin and Silhouette— the most privileged readers in the world!

For more information about Harlequin and Silhouette's PAGES & PRIVILEGES program call the Pages & Privileges Benefits Desk: 1-503-794-2499

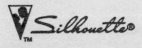

SPT-PP159